THE JUDAS BLADE

Autumn, 1671. War looms with Holland and discontent with England's dissolute monarch, Charles II, increases. Meanwhile, at the Duke's Theatre, the celebrated actress Betsy Brand is financially troubled and obliged to undertake a dangerous venture as a spy for her country. But a fact-finding mission to the Low Countries soon turns into a deadly game, in which Betsy must use all her acting skills. Though she meets her match in Captain Mullin, a reckless fellow-agent, the two find they must work together to confront an unseen killer, and unravel a plot that strikes at the very heart of England itself . . .

Books by John Pilkington
Published by The House of Ulverscroft:

AFTER THE FIRE

John Pilkington has written plays for radio and theatre as well as television scripts for the BBC. *The Judas Blade* is the second novel featuring heroine Betsy Brand. Born in Lancashire, he now lives in Devon with his partner and son. You can find out more about him at:

www.johnpilkington.co.uk.

JOHN PILKINGTON

THE JUDAS BLADE

Complete and Unabridged

ULVERSCROFT
Leicester

First published in Great Britain in 2011 by
Robert Hale Limited
London

First Large Print Edition
published 2012
by arrangement with
Robert Hale Limited
London

British Library CIP Data

Pilkington, John, *1948 June 11–*
The Judas blade.
1. Women spies- -Fiction. 2. Actresses- -Fiction.
3. Espionage, British- -Netherlands- -Fiction.
4. Netherlands- -History- -*1648 – 1714*- -Fiction.
5. Great Britain- -History- -Charles II, *1660 – 1685*- -
Fiction. 6. Historical fiction. 7. Large type books.
I. Title
823.9′2–dc23

ISBN 978–1–4448–1354–8

Published by
F. A. Thorpe (Publishing)
Anstey, Leicestershire

Set by Words & Graphics Ltd.
Anstey, Leicestershire
Printed and bound in Great Britain by
T. J. International Ltd., Padstow, Cornwall

This book is printed on acid-free paper

1

On an afternoon in October, Mistress Betsy Brand left the Duke's Theatre alone and walked along Water Lane towards Fleet Street. She was in sober mood, which had nothing to do with the play in which she was appearing. Nor did it concern the new role she had been given, in a comedy by the playmaker Mr Shadwell. In fact it was not a professional matter at all: it concerned her father.

Betsy had received news the previous evening which weighed heavily upon her. To her surprise, her sister Mary, low in spirits, had appeared at her lodgings, the house of Dr Tom Catlin in Fire's Reach Alley. The surprise was twofold: for one thing Betsy's older sister, who had made a good marriage and was the mother of two healthy children, was one of the most cheerful women she knew. For another, Mary rarely visited her. Betsy, unmarried and a prominent *woman of the theatre*, had long been a cause of embarrassment to her family. The reason for her sister's arrival, however, soon became clear: it seemed their father William Brand was in serious debt.

'Mother's beside herself,' Mary had said, shaking her head. 'Father's past his sixtieth year now . . . we cannot see how he'll pull himself out of this mire he's fallen into.'

'I do know how old he is, Mary,' Betsy had replied. 'And despite what you might think, I see him sometimes — when he consents to see *me*, that is.' The two women were sitting in Tom Catlin's parlour, the doctor having excused himself so that they might talk freely.

'Well, you know his position is difficult,' her sister had said. 'He tries to keep up acquaintance with friends from happier times, yet many of them ignore him. While those he's obliged to deal with mock him, thinking him a poor man of business . . . ' She bit her lip. 'If only he'd been more prudent, before the Great Fire . . . '

'Oh, flap-sauce!' Betsy's patience never lasted long in her sister's company. 'Father fell out with his superiors long before that — he was never a tactful man, was he? His losing a few documents during the Fire was all the excuse they needed to force him from his post.'

'Betsy, how could you!' Mary spoke as if she were reproving one of her children. 'Father's an honest man, who served the Crown faithfully — '

'Indeed — too honest,' Betsy retorted. 'You live a comfortable life out at Chelsea,' she went on. 'Here in the town — and especially at Court — different customs prevail. Guile is the most important asset a man can have nowadays — that and a droll wit, along with a lack of scruples. Father's an innocent soul from a bygone age, Mary. He's not moulded for the world of commerce. Now I think upon it, I'm not surprised he's fallen behind with his creditors. Like his customers, they've probably cheated him for years.'

'Sister!' Mary gazed at her as if she were a stranger. 'Great heavens, what has become of you?'

'Oh, I know what you think,' Betsy said. 'But you shouldn't believe all you hear about actresses — '

'I don't mean that! I know you're not a Nell Gwyn, or a Moll Davis . . . ' Her sister sighed. 'My dear, you seem to think so badly of everyone. One hears such lurid tales of the King and the Duke, and their libertine friends who patronize the theatres . . . is it they who've soured you?'

'Soured me?' Betsy was taken aback. 'What . . . do you think I've become such a cynic?'

'Well . . . perhaps not.' Her sister put on a wan smile. 'Look at us — we seldom meet, yet here we are railing at each other as we did when we were girls. Yet we always kissed and made up in the end, didn't we?'

'We did,' Betsy admitted. 'So let's put all this aside now and think of Father. Tell me plainly: how much does he owe?'

Mary hesitated, then, 'As I understand it, his debts amount to about fifty pounds.'

It was a shock. And thinking of it now, as she emerged from Water Lane by St Bride's, Betsy was plunged into gloom. Fifty pounds amounted to almost two years' wages for an actress like herself. She'd mulled over the figure throughout the day, and knew it was an impossible sum. None of her friends had that sort of wealth, though she had refrained from saying so to her sister. Instead, when Mary took her leave with vague promises about calling again, Betsy had told her not to worry. She'd even mentioned rich acquaintances like Lord Caradoc, the Master of the Revels, whom she might approach — if not for a loan, then at least for advice. Yet she knew the outlook was bleak. And the thought of her ageing father being thrown into a debtor's prison filled her with worry.

At Fleet Street she halted, assailed by the clop of hoofs and the noise of carts rumbling by. As she waited to cross, her thoughts turned again to Caradoc. The wily lord, whose fondness for the theatre was merely a diversion from his other interests, was the most important person Betsy knew. And though she was well aware that his attentions were less than honourable — she hadn't forgotten his leery smile and his hand upon her knee that day when she'd sat in his coach — he had always been kind to her. When he'd promised to get her friend Jane Rowe's rascally beau released from the Fleet Prison, he had been as good as his word. Musing on that now, Betsy felt a pang of unease: Lord Caradoc had performed the service, he said, as proof of his good will. In return, Betsy had all but agreed to his secret request: that she use her skills as an actress and turn intelligencer, in the service of her country.

Since then the best part of a year had passed. And though she had seen his lordship several times, he had not broached the subject again. For a while Betsy had felt ashamed for letting him think she would acquiesce so readily. Instead, only too eagerly, she'd allowed her work at the Duke's Theatre to fill her days, and the matter had gone cold. Or so she thought — apart from those occasions when Caradoc had cause to visit Dorset Gardens, and she had found him gazing pointedly at her from a distance.

She shook herself: no, it wouldn't do. She was an actress, who had risen by talent and hard work, from playing small parts to gaining an important role in the company's new piece. What did she care, or even know, about politics? And even if the famous playmaker Mrs Behn had been a spy for a short time, as Lord Caradoc claimed, what was that to Betsy? Frowning, she stepped into the street.

'Oi, Mistress Head-in-the-Clouds — watch your back!'

Startled, Betsy whirled round to find a brewer's dray bearing down upon her, the fat driver shaking his whip. With a yelp she dodged the nearside horse, grabbed her skirts and gained the other side of Fleet Street — just in time.

'*You* watch it, you big tub of lard!' she shouted back. 'Or do you want a body under your wheels?'

The driver roared with laughter. 'I wouldn't say no to yours, my lamb!' he cried. 'But not under my wheels!' He was still laughing as he drew away, urging his plodding horses towards the Fleet Bridge.

In spite of herself, Betsy felt a smile coming on. 'Cods,' she breathed. 'Perhaps my sister's fears are well founded after all . . . am I become as coarse as any woman of the streets?'

Drawing her bertha about her shoulders,

she walked the short distance to Fetter Lane, turned in by St Dunstan's and was soon nearing Catlin's house in Fire's Reach. But when she arrived at the door, she found someone blocking her way.

'Live here, do you?'

The speaker was a big man in a rough serge coat. To Betsy's alarm, he carried an oak truncheon.

'I do,' she replied, in her most imperious tone. 'And who are you?'

'John Dench, bailiff,' came the reply. 'And I've stood here long enough. I know there's folk within — so tell 'em I'm not leaving until I've had satisfaction!'

'Satisfaction?' Betsy looked the man up and down. 'If you mean you're here on behalf of creditors to Dr Catlin, I fear you'll be disappointed. He seldom returns home before nightfall, and sometimes long after — '

'I said I know there's folk within, and I meant it!' Dench retorted. He levelled his truncheon at the window. 'See — mark you that!'

Betsy looked, and her heart sank. Peg Brazier, Tom Catlin's rebellious servant, was peering round the window frame. At once she ducked out of sight, but she was too late.

'How much do you want?' With a sigh, Betsy fumbled in her gown. 'Or rather, what sum would persuade you to depart and return next week? No doubt circumstances will have changed by then, and my landlord will be able to settle his account.'

The appearance of Betsy's purse placated Dench somewhat. 'Well . . . I don't know if I should,' he muttered. 'I'm charged by Kitts the bootmaker to recover the sum of four guineas. Anything less would be — '

'Here's a silver crown on account,' Betsy said. 'And another shilling perhaps, to compensate you for your trouble.'

She fixed the bailiff with her most brazen stare. It had quelled lesser men, and it did not fail now. With a glance up and down the street, Dench tucked his truncheon into his belt.

'On account, then.' He shook his head reluctantly, but the show was wasted on a professional like Betsy. 'Kitts won't like it, but if you say I can expect the rest next week then I'll take your word, miss.' He smiled knowingly — which was a mistake.

'*Miss?*' Betsy stared at him. 'Just who — or what, do you think I am?'

The bailiff's smile faded. 'Why, I didn't think nothing — '

'Yes you did!' To her own surprise as well as Dench's, Betsy's temper had flared. 'You thought I was the doctor's kept woman — or even a trull. Well hear this, Mr Dench: I'm neither. I'm Mistress Brand of the Duke's Theatre. And there are those I could call on, who'd send you back to Kitts the bootmaker with a sore head. Now — here's your money!'

And she thrust the coin at him, so abruptly that the man flinched. For a moment he regarded Betsy as if she were a Bedlam inmate, before snatching it.

'A pox on you, then!' He glowered — but with a swish of her gown, Betsy swept past him and mounted the doorstep. In seconds she had lifted the latch and was disappearing into the house, whereupon Dench called out, 'Wait — another shilling, you said!'

But all he got in return was a sound familiar to men of his calling: the slam of a door. Instinctively he raised his fist to hammer, then on second thoughts lowered it again.

In the house, Betsy and Peg waited breathlessly on the other side of the door. When at last they heard the thud of heavy boots moving away, both let out sighs of relief.

'I daren't open up to that one,' Peg said, jerking her thumb. 'He's the hectoring sort — won't leave until he's got a result.' She frowned. 'What did you tell him?'

But Betsy started towards the stairs. 'Will

you bring hot water to my room, Peg?' she said quietly. 'I'd like to wash.'

⋆　⋆　⋆

Doctor Tom Catlin returned home late that evening, after Betsy had taken her supper in the kitchen. As was his frequent custom, he called his friend and lodger down to share a cup of sack with him. So there in the parlour, where she had sat with her sister the evening before, Betsy told him of her father's troubles. And, tired though she was, after she was done she felt better. Then, most people who talked with Tom Catlin would have said that. For a man, Betsy had always maintained, he was a good listener.

'Sadly, good William Brand isn't the only one to get himself into debt,' he observed. They were seated by the fire, the doctor in waistcoat and shirt sleeves, Betsy in a plain nightgown. 'Peg's told me of your encounter with the bailiff . . . ' Embarrassed, he looked away. 'I'll deduct a crown from your rent.'

'Please don't concern yourself with that,' Betsy said. She took a drink, then added, 'My father isn't the only man I know who thinks of his customers first and his profits last. When are you going to charge enough to cover your own costs?'

'Come, Betsy — you know how poor many of my patients are,' Catlin replied wearily. 'What should I do when called to the bed of a sick man, or a woman in the pains of a difficult childbirth? Demand payment, before I lift a finger?'

'Most of your fellow physicians would,' Betsy said. 'But then, we've trodden this ground before, have we not?' She lowered her eyes, and gazed into the fire. No matter how straitened his circumstances, Tom Catlin always had a good sea-coal fire burning.

'I saw Mr Betterton today, in Covent Garden,' the doctor said, to change the subject. 'I gather you're to take a prestigious role at the Duke's.'

'I'm playing Lady Waspish,' Betsy told him, with a wry smile. 'And I hope you'll make no comment on that.'

Catlin maintained his sober demeanour. 'Would I dare?' Then, almost as an afterthought, he added, 'I may as well tell you my news too, Betsy: it's possible I might have to sell this house.'

Betsy turned sharply — but at once there came a loud clang from beyond the door. Catlin looked round.

'Peg?'

A muffled oath was his answer. Getting to his feet, he strode to the door and flung it

11

wide — to reveal Peg on her hands and knees, dabbing at the floor with a cloth.

'It's naught to fret about,' she muttered, peering up at him. 'I was bringing a jug of slops down, and — '

'Save your excuses!' To Betsy's surprise as well as Peg's, Catlin was angry for once. 'You were listening again!' He raised his hands helplessly, then let them fall. 'So, you've heard the worst — am I correct?'

But the expression on Peg's face was all the reply he needed. With a stifled oath of his own, her master turned away. Looking forlorn, Peg got up and stepped into the room. The doctor had returned to his chair, from where he looked at each of them in turn.

'I hadn't meant to announce it just yet — and certainly not in such precipitate fashion,' he said, calming himself. 'But now that you both know . . . ' He gestured to a pile of papers on his bureau. The stack of unpaid bills was such a feature of the room that Betsy rarely noticed it, as a rule. Though now that she looked, it seemed to have grown taller of late.

'I won't mince words,' Catlin said. 'In brief, I'm a pauper. Though in case you think I've turned spendthrift that payment due to Kitts that occasioned the visit from our Mr

Dench, wasn't for boots: it was for leather straps, to confine a patient with the falling sickness. That and a new instrument case . . . ' He gave a shrug. 'What does it matter? He's just one of many who've grown tired of waiting for their money. Coal-merchants, butchers, the wig-maker . . . ' He eyed Peg. 'I've no need to tell you, have I?'

Peg was fussing nervously with her cap, which was frayed enough already . . . and that simple gesture was enough for Betsy. It had been a trying day, and her usual resilience was strained. All at once she felt close to tears, but skilfully turned it into a cough.

'Speaking of coal-merchants' — she flapped her hand, as if wafting smoke away — 'that last delivery was hardly of the best quality, was it? The man should accept half-payment on principle.' And thinking fast, she fell into the role she was about to play: that of the outraged Lady Waspish.

'As for wig-makers.' She stuck up her nose, and looked disdainfully at Tom Catlin. 'Yours doesn't deserve payment, sir, for that . . . doormat you wear. Why, the man should be dragged through the streets in disgrace!'

There was a brief silence, then the tension broke. Peg sniggered, tried to stifle it, but failed. In a moment she was bent double with laughter, putting a hand to the door-frame to

13

steady herself. That made Betsy laugh too, though hers was more subdued. She waited until Peg managed to control herself, whereupon both women looked warily at Tom Catlin. Finally, to their relief, he relaxed and shook his head.

'Perhaps I should give thanks that humour, at least, isn't in short supply,' he said drily. Despite everything, a smile tugged at his mouth. 'And yet . . . ' The smile faded. 'I fear we cannot escape the truth.' He looked at Peg. 'Don't fret. If it comes to the worst, I'll see you get a place somewhere else. I have friends who would do that much for me, at least — '

'I don't want to go somewhere else!' Peg was suddenly aghast. 'This is my home. I . . . I couldn't countenance it!'

'*Countenance?*' Catlin echoed. But Peg's fingers worked at her apron, and now she seemed lost. Or, to Betsy's eyes, she looked every inch the spindle-thin waif the doctor had plucked off the streets, all those years ago.

'You know I'll go wherever you go,' she said anxiously. 'Even to the Americas — you wouldn't leave without me, would you?' But when her master didn't answer, she turned quickly and went out.

The other two heard her footsteps patter

down the hallway to the kitchen, and for a time neither looked at the other. However, when the doctor finally turned to Betsy, he was surprised to see her wearing a very different expression. She had come to a decision, but she was not about to reveal it. She knew only too well that if her friend learned the truth, he would have been dismayed. Instead she ventured a question.

'How long will it be before you decide?' she asked. 'I mean, about selling the house?'

'A month, perhaps two . . . ' Catlin shrugged. 'I hope you'll not lose any sleep over it. If I must take such a course, I'll help you to new lodgings.'

'Well, that may not be necessary.' Betsy was looking into the fire again — and now the doctor's eyes narrowed.

'What are you concealing from me?' he demanded. 'If you've got one of your foolhardy schemes in mind — '

'There's no scheme.' Betsy rose to her feet. 'Now, will you excuse me if I retire? I need to think for a while — and I promise not to lose any sleep.' With that she made a theatrical curtsy, as she did whenever she wished to amuse him, and went out.

But, as she climbed the stairs, her manner changed. For only now did it dawn on her that she'd known since yesterday what she must do. This evening's events had merely forced her to face it, and now that she did so, she was uneasy. Yet her course was clear; indeed, she could see no other. And by the time she entered her bedroom she had managed to push fear aside and think about what to wear the next morning, when she paid a visit to Bredon House in Piccadilly — the London residence of Lord Caradoc.

There at last Betsy would honour her promise, and offer her services to the noble lord as an intelligencer — provided the payment was enough. Though what it might involve, she hardly dared imagine. In fact, if she had known, she told herself much later, she would have had second thoughts — and third ones too.

For it was as a result of her decision, and her private conversation with Lord Caradoc, that one week later Mistress Betsy Brand found herself committed to the King's Bench prison.

2

As London's prisons went, the King's Bench in Southwark wasn't the worst. At least Betsy wasn't sharing a cellar with a score of thieves and rogues, she discovered, as she would have done at Newgate. Some of the inmates were debtors, some were felons, while others had seemingly been put here for little reason, not knowing when they might be released. Meanwhile they endured the same privations as prisoners elsewhere: harsh treatment, cold rooms, food that would have sickened them had they not been so hungry — and an ever-present air of menace.

The atmosphere swirled about Betsy from the moment she was admitted. Hidden eyes seemed to be watching as a taciturn guard steered her through dank passages, holding her arm in a claw-like grip. Finally he unlocked a door and pushed her into a square room occupied by several others.

'Who's this, Foggy Moll?' A lank-haired man in a suit of faded fustian sneered at Betsy from the floor. The others eyed her low-cut gown divided to show a red underskirt, her painted face and unbound hair, and knew her at once for what she was. What they didn't know was that it was a role: the most fitting one Betsy had been able to think of. Though it was not one she could put aside each afternoon, after a performance. For as long as she was in this place, she must not lose character — and here was her first test.

'You couldn't afford Foggy Moll, greasy-locks,' she threw back in her best Cheapside accent, ignoring the squeal of the rusty lock behind her. 'Nor me, for that matter.' She threw a disdainful look at the straw-strewn floor and greasy pallets. 'I don't think much of the furniture. Where do I sleep?'

A wheezing voice spoke from the wall, beneath the barred window. 'You'd best lie beside me, dear. We'll warm each other, if you're not a-feared of my sickness. And at least I won't be fumbling your placket.'

Turning, Betsy saw a shrivelled figure in a tattered shawl: the only other woman in the cell. Aside from the one who had spoken, there were two other men. One was a flabby, pink-cheeked fellow, who looked a little too well dressed to be in prison. The last occupant was a man in his forties, plainly garbed, who sat alone. Betsy glanced at each of them, then moved to the woman's pallet and eased herself down.

'What time's supper?' she asked.

The pink-cheeked man spoke up in an educated voice. 'I fear you'll find it somewhat poor, madam,' he said. 'If it arrives at all, that is. But tell me, what misfortune brings you into our company?' When Betsy told him, he frowned. 'Disturbing the peace — is that all? Why didn't they commit you to Newgate?'

But she had rehearsed her tale. 'No doubt they would've done,' she answered, 'except I was in the wrong place.' She tapped her nose. 'Whitehall business. Too close to the King's presence — they don't like that. Stuck me in the gatehouse for a night, then brought me here.'

'King's presence?' The man in fustian threw her a scornful look. 'Don't spin fables! Royal mistresses live like queens, with coaches and servants and all. They dress in silks and velvets, not poor taffeta — '

'Whitehall business I said, not royal,' Betsy retorted. 'There's others live there too — you think they're all as rich as King Charlie?' She sniffed. 'I work Moorfields as a rule. Only I've a cull — a keeper of hawks at the King's Mews by Charing Cross. I was with him . . . got unlucky, that's all.'

She wiped her nose with her sleeve, looking round defiantly. To her relief nobody challenged her further; instead they quickly

19

lost interest. The man in fustian turned to his companion and picked up a wooden shaker. He rattled it, then tossed the dice to the floor, prompting a groan from the other. Suddenly the woman in the shawl coughed; a rasping, rattling cough that jarred the nerves.

'You need a drink, Mother,' Betsy said. 'Is there no water?' But for answer, the other gestured weakly to a tin jug.

'Gone . . . ' she sighed, then startled Betsy by leaning close. 'But *you* can get served in here — if you'll serve others. Let the gaolers know you'll lift your skirts and you can get anything you want . . . ' She broke off, croaking. '*You* know.'

In reply, Betsy gave a nod. Then all at once she found a pair of sharp eyes upon her: those of the man who had not yet spoken. Immediately he looked away, but not before she had given another loud sniff. 'Seen enough have you?' she demanded. And with that she turned aside, closing her eyes.

But her pulse had quickened, and not only because of the dangerous role she was playing. She had expected she would be at pains to defend her body in prison; what she hadn't expected was to attract the attention so soon of the man she was here to watch. Because she had caught a glimpse of something she'd been instructed to look for: a

20

birthmark on the back of his right hand. She saw it now in her mind's eye: plum-coloured and shaped like a hammerhead, Lord Caradoc had said.

As if from weariness, she slumped against the wall. But her mind was busy, thinking what to do next. For the sullen man who looked like a down-at-heel shopkeeper went by the name of Venn.

And he was believed to be a traitor.

★   ★   ★

That first night in the prison, Betsy could not have slept if she'd tried. As darkness fell she grew more aware of the noise — sounds she'd heard since she had arrived but barely noticed: muffled cries and whispers from beyond the door, not to mention the noises in her own cell. The men slept fitfully; snoring, shifting, sometimes muttering to themselves. The sick woman coughed and wheezed. Betsy lay beside her using her gown as cover for them both, and refusing to think what might be lurking in the foul-smelling straw beneath her. Lice and fleas were the least of her troubles: instead she thought over the instructions Lord Caradoc had given her, only the day before.

'This man Venn practises as an apothecary,'

21

his lordship had said. 'Yet he is more. He's an enemy — a secret Cromwellian, one of those bitter men who yearn for the days of the Good Old Cause. I speak of the Common-wealth, Mistress Brand: a time people like me would like to forget, if others would let us!'

To that, Betsy had merely nodded. Caradoc would have been displeased to know that her views on that subject were more equivocal than those of his class. Furthermore, she could guess what he might think of the republican sympathies Tom Catlin sometimes espoused: not every Englishman viewed the restoration of the Stuart monarchy with joy. But, for better or worse, she had given her word to serve the Crown, and she would keep it. So she'd listened carefully to Caradoc's words: how she must win Venn's trust, by whatever means she could; how she must then *draw him out*, using the cover information given to her, and commit to memory every word that fell from his lips. The man had been imprisoned for a trifling matter, yet he would be on his guard, which meant Betsy would need her very best acting skills. If possible she must learn who his associates were, and of any plots they might be hatching — real or imagined, Caradoc had added with a smile. Though these were uncertain times, the rabble of ex-soldiers, fallen government servants, puritan Fifth Monarchists and other malcontents that made up the republican movement posed no serious threat to England's safety, he insisted. And yet, loyal servants of King Charles never rested . . . and it was at that moment that Betsy had fully realized what she was about to do: act as an informer.

It was an uncomfortable thought. Now, lying in the pitch dark, she forced herself to think of the payment Caradoc had promised her; money which could help her father in his predicament, and perhaps her landlord too. Though his lordship had not been specific about the amount: that, he said, depended upon results. Nor had his parting shot been of much comfort: this was low-level intelligence work, which was assigned to inexperienced operators like Betsy. Though if she proved herself able for the task, then perhaps . . .

Her thoughts were broken by her companion coughing again. Betsy turned over on the pallet, trying to shrug off the feeling of foreboding that had settled upon her. She longed for morning, when prisoners were allowed to walk in the yard, even to mingle. That could be her first opportunity to strike up a conversation with Venn — or so she hoped. Afterwards she would have only her wits to rely on, along with luck.

★ ★ ★

The prison yard was a paved square, with the main building on one side and a high wall around the others. There was no shelter, the disadvantage of which was soon obvious: a drizzle fell, soaking the clothing of those who ventured out. This being but a trifle compared to their other privations however, most people were outside. Betsy saw some moving restlessly about, flitting among their fellows. Others idled by the walls, while some walked the wet flagstones. The gaolers stood in pairs, truncheons as well as keys at their belts. One or two threw meaningful looks at her, which reminded her of the words of her cellmate: it would have been all too easy, she knew, for an attractive woman of her years to gain favours here.

Keeping her face averted, she took a turn of the yard, seeking a moment to approach Venn. She had yet to hear the man speak: that morning, when a pail of gruel had been brought into the cell, he had taken his share without addressing anyone. The other two men, who passed the time dicing and bickering, had seemingly grown accustomed to his ways and ignored him, as he did them. But now she saw Venn alone near the wall, eyes downcast. With a swift look round, she seized her chance and approached him.

'I prefer the Royal Exchange,' she said. 'There's cloisters there — keep the rain off, anyway.'

There was no answer, but she expected none. And, as if oblivious of the other's silence, she chattered on: 'Been here a while, have you? Know when you're getting out? Me, I reckon on two days at most. I've got friends, see. Make a fuss in the right circles . . . ' She tapped her nose. 'I don't carry a poniard under my skirts like some. Don't need to. Never short of places to sleep.' Then, seeing that the other was on the point of walking away, she played her first, all-important card.

'Take Thomas Prynn — drinks in the Red Buck in Coleman Street,' she said in a low voice. 'He's a friend. And he wants to be remembered to you — Mr Venn.' Then she waited, eyes lowered. A moment passed . . . and finally Venn spoke.

'Never heard of him.'

He began to move off, but when Betsy made as if to follow him he stopped. 'I don't want company,' he muttered.

'I know it.' Betsy allowed a note of urgency to creep into her voice. 'And that's not why I'm here.'

But the other was not to be drawn. 'It's

naught to me,' he said. '*You're* naught to me. Go and trouble someone else.'

'You sure about that?' Betsy countered, and was rewarded with a fleeting look of uncertainty on Venn's part. 'I'm not here to waste time,' she said quickly. 'Do you want further tokens?' And to the man's annoyance she took his arm as if to walk with him. He pulled it away, but she ignored the gesture.

'Five of you met at Tom Prynn's house, a fortnight ago,' she breathed, bending close to him. 'You drank a toast — and it wasn't to the King, was it? Shall I say who it was to?'

She was outwardly calm, but it took an effort. She had already used up most of the information, gleaned from informants, with which Caradoc had provided her. Soon she would have to make things up, which would be difficult — but the next moment it was all she could do not to cry out, as a hand was suddenly thrust between her legs.

'Tell me, then.'

Venn pressed his body against hers, while his gaze swept the yard. Then he shoved his face close to Betsy's, so that she smelled his sour breath — and all the while he gripped her crotch through her skirts.

'Who did we drink to?' His voice was soft, but his eyes, when she forced herself to meet them, were hard as flints.

'The Blessed Oliver — our Lord Protector!' She gasped. 'Whose body was cruelly plucked from its grave and desecrated . . . ' She swallowed, fighting the bile that rose in her gorge; and at last, to her relief, Venn withdrew his hand.

'I see you're no Moorfields jilt,' he said. 'So tell me: who's this Thomas Prynn? And who says I was at his house?'

'A man named Phelps told me,' Betsy answered shortly. But she was in turmoil: Venn had only to ask the names of the other men present at that supper, and she would be lost.

'And what's he to you?'

Not for a second had Venn taken his eyes off her, and now she knew no answer she could give would do. The only course she could think of was to throw caution aside, and get angry.

'Damn you and your suspicions!' she hissed. 'I'm on your side, you hard-faced cur! And of course I'm not a whore — didn't you see through that yesterday?'

'Well then, who are you?' Venn's voice was harsh. But Betsy trusted her instincts, and sensed she was halfway to convincing him. She was about to answer, whereupon . . .

'Do you need any help, Mistress?'

She snapped round as a huge figure

lumbered up, dripping with rainwater. At once Venn jerked aside — but too late. A meaty hand shot out, grasped him by his coat collar and almost lifted him off his feet.

'I saw this one grab you, the way no gentleman should've done,' the speaker mumbled, in a deliberate fashion. 'Give me the word now, and I'll break his head.'

She stared up at the giant. He was young: not more than twenty-five, she guessed. His blond locks were plastered to his broad face, which was red with indignation. He wore a leather jerkin like a slaughterman's, over a grimy shirt through which his muscles bulged like cushions.

'Well, see now — there's no need . . . ' she began, dismayed to see a guard watching them. Other people too were looking in their direction. 'It was in jest . . . nothing more.'

The blond colossus, however, did not move. His eyes, which were bright blue, swivelled towards Betsy. 'Jest?' he repeated. 'Didn't look like it.'

'Get off me, Wrestler!' Venn had found his voice at last, and was struggling to pull himself free. 'There's no harm done — this woman's a friend. Ask her yourself!'

But the other wouldn't let go. 'Odd thing for a friend to do, manhandling her like that,' he grunted.

'Er . . . Mr Wrestler.' Betsy put on a smile. 'I'm most grateful — you're a true gallant. But — '

She broke of, for footsteps were approaching. And at last the big man released his captive, whereupon Venn spoke to the warder who hurried up. 'No harm done,' he said. 'Just a tiff.' And with that he walked briskly away. The guard watched him go, then glared at Betsy.

'It's true,' she said. 'I'm new, and I'm — '

'I know who you are!' the warder retorted. 'And *what* you are.' He turned to the wrestler. 'I warned you, this isn't the Bear Garden. Next time, you'll get a lashing!'

'Please,' Betsy forced a smile. 'This man's done nothing wrong — ' But when a truncheon was thrust under her nose, she gulped.

'Don't wrangle with me!' the jailer growled. 'Your kind always bring trouble — get back inside!' And after giving her a shove, he stalked away.

Betsy's heart was pounding. With a last look at the giant she started off, but to her alarm, the man drew close.

'You need to take more care in the King's Bench,' he murmured, in a different voice. 'Folk aren't always what they seem.' And when Betsy looked up sharply, he dropped his voice to a whisper.

'I'm here to help you. My name's Peter Crabb, and I serve the same masters as you. It's I who'll fix your escape when you're ready. All you need do is pass me in the yard, and tell me you saw a white rat.'

And with that he turned abruptly, and was gone.

3

Three more nights passed in the prison, and by the morning of her fifth day, Betsy was close to despair.

It wasn't the smells, the dirt or the hunger, or even the lice she had picked up from her wretched companion that troubled her; she had grown used to those. It wasn't the dark looks she got from her male cellmates, or the leering glances of guards, who wondered why she had yet to offer herself in return for an easier life. Nor was it the sullen silence of Venn, who had not spoken to her since their encounter in the yard. The biggest strain of all, she found, was keeping up her performance as a common trull who'd been unlucky.

In those few days Betsy had learned a lot about prison — and about herself too. So far her resolve had held firm, which was a comfort; thinking about why she was here helped. And if her spirits flagged, especially at night, she managed to revive them in the daytime when she walked the yard, the rain having given way to sunshine and clouds. The lack of food was a worry: she knew she couldn't live like this much longer without growing weak. A greater fear was illness: even if she escaped whatever disease the shrivelled woman had, she might contract another. An alarming number of the prisoners were sick, she discovered.

But what surprised Betsy most was discovering how soon she had tired of her role, and how she yearned to cast it off. For as long as she could remember she had wanted to go upon the stage. And though the life was hard at times, she wished for no other. Her friends, all those she loved apart from Tom Catlin and Peg, were people of the theatre. Even the noisy London audience with their boos and catcalls — they too were a part of her life outside. Now, each time she used the vile, stinking prison jakes, or forced down another mouthful of watery gruel, or scratched her own skin, her desire to stop acting grew. She began to long for home, and for comfort. To wash herself, put on a clean chemise and stockings, and have Peg dress her hair. In a very short time, such luxuries had begun to seem impossibly remote. In fact, thinking of them only made her feel worse. Which was why, on the fourth day, she made a decision. Somehow she must contrive to speak to Venn again soon, and get something out of him: anything that would serve to show Lord Caradoc she'd tried her best. If not, she would have failed; whereupon her only course, it appeared, was to find Peter Crabb and tell him she'd seen a white rat.

Like Venn, the young giant had not been near her since that first morning. And though she saw him outdoors, he always refrained from looking her way. Today — it was Friday: she had been careful to count the days — was no exception.

Eyes down as usual, Betsy moved listlessly around the yard. In her pocket was a crust of hard bread which she'd saved for later. The air was chilly, but she no longer noticed. A layer of grime coated her body, which perhaps protected her a little. She sniffed, realizing she no longer noticed how her clothes stank. And she realized something else: the disdainful sniff she'd adopted for her role had become part of her too. Idly, she wondered if she would lose it when she finally got out of here; assuming she did get out, of course.

She stopped. Suddenly she heard Peg, warning her about *falling into the mulligrubs* — one of her favourite expressions. Then she pictured Tom Catlin in his russet waistcoat . . . and before she knew it, her eyes filled. Neither Tom nor Peg knew where she was. She'd been forced to concoct a tale about staying with an actress friend who was ill — more deceit. Though even those lies paled compared to the ones she had told Betterton and others at the Duke's Theatre — at the thought of which, she bent her head in shame. There in the yard she dug her nails into her palm, while tears ran down her cheeks. She was wiping them with her sleeve when a low voice spoke at her shoulder.

'I had to wait, to be certain. I'd have given it more time, if I could. But we'll speak now, if you're willing.'

Slowly and rather dully, Betsy lifted her head to find herself face to face with Venn. Instead of replying, she merely stared at him.

'You've stayed longer than I thought,' he said. His eyes roved about anxiously. 'You must understand: I can't trust anyone. But I don't have a deal of choice, so we'd better talk. You said you knew Tom Prynn — but how did you know me?'

'The birthmark.' Betsy's mouth was dry. But faintly, almost reluctantly, hope stirred within her. 'On your right hand. The hammerhead.'

Venn nodded quickly. 'And Tom — what can you tell me of him? Is he a dark man, or is he fair? Tall, or short? Speak now — I must be sure of you.'

'He's neither.' Betsy eyed him. 'He's of

34

middling height — and what hair he's got is white. Does that answer you?'

Then she waited. Venn couldn't know that she had just used up the last fact she knew about Thomas Prynn, a man she'd never set eyes on; but mercifully, it was enough.

'Thanks be to God!' Suddenly, the other sagged. 'Your pardon, mistress, for what I did when you accosted me,' he muttered. 'I was angry — I thought you were . . . well, you can guess, can't you?'

Weak with relief, Betsy gave a nod. The change in the man was remarkable: he now looked desperate. She found herself looking round too, almost as anxiously as he had done.

'It's forgotten,' she lied, thinking fast. 'I . . . I've got no news, as such. Have you?'

'I have — and in God's name, I'm mighty glad to tell it!' Quickly Venn took her arm. 'Walk with me,' he said. 'I may not get another chance — likely one in our cell's a trepanner. I thought it was you . . . ' He screwed up his eyes. 'I daren't rest,' he went on. 'I spend the nights with this in my sleeve.' Glancing down, Betsy saw the glint of a pocket dagger, which he quickly stowed away. And though she had no idea what a trepanner was, she kept quiet; the man was as eager to talk as she was to listen. At once, they began walking.

'First, tell me your name,' he said.

'It's Beatrice.' She used the cover name given her by Caradoc.

'Well, Beatrice,' — Venn squeezed her arm — 'I pray you have the means to get word outside — for I can't.'

'I have such,' Betsy told him, hoping he wouldn't ask her for details. But he was too impatient for that.

'Then listen well,' he said, 'for there are matters that must be addressed. I would have passed word on, if I hadn't been taken. You must tell Prynn — or John Phelps, or any of them. They'll have to move swiftly.'

He walked faster, forcing Betsy to keep up. But at what followed, she grew anxious. For soon the man was babbling.

'Our man's still in the Provinces,' he said. 'I believe he's safe, but the country's full of holes — like a Dutch cheese!' He grimaced, which Betsy guessed was the nearest he came to smiling. 'Someone must go there: to Delft, I think. They must find him — he may be dressed as a priest. Tell him the projection's still set for late November, but the venue's been changed from N to D — the Roman Plate. The family will be nearby, but I don't know where.' He turned to Betsy. 'Now do you mark that, Beatrice?'

'I believe so.' Betsy swallowed. 'Your man's

likely in Delft, dressed as a priest. The projection's set for late November, D not N . . . ' She hesitated, whereupon Venn broke in.

'The Roman Plate! Do you have *that*?'

Though she nodded, Betsy's pulse was racing. She was hungry and weak, and her mind was not at its sharpest. 'And the family . . . ?' she began.

'Never mind . . . he won't see them. They'll find him. Now heed me, because this is most important.'

Venn glanced round furtively, and to her alarm she almost laughed. The man looked every inch the stage conspirator, as played by the weakest of actors, but then unlike Betsy, he was no player. She gave a sniff and bent close.

'There are trepanners among the Dutch too — famblers and decoys of every sort,' Venn said. 'Our man must tread more carefully than ever, or it'll all be over before it's begun!'

'Before what's begun?' The words were out before Betsy could stop them. Inwardly she cursed: asking such questions would arouse his suspicions. But to her relief, the other was already talking.

'I've a friend who'll bring news from abroad,' he said. 'Tomorrow — or that's my prayer.' Abruptly he stopped walking. 'Come to me near the end of the day, before lock-up. I should have something then. You must get word out — can you do it?'

For answer Betsy put on her brazen look, flicking her gown aside briefly. 'What I said, when I first came here, it wasn't all bluff,' she murmured. 'I know one of the turnkeys. I can get more than just news out: I can get myself out, if I wish — '

But quickly she broke off. For if she had expected some sort of approval, she found she was badly mistaken. Instead Venn drew back, frowning. 'You would truly play the whore?' He peered at her. 'I could never ask such! These creatures in here would use you cruelly, then cast you aside. Is there no other way?'

She blinked: despite everything, the man was a prude! All at once she recalled Caradoc's term *Cromwellians*. Perhaps some of them hankered for more than the fall of the monarchy, she thought: they wanted a return to a Puritan past, too.

'I pray you, don't judge me so readily,' she answered. 'I merely speak of promising more than I would deliver.' She bit her lip, and sounded resentful. 'Do you not yet trust me?'

For a moment Venn regarded her, before lowering his eyes. 'I do — what choice have

I?' He sighed. 'But tread warily — your gaoler may play you false.' Then, at another thought, he jerked a thumb over his shoulder.

'And beware that oaf, the Wrestler! You know no more of him than you do of anyone else here. Why did he take such pains to play the kindly rescuer — have you thought on that?'

'Well, I confess I had not,' Betsy replied, maintaining a casual air. 'I'll be more careful . . . I was flustered that day.' She put on a hurt look. 'That was your doing, wasn't it?'

At that Venn's face fell, and to Betsy's surprise he slammed his fist against his thigh. 'Again, I ask your pardon,' he said bitterly. 'This pit of wickedness has tainted even me.' He met her eye. 'Find me tomorrow, then whether I have the news I wanted or not, get yourself out by whatever means you can. Otherwise at best you'll sicken, Beatrice. At worst . . . ' He gave a shrug. 'There's no knowing when I'll be set free,' he added. 'The charge was false. And I still swear there's a trepanner here, set to watch me. So trust no one!'

Then turning away from her, he walked off.

Head spinning, she began shuffling about the yard once again. An hour seemed to have passed, though it was only a matter of minutes. But in those minutes, all had changed. She kept her eyes down, for despite everything she was excited. She'd learned more than she ever expected — and if much of it made little sense that was not her fault. Caradoc or others must puzzle out the information — her task, she realized with rising elation, was almost done! One more night and day, and then she would act as Venn had told her: whether he had more information or not, she would find Peter Crabb and give him the word. And soon after that she would be free. It was almost too much. Which was why, when she returned to her cell, she was at pains to look glum, and to work harder than usual at playing a hard-bitten trull.

*   *   *

But on the following afternoon came news that threw everything into disarray.

It was carried on whispers that travelled to every part of the King's Bench: from cell to cell and outside to the yard, where people received it in various ways — some with alarm, some with indifference, others in shocked silence.

Venn had been found with his throat cut.

4

The discovery shook Betsy to the core.

All morning she had wandered the yard, exchanging a word here and there but generally keeping to herself. In the afternoon, however, she grew uneasy when she noticed that Venn seemed to be absent. Her other cellmates were taking the air, like all those whose faces had now become familiar to her. Thus far the day had been no different to any other: the prisoners rising at the opening of the doors; the man in fustian — whom Betsy now knew as Dyer — and his companion grumbling and dicing; Venn silent as ever. Apart from Sarah, the sick woman, as soon as permission was given they had all left the cell.

Betsy had avoided looking for her informant, meaning to wait until the last moment as he'd told her. So that afternoon, when a ripple of excitement began to spread, at first she felt only curiosity. Seeing Dyer standing with another man, both wearing expressions of alarm, she wandered over to them.

'What's ruffling everyone's feathers?' she asked with a sniff . . . then received a surprise. Because for once Dyer didn't answer her in his usual contemptuous tone. Instead, with a shake of his head he delivered the news.

'It's Venn, the silent one,' he said, in a voice of disbelief. 'He's dead — murdered!'

All about the yard, voices were rising. Even those who habitually stayed apart were gathering. Betsy turned aside, trying to collect herself. After that she merely listened, as the grim picture took shape.

Venn had been found in the jakes only minutes ago. He was lying in a pool of blood, and holding a pocket dagger — his own, Betsy surmised. Whoever cut his throat had placed it in his hand, to make it appear that he'd taken his own life. That notion, however, didn't hold water: the prisoner, some warders knew, was left-handed, while the weapon was in his right hand. The one with the birthmark, Betsy thought, still struggling to take in the news. Then she realized someone was addressing her.

'Did you hear me? They'll suspect us — those of his cell!' Dyer was staring at her in fear. 'God knows I detested him, but murder . . . ' He shook his filthy locks. 'It'll bring disaster upon us all!'

'Don't talk like a fool.' Quickly Betsy summoned her anger, fighting off the fear that threatened to grip her. 'We've been outdoors the whole day . . . all save Sarah, and she's so weak she can hardly stand, let alone kill anyone.'

'Yet people will point the finger!' Dyer countered. 'What of you, for one? You were talking to him yesterday, walking arm-in-arm, I heard. He's never said a word to anyone before — what was it about?'

Though her heart jumped, Betsy's reply was swift. 'What do you think?' she snapped. 'If I don't do business here soon, I'll starve.' She threw him a scornful look. 'But don't go thinking I'd let *you* near me!' And with a toss of her head, she swept away.

But by the wall she stopped, gazing across the yard. Most of the guards had gone indoors, while those who remained were tense, gripping their truncheons. Then she saw the figure of Peter Crabb, standing a head taller than those near him, and at once she knew what to do. Indeed, it was the only thing to do, now that her reason for staying here had been taken away, and in such a terrible manner. Picking up her skirts, she circled around until she stood in the big man's field of vision, then caught his eye.

'Wrestler!' she called. 'Over here!'

The other men in the group glanced at her, before resuming their conversation. With a casual air, Peter Crabb left them and ambled towards her, whereupon her words spilled out.

'I've seen a white rat,' she breathed. 'Can you get me — ?' Then she yelped, as without warning the giant grabbed her arm and pulled her roughly aside.

'You dirty blowze!' he cried. 'I should have steered clear of you — now leave me be!' With that he pushed her away, but as he released her he lurched, as if he had lost his balance.

'Tonight,' he whispered. 'Be ready!' Then he lumbered off.

★   ★   ★

That night, her fifth in the King's Bench, was the longest Betsy had endured since she had arrived. Then, she expected as much — though she had not expected the silence.

The death of a prisoner was hardly a rarity — but cold-blooded murder was, especially by daylight. *Trust no one,* Venn had told her; the sentiment had bitter currency now. Presumably the murderer was still within these walls — was that why the place was eerily quiet? There had been no further news since the discovery of the body; nor were there whisperings along the passage this night. Apart from Sarah's coughing there was

44

no sound in her cell either, save for the rustling of straw. The death had stunned them all, but through the evening nobody spoke of it. Even Dyer and his younger companion, whose name was Gorton, barely addressed each another. Instead they had lain down, huddled on their pallets against the walls, each seemingly busy with his own thoughts.

Venn's pallet had been taken away, his corner left bare. Those in the cell shunned the spot, as if the ghost of the dead man might haunt it. But after dark, Sarah, who had heard the grisly news without comment, spoke to Betsy.

'It happens in here,' she whispered hoarsely. 'There's nowhere to hide. Them with grudges or scores to pay off — they can always take their revenge, if they've a mind.'

The two of them sat against the wall, pressed together for warmth. Betsy was on edge, and could not help flinching when Sarah's hand sought hers in the dark. But she took it, feeling its coarseness, and the bony fingers that closed about her own.

'I'll be next, my duck.' Sarah's voice was thick with phlegm. 'There's doom in this cell. So listen to me: don't keep 'em waiting any longer, or they'll come for you.'

'For me?' Betsy echoed. 'Who do you mean?'

'The turnkeys,' was her reply. 'You've stretched your luck, girl. They won't wait for ever. Lift your skirts . . . ' Sarah coughed, her voice weakening. 'You can get yourself took to a better room. You'll have food, fresh linen — I told you, anything you want . . . ' She began wheezing, which prompted a curse from across the room.

'Shut your mouth, you vile heap of rags!' Dyer spat his venom through the dark. 'Let me sleep, can't you?' Angrily he turned on his pallet. From Gorton there was no sound.

After a moment Sarah withdrew her hand, but before letting go, Betsy squeezed it. She was moved, more than she could have foreseen. This dying woman, whose crime Betsy never learned, had been her only comfort. She would have liked to tell Sarah that she *was* getting out — this very night, if Crabb was as good as his word. Instead she touched her companion on the shoulder, bidding her lie down. Then she settled back to wait.

It was an ordeal, of course. As on her first night in the cell she did not sleep, tired as she was. Doggedly she remained by the wall for hours, until finally, with the men snoring, she judged the moment was right to move. Carefully she rolled off the pallet, shivering at the touch of cold stone. And after that, she crawled.

She had no difficulty in finding her way, for like the others she knew every square inch of the room; every mark on the walls, each crack in the flagstones. Soon, with only a little rustling of straw, she had manoeuvred herself to a place beside the door. And there she sat, hunched in her gown, hands clasped about her knees.

That last hour, she decided, was the worst. Yet she withstood it, strengthened by hope, until she sensed that dawn was approaching. At times she had to fight despair, thinking of all that might go wrong. Could she be certain Crabb would arrange everything as he'd claimed? Could she even trust him? She pictured the big man as she had first seen him, bearing down upon Venn — which brought the latter's words back: *You know no more of him than you do of anyone else here . . .*

She stiffened: she could not afford to think like this. Savagely she jabbed her palm with her nails; it had helped her gather her wits before, and it did so now. Venn was dead and gone, she told herself through the pain. But what he had told her — his testimony, as she thought of it — was burned on her memory.

Once again, as she had done many times

47

that night, Betsy went over his garbled account as if rehearsing a speech for the theatre. And it was that which helped her endure the final minutes, when at last the moment came for her deliverance. Though it came not with stealth, as she had somehow imagined, but with a bang on the door only inches from her ear, and the rasp of the lock. The door opened, waking everyone, and a voice called out.

'Where's the harlot?'

A lantern's beam swept the room, blinding Betsy as it fell upon her, then a shadow loomed behind it. 'Get up, woman. You're coming with me!' And before she could move, the guard seized her shoulder and pulled her to her feet, slamming her against the door.

The pain made her gasp, before one thought overwhelmed her: she was getting out. And the next moment, to her own surprise, she was shouting! Only later did she realize that she had played her role so long, it must have become second nature.

'Get off!' she yelled. 'I'll spike your eyes, you stinking rogue! Where are you taking me — ?'

A crack across the mouth silenced her. Tasting blood, she was shoved outside. The cell door slammed, the lock squealed, and she was being dragged through the echoing passages of the King's Bench, blinking yet wild with elation — until a sudden pang of doubt struck her, chilling her to the bone.

What if this isn't Crabb's doing? she asked herself. *Suppose Sarah was right: the turnkeys are going to violate me . . .* and to her dismay, her legs buckled. But even as they slipped from under her, and the guard cursed at the sudden weight, she heard a voice that wasn't his. In fact, it seemed familiar . . . She struggled to right herself, but her strength had gone. Half-dazed with fear and pain, she found herself set on her feet by a pair of strong arms, while from nearby came the squeal of a bolt being slid. She was yanked through a narrow doorway, and a gout of cold air hit her. She was outside! Then a door slammed, and she was in darkness. Breathlessly she looked round, to see a huge shape leaning over her.

'It's me, Crabb — you're free.'

Shakily Betsy reached out and, as if to make sure he was real, she touched him. 'Free?' she muttered vaguely. 'Then . . . why did the warder have to be so rough?'

'To make it look right,' came the reply. 'Are your legs working now? There's a boat waiting.'

A boat? she struggled to take it in. They were in a narrow street, in the shadow of the prison wall. 'Where are we going?' she asked.

'To Tower Wharf,' Crabb told her. 'Lean on me if you like . . . but come on!'

★　★　★

The night was cold. Betsy shivered in her filthy gown, but she didn't care. Freedom, after those days in the King's Bench, was the sweetest thing she had ever tasted. Dawn was breaking as, walking at the best pace she could manage, she and her rescuer threaded their way through the grimy streets of Southwark, to emerge by the river. To her left the bridge loomed, while across the Thames lights twinkled . . . and at the sight of it, she could have wept.

But there was no time to give vent to such feelings. As Crabb had promised, a boat was waiting at a jetty, its stern lantern lit. Still shivering, Betsy clambered down the steps, grateful for the hands of the waterman who helped her aboard. She sat down, lurching as the young giant's sudden weight almost capsized them. But soon he was seated beside her, exchanging words with the boatman. The man put his oar to the jetty and pushed, and in a moment the vessel was propelled into the current. Then they were out on the river and at last, Betsy sagged with relief.

'I can only thank you, Wrestler,' she said. 'Though it's not enough — not by a mile.' She looked up at Crabb, as a thought struck her. 'You didn't tell me you were coming too . . . ' Then she recalled his words, on her first day in the prison. 'But if you serve the same masters as me — '

'Not now, sweet Sister.'

Crabb bent close to her, gripping her arm. He was smiling, but his eyes flew to the boatman who, head down under his hat, was heaving at the oars. 'We'll talk when we get home,' the young man went on. 'You're weary, and our father's waiting.'

Weak though she was, Betsy understood; and suddenly a weight came down upon her — one she had thought she was free of. 'As you wish, Brother,' she answered. Closing her eyes, she allowed herself to lean against his solid bulk, as unyielding as a tree-trunk. Then, as so often in recent days, she chided herself silently for her carelessness.

She wasn't Betsy Brand, not yet: she was an agent of the Crown, if only a temporary one. Secrecy was her watchword and, as in the prison, she could not let her guard slip. *Trust no one* . . . now Venn's words filled her with foreboding.

But later, when they reached Tower Wharf and climbed up to the quay, she began to feel better. In fact, by the time she was accompanying Peter Crabb through the London streets, with chimney smoke swirling and people already astir, her spirits had risen considerably. Leaving the riverside, they walked by Tower Street to Mark Lane, then turned into Crutched Friars. From there they passed through the warren of alleys that gave on to Fenchurch Street, before rounding the corner into Leadenhall. There at last, outside a very ordinary looking house, Crabb halted and turned to her.

'We're here,' he said. And only then, standing in the early morning light, did he observe Betsy properly for the first time. 'There's blood at your mouth,' he added.

'It's no matter.' She glanced at the house, which was shuttered. 'Where have you brought me?'

Instead of answering, Crabb rapped on the door. He rapped twice, waited, repeated the pattern, then knocked four times. 'It's just a house we use,' he said at last. 'They'll have clothes for you, and water for washing. After you've supped and rested you'll be ready to talk.'

'Talk to who?' Betsy asked absently — then gave a start as the door opened. A young maidservant in a plain apron and cap stood there, bobbing nervously.

'Welcome, sir and madam,' she said. 'Your rooms are ready.' With a polite smile she drew back, allowing them to enter. Betsy found herself in a flagged hallway with a staircase. Dog-tired, and only too aware of how she looked as well as smelled, she faced Crabb.

'Did you speak of clothes, and water for washing?'

'I did.' All at once, the young man smiled: not the warning smile he had used on the boat, but a real smile. He even allowed himself a sigh of relief: that of a man who has faced a daunting task, and seen it through. Turning to the servant, he opened his mouth — then gave a start.

Fortunately he possessed quick reactions; or so Betsy would think later. For the present all she did was stagger and fall, while her surroundings swam dizzily about her. But before she could hit the floor she was caught, by the same pair of strong arms that had brought her from the King's Bench prison to safety.

And after that she was dimly aware of being carried, before blackness settled over her, and a blissful oblivion.

5

Betsy slept heavily, finally waking with a jolt. She looked about . . . then remembering that she was no longer in the prison cell, sank back upon the pillow and gave herself up to overwhelming relief. But a moment later she tensed: something was odd. She felt her body, and found she was wearing only a linen shift. Uneasily, she sat up.

She was in a small room with drawn curtains, through which a streak of daylight showed. The only furniture was a chair, piled with what looked like bedding. Turning the coverlet back, she got up quickly . . . too quickly. Her legs wobbled, and with a thud she sat down on bare floorboards. And there she stayed, leaning back against the bed, until the door opened.

'Is anything wrong, mistress?'

Feeling rather foolish, Betsy looked up to see someone walk in. The figure went to the window and pulled back the curtains, revealing herself as the young maidservant who had admitted her to the house. 'I heard a noise,' she said. 'Are you hurt?'

'I don't believe so.' Betsy managed a smile.

'I'm just a little weak . . . would you mind helping me?'

The servant came forward and took her arm. Putting her other hand on the bed, Betsy heaved herself to her feet and stood, somewhat shakily.

'My thanks.' She eyed the girl. 'Was it you who washed me?'

The other nodded. 'You were insensible. I had to cut your clothes off before I could soap you. I burned them — they were fit for naught else.'

'Again, thanks.' Betsy glanced at the chair, which she now saw was heaped with women's clothing. 'Are those for me?'

'Yes, mistress. It's only fripperers' ware, but clean.' Moving to the pile, the girl took a petticoat and held it up to the light. 'If you rummage, you'll find garments to suit . . . there are shoes here too.' She looked round. 'You'll be hungry — there's a herring pie in the kitchen.'

As if in answer, Betsy's stomach rumbled like thunder. 'That sounds splendid.' She glanced out of the window and saw that she was on the first floor of the house. From below, street noises rose.

'Wrestler . . . did he carry me up here?' she asked.

'Mr Crabb's downstairs, with Mr Lee,' the

girl replied, nodding. 'Mr Lee has let you rest, but I wouldn't keep him waiting much longer. It's past two of the clock — you've slept for over seven hours.' With a shy smile she started for the door, whereupon Betsy stayed her.

'Who is Mr Lee?'

'He's our master. An important man.'

'And your name?'

'It's Eleanor,' came the reply.

Betsy gazed at her absently. Only now were yesterday's events coming into sharper focus. She put a hand to her lip, and found it was swollen.

'I cleaned the dry blood from your mouth,' Eleanor told her. 'I've some witch-hazel downstairs, will help it heal.'

'You're a treasure, Eleanor,' Betsy said, much to the girl's embarrassment. 'I'll dress and come down to the kitchen. Then I suppose I had better go to Mr Lee.'

'Indeed you must,' the girl said. 'And I'd choose a different garb from the one you had. Mr Lee's very proper.'

With that she hurried out. Thoughtfully, Betsy moved to the chair and began to pick through the clothes.

★   ★   ★

The Important Man's real name was not Lee, of course; she had already suspected that. When she found out who he was, however, she was surprised and impressed.

'Lord Caradoc speaks highly of you, mistress,' he said, peering down at her; he was a tall man. 'Yet it remains for me to judge whether you've earned the trust placed in you — do you follow?'

Stiffly, Betsy signalled assent. She had rested, been washed clean, dressed herself in clean clothes and eaten a good meal; things she had longed for inside the King's Bench. Yet now, seated in this candlelit room with the windows shuttered, she was ill-at-ease. The well-dressed, imposing man in the black periwig, who had received her somewhat coolly, was one reason: the other was the presence of Peter Crabb, sitting in the corner. He no longer played the dim-witted bruiser Betsy had known in the prison. Now he was regarding her keenly, which made her uncomfortable.

'Ask me what you will, sir,' she said, meeting Mr Lee's eye. His accent was unfamiliar, though she knew it hailed from the far north. 'For I've much to tell . . . ' But she broke off when he held up a hand.

'Soon,' he said. 'First, I have things to say to you.'

He was standing near the window, where he had been since Betsy entered. Now he moved to a small table on which lay papers and writing materials, and sat down beside it.

'I'm Joseph Williamson,' he said. And when Betsy showed her surprise, he added, 'I see the name's known to you.'

'You're Lord Arlington's deputy,' she murmured, naming one of the Cabal — the King's closest ministers.

'His Under-Secretary,' Williamson corrected. 'But you will know me always as Mr John Lee.'

Putting on a respectful expression, Betsy gave silent thanks to Eleanor for telling her to wear suitable clothes. This severe man had no time for flummery, she thought, and no doubt little for actresses. She could only hope the plain russet gown and black bertha would serve. She glanced at Peter Crabb as another thought struck her — then saw that Williamson had anticipated her.

'You guess correctly,' he said. 'Crabb is not this man's real name. As you will use that of Beatrice . . . provided, that is, you continue in my service.'

'*Your* service, sir?' she echoed. 'I thought I was in the employ of Lord Caradoc.'

'Then you were mistaken,' came the swift reply. 'His lordship is a loyal friend, and has often helped our office in the past, but the gathering of intelligence is my task.'

'You mean . . . spying?' Betsy blurted out.

A frown crossed Williamson's brow. 'I advise discretion, Beatrice,' he murmured. He picked up a sheet of paper and ran his eyes down it. 'However, Crabb's report is favourable. You have acquitted yourself well inside the King's Bench — far better than I expected.'

Betsy looked at Peter Crabb, who threw her a brief smile. 'Some of us had work to do while you slept,' he said — whereupon she sat up sharply.

'Is that what you were doing inside the prison?' she asked. 'Spying on me?'

Williamson answered instead. 'It's not important,' he said shortly. 'Crabb can answer your questions later, if he's a mind. You and he will be spending some time together — that is, if you agree to work for me.'

But now, Betsy was forming a picture. 'Do you mean to tell me the days I spent in that vile place were merely a test of some kind?' she asked. 'Then, what of Venn? And what of — ?'

The other raised his hand again. 'Please. I know what you have endured, and yet — '

'Do you indeed, sir?' In spite of the man's status, Betsy's temper was rising. 'Do you also understand the dangers I faced there? Exposed to sickness, let alone hunger and cruelty — '

'Enough!' Williamson was impatient now. 'I know very well what the prisons are like,' he snapped. 'As do my agents, most of whom have suffered far worse hardships than you in the service of His Majesty — even paid with their lives.'

Silence fell. With an effort Betsy calmed herself, whereupon the man continued in a softer tone, 'Believe me, mistress, when I tell you that your stay in the King's Bench was more than a test — far more. I'm not so well supplied with agents that I can afford to waste such opportunities as may arise.' He paused, then: 'You spoke with the conspirator, Venn. Are you ready to tell me all that he told you?'

'I suppose I am,' Betsy answered after a moment. 'Although I believe I could have learned more, had he not been murdered. He was awaiting important news, he said. But I've committed every word he said to memory.'

'Good!' The under-secretary leaned forward so suddenly that Betsy blinked. There was a gleam in his eye that seemed out of character. This man relished his work, she thought. On impulse, she spoke up.

'Why did you say Mr Crabb and I would be spending time together, if I agreed to work for you?'

Williamson paused, then, 'Are you telling me that you would consider doing so?'

Now Betsy was silent. All of a sudden, the situation seemed fantastical. Only hours ago she had been sat in a damp, filthy cell, shivering with cold. Now she seemed to be discussing her future with a member of the government.

'Would I have to go to prison again?' she asked finally, to which the other shook his head.

'That isn't what I had in mind.'

'Then, what did you have in mind?'

'A very different role — one you would no doubt find more congenial.' Williamson glanced briefly at Crabb. 'But the choice is yours. After you've given me your intelligence, you may take your payment, leave here and return to your life in the theatre — if you must. Though you'll remain sworn to secrecy with regard to all that's passed — on pain of death.'

'And . . . if I were willing to continue in your employ?'

'Then you would make me a contented man. Especially as I have no other female agents at the present. You could prove

61

invaluable . . . And with regard to payment, you would not find me ungenerous.'

'Indeed?' Betsy lowered her gaze. Thoughts of her father's troubles, and those of Tom Catlin, flitted across her mind to be replaced by another notion. Despite all she had endured — including the tiresome role of a Moorfields trull — she felt excited. Williamson was speaking of acting, but not for an audience of city fops. Nor would this be acting from words penned by others, but those fashioned by herself to meet many occasions — occasions in which failure could mean real danger. She swallowed, and looked up to find both men watching her closely.

'I would like a sum in advance,' she said, making her voice flat. 'Paid not to me, but to Mistress Mary Luxton in Chelsea. She is my sister.' Then, taking Williamson's brief wave of his hand for assent, she added, 'Upon that, Mr Lee . . . '

'Upon that?' Williamson's tone matched hers.

'We are in agreement,' she finished.

'Then, you have my word,' he said. 'And if that concludes the wrangling, I'd now like to hear all that Venn told you before his untimely death — and I mean everything. Is that clear . . . Beatrice?'

'It is, Mr Lee,' Betsy replied. And with that,

she began her testimony.

It took less time than she thought. To her relief, she found that most of it made sense to the under-secretary. Moreover, as she recounted Venn's hurried words to her from memory, the man's interest grew until he was hanging on every word. When she had finished, however, he sat back abruptly.

'This news he expected, from outside the prison. Have you no clue as to what it concerned, or who the bringer might be?'

Betsy shook her head. 'He spoke of a friend. I thought it might be a gaoler.'

'Then the pathway isn't mapped — indeed, it's as dark as pitch.' Williamson frowned at Crabb, as if it were somehow his fault. 'If only we knew who killed the wretch, we'd at least have a trail to follow. Could you learn nothing from your turnkey?'

Crabb shook his head. 'No known associate of Venn's was in the prison,' he said. 'I'd swear to that. As for the guards . . . ' He shrugged. 'I wouldn't trust a single one of them.'

Williamson's eyes shifted towards Betsy, but he wasn't looking at her. She sensed a sharp mind, sifting and calculating; and at last he seemed to reach a decision.

'Well, then — you know where you must go next?' he said, turning back to Crabb. The younger man nodded, though he looked far from pleased.

'Will you instruct Beatrice in her part?' he began, 'Or — '

'You can do that on the journey,' Williamson answered. 'It will give you time to practise your roles. I'll send Eleanor too.' He faced Betsy, who was now feeling quite alarmed.

'Journey?' she repeated. 'Where am I — where are we going?'

'Isn't that obvious?' Williamson retorted. 'We need to find this bogus priest, discover what mischief he's planning — this *projection* Venn spoke of. You must take ship for the United Dutch Provinces — there are boats from Dover. You'll go as a gentlewoman, with the others as your servants. You should leave in three days at the most.'

'So soon?' Betsy started. 'But if I'm to play a lady, I must make ready. I'll need clothes . . . I should go home.'

'You have three days,' the under-secretary repeated. 'Crabb will meet you, at a place of your choosing. He'll have a purse of guilders, and my instructions, which you should study when you reach your destination. Now, if you've no further questions, I have much to do!' And with that dismissal he looked away. Flipping open an inkwell, he seized a quill, dipped it and at once began writing.

In silence, Betsy rose. Crabb was already on his feet. Moving to the door, he opened it and made a bow. 'Your servant, madam,' he said gravely. Whereupon with barely a glance, she walked outside to the hallway.

'Shall I find a chair to take you home?' The blond giant closed the door and stood by respectfully. Yet when Betsy turned to him she saw no mockery in his gaze — instead, she found something quite different.

Cods! she breathed. *As if I didn't have enough to fret about* . . . but keeping a straight face, she nodded. Once he had gone out, however, she went to the staircase and sat down heavily on the bottom step.

She was filled with foreboding, though not by what she had seen in Peter Crabb's eyes. The young man, it seemed, was besotted with her, but that was something she could deal with. Far more alarming just now, was her rash decision in agreeing to become a spy for King Charles's Government!

In three days she was to travel to the Dutch Provinces as a gentlewoman. She would have to make more excuses to Tom Catlin and Peg, and send a message to Betterton . . . She gulped. She had never been on a ship in her life — never left England. For a moment, she thought about going back into the room and telling Williamson that she had changed her mind — that the whole thing was absurd.

But she didn't.

Instead, three days later, she found herself crossing the grey, freezing expanse of the North Sea on a heaving vessel, racked with a violent nausea. And as if that weren't enough, when she finally staggered ashore after dark onto the quayside of a small West Flanders town, there was no one to meet her.

Tired and weak from sickness, she stood on the windswept cobblestones huddled in a fur-trimmed gown, watching the last of the other passengers disembark. Finally, when those who remained were only seamen speaking incomprehensible Dutch, she faced Peter Crabb and Eleanor.

'Well,' she muttered, 'I take a dim view of the welcome. Now what's to be done?'

6

The inn at Nieuwpoort was small, but comfortable enough. While the two women waited at the harbour, Peter Crabb went to find accommodation, returning quickly. There was a place not far away, he said; the innkeeper even spoke some English. So in better spirits the party, which now consisted of a well-dressed lady and her baggage-laden servants, made their way by quiet streets to a steeply gabled house on one side of a little square. Once indoors, Betsy and Eleanor retired to their chamber while Crabb went down to order supper.

In the room, which was dominated by the large bed, Eleanor began unpacking for the night. Because of Betsy's seasickness, there had been little time for the two to speak on the journey. But the girl rarely said more than she needed to in any case, and appeared content with her place as a lady's maid. Her bed would be a truckle, which pulled out from beneath Betsy's. While she busied herself, Betsy sat down by the window and broke the seal on her instructions from Williamson. But, as she peered at the sheet bearing her new master's scrawled hand-writing, she began to frown.

Once memorized, this paper is to be burned. Its contents may be discussed only with no. 76 (Crabb) and the man who will make himself known to you. He is no. 51, and may use the name Girvan.

Girvan knows the country and speaks the language. You will appraise him of what you know: that is, all you learned from Venn. You and he must then work together, travelling as husband and wife, to discover the priest, whether he be in Delft or elsewhere. You may pretend republican sympathies, as you did to gain Venn's trust.

Once the Projector is found, Girvan will deal with matters of interrogation. If he has further need of you, you must remain in the Provinces until all tasks are completed. Then you will return home at once and come directly to me. On no account must you go to The Hague, or have any dealings with His Majesty's ambassador. Report only to me.

God keep you safe.
John Lee

Slowly Betsy lowered the document. Then, aware that Eleanor was watching, she looked up. 'It seems I'm to acquire a husband,' she said quietly.

'That's no surprise, madam,' came the reply. 'It's the easiest way to travel.'

'Is it?'

'A woman alone here would attract attention,' Eleanor said. 'Some hide among the Papists, even pretend to be nuns. But we may need to move about, so . . . ' She gave a shrug.

'Then, where's this man who was to meet us?' Betsy wondered. 'We can't stay here in Newport, or whatever it's called.'

'I believe he'll come, sooner or later.' The girl was moving towards the door. 'Now I'll go and find water for washing.'

'No — wait.' Betsy got up, went to the fireplace where a small fire blazed, and placed Williamson's letter on it. As it burned to ashes, she turned to Eleanor.

'I don't know how much you've been told about me,' she said, 'but I'm still finding my way in this venture, hence . . . ' She sighed. 'I'll confess I've never taken much interest in anything outside the theatre, apart from scandals, the doings of the King and his circle. I see that I've much to learn so, will you instruct me?'

'Of course, if you wish it.' Eleanor looked taken aback. 'But I know no more than you. Mr Crabb's the one. He would have spoken to you on the boat — '

'Had I not fallen ill, soon after we left Dover,' Betsy finished, with a wry look. 'At least you and Wrestler were spared that indignity.'

Eleanor gave one of her quick smiles. 'I've been on a ship before,' she said. 'As for Crabb, he's never sick — he's like a slab of stone. Now, I'll fetch the water.'

She went out, whereupon Betsy went to the bed and lay down. Supper on its way and servants doing her bidding: this was a role more to her liking, she thought.

But the peace was to be of short duration.

In the middle of the night she was woken by a hand gripping her shoulder. She started, and found Eleanor bending over her. The girl was holding a candle, its flame trembling.

'You have a visitor,' she said with a shiver.

'At this hour?' Blinking, Betsy sat up — then started at the sight of another figure looming behind. But it was only Peter Crabb.

'The fellow's outside,' he said. 'I told him you needed to rest, but he wouldn't wait. He's the one who should have been at the quay, says he was delayed, but I smell strong drink on his breath.' The young man was tense, Betsy realized, bending his head to avoid the low ceiling, while carefully avoiding looking at her in her shift.

'Did he give a name?' she asked.

'He refused,' Crabb replied stiffly. 'Said he'd speak to the English lady, not her lackey. But I wouldn't let him come in here — nor will I, unless you order it.'

'Well, if he's the one we were expecting, I suppose I have little choice,' Betsy said. 'Give me a few minutes.'

With a nod Crabb went out, whereupon voices were heard from beyond the door: his and another's, somewhat indignant. Hurriedly Betsy got out of bed, found a nightgown and pulled it on, then sat in the chair by the window. Having lit more candles and gowned herself, Eleanor stood beside her.

There was a knock, and Crabb put his head round the door. At a sign from Betsy he came in — only to be brushed aside by a bulky figure in a bombazine cloak, who strode into the room hat in hand. At sight of Betsy he made an elaborate bow, so low that his periwig almost brushed the floor.

'Your servant, madam!'

Straightening up, the newcomer favoured her with a broad smile. 'My heartfelt apologies for not attending on you sooner. I

71

was detained by important business.'

There was a brief silence, broken by Crabb closing the door and bolting it. There the colossus stood with arms folded, regarding the visitor stonily. Eleanor too was watchful.

'Then you are excused, sir,' Betsy regarded the gentleman — for such he appeared — with all the dignity she could muster. 'Might I know your name?'

'Of course — I am Captain Marcus Mullin!' Still smiling, he looked deliberately at Eleanor and held out his hat. After a moment's hesitation the girl came forward, bobbed and took it from him.

'Well, Captain Mullin, may I offer you some wine?' Betsy indicated a jug and cups on the table, where they had remained since supper.

'Thank you, but I'll pass,' the other replied, with a disdainful look. 'The Flanders wine is quite unpalatable.' He glanced round, unfastening his cloak, then threw it on the bed where Eleanor had placed his hat. Seeing that the only other seat was a plain stool, he caught it up with one hand, brought it over and sat himself down facing Betsy. Across the room, Crabb stirred.

'So, how was your journey, madam?' Mullin's eyes found Betsy's. He was a handsome man, sporting a thin moustache of

72

the kind favoured by the King. 'The crossing can be rough at this time of year . . . I hope you were not discommoded.'

'Not at all, sir,' Betsy answered. She was tense, for she realized that she had no idea how to proceed. To her relief, Peter Crabb spoke up.

'We're friends of Mr John Lee,' he said, taking a step forward. 'As are you — or so I believe. Perhaps you'd oblige me by giving the password.'

A perplexed look came over Mullin's features. 'Password?' he echoed, swivelling round to face Crabb. 'I don't know what you mean, fellow.'

The young giant bristled; and now the tension between the two men filled the room. Betsy and Eleanor exchanged glances.

'This man goes by the name of Crabb, sir,' she said quickly. 'He also bears a number . . . seventy-six. Would you like to give me yours?'

'Oh, that!' Turning back to Betsy, Mullin waved a hand airily. 'It's fifty-one . . . or it was, last time I used it. Does that satisfy you?'

'It might,' she answered. 'Perhaps, now that you're here at last, you'll tell me what orders Mr Lee has given you. You do have orders, I presume?'

'I might.' Mullin's smile was back.

'However, I don't propose to discuss such matters in front of your servants. Would you care to dismiss them?'

Betsy threw a swift look at Crabb, but at once Eleanor spoke. 'We'll wait outside, madam,' she said. 'If you have need, just call.'

With that she moved to the door, where she stopped. Crabb stood rigid, and Betsy recalled her words: he did indeed look like some figure of stone. Wordlessly he met Betsy's gaze — and her heart softened. He would protect her, he seemed to say, and she knew it was true, as she knew he could have picked up Marcus Mullin and squeezed the life from him. But when she nodded, the young man turned aside, unbolted the door and threw it open. In a moment he and Eleanor had gone out, leaving Betsy alone with her visitor.

'Well, what a performance your friends gave!' To Betsy's discomfort Mullin relaxed, stretching out his legs — and delivered the *coup de grace.* 'In fact it was almost as good as one of yours — Mistress Brand. How's dear Betterton, by the way?'

For a moment Betsy froze, then realization swept over her.

'Oh, cods . . . ' She raised her eyes to the ceiling. 'I should have known: you're an actor!'

'I was,' came the reply. 'Played at the King's, a few years back. You weren't on the stage then, but I've seen you since at the Duke's. You were a convincing trull, as I recall.'

'Do you indeed!' Feeling an utter fool, Betsy glared. 'And who are you? For you're surely not a captain of anything, I'll wager — any more than your name's Girvan, or Mullin!'

'Ah, there you're mistaken.' Mullin laughed — the sort of hearty laugh only actors used. Then abruptly he got to his feet. 'Perhaps I'll risk a mouthful of wine after all,' he said, moving to the table. He picked up the jug and sniffed at it. 'Better than horse-piss, I suppose . . . Will you partake, too?' Without waiting for a reply, he poured two cups and brought them over. In spite of herself, Betsy accepted one and took a fortifying drink.

'You inferred that I was mistaken,' she said drily.

'Oh, yes . . . ' The other sat down again, drank and pulled a face. 'Vile, as I thought!' He grinned at Betsy. 'I *am* a captain. Before I went upon the stage I was a captain of horse . . . it proved very useful, in certain roles.'

'Villains?' Betsy suggested. 'Or charlatans, perhaps?'

'Naturally! But nowadays I act for King

and Country . . . as I see you do, Brand. Did Lord Caradoc recruit you?'

Though fuming, Betsy managed to keep her anger in check. 'That's not your affair,' she said icily. 'And I'll ask you now to tell me what orders Mr Lee gave you, so that I know — '

'Mr Lee?' Mullin broke in. 'You mean Williamson, the bootlicker.' He gave a snort. 'There's no need to work from the book with me, Brand. I've been at this game too long.'

'It's *Mistress* Brand!' Betsy snapped; then her face fell. 'I mean, it's Beatrice. And I'm to call you Girvan, I think.'

'Oh?' The other sat up. 'Surely your orders say otherwise. When a male and female agent work together it's usual for them to pass as husband and wife, to allay any suspicions. Which would make us Captain and Mrs Mullin, would it not?'

An uneasy feeling was stealing over Betsy. 'I suppose it would,' she began. 'But even if that were your real name — '

'It's as good as any other, isn't it?' Mullin drained the last of his wine, made a sound expressive of disgust and plonked the cup down on the floor. 'Well now, *Mistress* Brand,' he went on, 'while I'm tempted to ask for the latest theatre gossip, I suppose we'd better get down to work, don't you?'

'Not just yet,' Betsy answered coolly. 'Firstly, I'd like to clarify my role — '

'You mean, as my wife?' The other raised his eyebrows. 'Would that present difficulties?'

But it was his turn to be startled as Betsy jumped to her feet. 'Don't try your tiring-room tricks on me, Mullin!' She snapped. 'I'm nobody's jilt — and if you think we're sharing a bed, it's you who is mistaken!'

'My dear woman, how badly you must think of me.' Mullin put on a shocked expression. 'Your person will be perfectly safe in my company — you have my word upon it.'

'Your word?' Betsy echoed. 'I doubt it's worth a fig. You weren't here when we arrived. Instead you turn up in the dead of night smelling of brandy, and strut about as if you owned the place — which we both know was merely a performance. Furthermore Peter Crabb's not my servant, he's an agent, with whom you're already at loggerheads with — '

'That hulking brute?' Mullin sniffed. 'It's jealousy on his part. He wishes he were the one to play your husband — as I think you've probably guessed.'

'Even if that were so, such ill feeling could

hamper us in our task, could it not?' Betsy countered. But under Mullin's sardonic gaze she sat down again. The fire had gone out, and the room was chilly. Pulling her gown about her neck, she tried to compose herself, whereupon the other sighed.

'Well now: regarding my lateness, I received word of your arrival only yesterday,' he said. 'I was in Bruges, which is why I couldn't get here sooner — the roads are muddy. As for the performance, I thought I'd begin as we must continue. Now, shall we proceed? I gather you have intelligence to share — even rumours of a conspiracy?'

With an effort, Betsy composed herself. 'I spoke to one of the Projectors in prison,' she said. 'A man named Venn. He might have told me more, but he was murdered — the very next day.'

'How unfortunate,' Mullin observed, frowning. 'No doubt one of his fellows got to him, after you were seen talking.'

'What do you mean?' Betsy blinked. 'Are you saying — ?'

'That you caused his death?' He gave a shrug. 'It's a common enough occurrence. Men like Venn live on fear, panicking at every trifle. They're more afraid of each other than they are of the Pope!' He gave a snort of laughter, then his frown deepened. 'And yet, this smacks of something bold, I'll admit. You'd better tell me what you know. Then I'll decide where to start looking.'

But Betsy was barely listening. Instead she pictured Venn, wild-eyed, pouring out his testimony in the prison yard. She heard Dyer, telling her she and Venn had been seen arm-in-arm . . . and now she faced the truth: the man's brutal murder might be due, in part at least, to her actions. Dismayed, she looked up to see Mullin watching her.

'It's best not to torment yourself with such thoughts,' he said gently, 'or you won't last another day in this game.'

'Game?' Betsy's temper rose again. 'That's what all this is to you, is it? Just another stage, on which to strut about.'

'Well, is it not the same for you?'

'No!' She shook her head, staring at him defiantly. 'I had other reasons for coming here.'

'Money, you mean?' He waved a hand dismissively. 'Well, of course. You think I'd be here otherwise, in the bog of Europe? Though in the matter of reward, dear Mistress Brand, I should warn you that you face disappointment. You'll get no thanks from Williamson for what you do. Moreover — to put it plainly — I haven't been paid in four months.'

'Oh, flap-sauce — you're merely trying to

annoy me!' Betsy cried. 'Mr Lee — Williamson if you must — wouldn't deal with me in such a manner. Nor would Caradoc! He's a . . . well, he's . . . ' But she was faltering, and they both knew it. Chest heaving, she looked away.

'Perhaps I should ask your pardon.' Mullin's tone softened. 'You're tired and unnerved . . . why shouldn't you be, on your first foray into this blighted profession?'

With a sigh, he stood up. 'It's almost dawn, and I haven't slept either,' he added. 'We'll confer in the morning. You'd best call your servants — I mean your friends.' He hesitated. 'Don't fret yourself — I'll smooth things with the big fellow. I may need him, if things turn sour.'

After a moment, Betsy stood up too. 'That's well,' she replied, though her mind was elsewhere. 'Until the morning.' She yawned. 'Before you leave, will you answer a question?' she said, thoughtfully. 'Can you tell me what a trepanner is?'

At first Mullin looked as if he would laugh. But instead he met her eye and said, 'A trepanner's many things: a swindler, a sharper . . . call him what you will. The sort who befriends others only to draw them out, then betray them.' And when Betsy stiffened, he gave a nod. 'You understand me. Such men

— and women — may be found in many places: prison is one. I've performed such services myself, more times than I care to recall.'

He moved to the bed, took up his cloak and hat, then walked to the door and threw it open. Immediately Peter Crabb appeared, filling the entrance. But at sight of Mullin taking his leave, he came quietly into the room.

With a careless air, Mullin threw his cloak over his shoulder. Then he checked himself, turned back and faced Betsy. 'Some call us the Children of Judas, madam,' he said, his expression bleak. 'A fitting enough term, is it not?' Then he went out.

Eleanor came in and stood beside Crabb. Both looked at Betsy, but she barely noticed them. Instead she gazed at Mullin's empty cup, on the floor where he had left it.

7

The next day, to her dismay, Betsy learned that she would have to take ship again. The town of Delft, it seemed, was some distance away, and travelling by road would be difficult. So the party, which now consisted of a Captain and Mrs Mullin and their servants, would embark from Neiuwpoort by coastal barque to the port of Rotterdam on the River Maas. From there it was but a short journey to their destination.

'It's for the best,' Mullin told her. 'The weather's fair, and we'll have time to converse.'

He, Betsy and Peter Crabb stood in the square, which was now bustling with life. The day was indeed fine, and Mullin appeared in good spirits for a man who'd had only an hour's rest. Peter Crabb, who had slept in the stables, said little. To Betsy's eye, Mullin's promise to 'smooth things' between himself and the young man was yet unfulfilled.

'Then it seems I've no choice,' she answered. 'But I can't promise to keep my stomach from rebelling.'

'Nonsense, this will be a pleasure trip.'

Mullin smiled at her, and at that moment Eleanor emerged from the doorway of the inn with her baggage. So without further delay the group set off.

The barque, it turned out, was open-decked, which in one way was a relief to Betsy. With a fresh breeze about her, she thought she might manage the voyage up the coast without mishap. When she found out how far Rotterdam was, however, she balked.

'Seventy miles? But we'll be at sea for days!'

'Two, I expect,' Mullin replied. 'We'll put in tonight along the way . . . speaking of which, how much money do you have?'

'I was given a purse of fifty guilders,' Betsy told him, which prompted a curse.

'That skinflint Williamson. He's no better than his master!'

'What do you mean?'

'I mean fifty guilders amounts to only five pounds. Our esteemed Secretary of State, Lord Arlington, is a miser — and so is his underling, that wily Cumbrian!'

'Well, this is no place to speak of it,' Betsy said quietly. They sat in the stern with the better-off passengers, women in hooded cloaks and gentlemen in feathered hats. Eleanor and Crabb were forward, among the other travellers.

'But it is,' Mullin countered. 'It's the perfect place. For none of these Hollanders understands English.'

'How do you know they don't?'

'Because I speak enough of their tongue to understand *them*.'

The boat was leaving the mouth of the River Yser now, and venturing into the open sea. As its sails filled, Betsy recalled Williamson's letter. 'Perhaps it's time you shared some of your knowledge with me,' she said.

'I'd prefer you to tell me what you know first,' the other replied.

Just then the vessel heaved. So, partly to keep her mind off the matter of seasickness, Betsy decided to give her fellow intelligencer a full account of her time in the King's Bench, with all that she had learned from Venn. When that was done, she spoke of the orders Williamson had sent, which puzzled her.

'Why do you think he was so insistent that I report only to him, and stay away from our ambassador?' she asked.

Mullin frowned. 'Well might you wonder. The truth is, Williamson likes to keep everything to himself. He may be Arlington's man, but there's little love between those two. Each hides intelligence from the other.'

At that Betsy gave a sigh of exasperation. 'Cods,' she muttered. 'Does no one trust anyone else in this bear-pit . . . this *game*, as you call it?'

'It's best to assume they don't,' the captain said. He gestured to the shoreline on their right, the boat having turned to starboard. 'Observe, if you will. It looks peaceful enough, doesn't it? This prosperous little country of tile-makers and tulip-growers? But dig deeper, and you'll find the place seethes with fear and unrest — and intrigue. Why, we've had spies here for over a century! As for our ambassador: Sir William Temple left for England months ago, and won't be back. Sir George Downing now sits in the Hague — the most rabid, Dutch-hating rogue you'll find anywhere. Would you care to guess why he's here?' And when Betsy shook her head, he bent closer. 'Because the King means to declare war on the Dutch.'

Slowly she raised her eyes to meet his. She'd thought he was in jest, but one look was enough.

'When?' was all she could say.

'Soon enough. He wanted to do it back in the summer, but he's been persuaded to wait until next year. Early spring, would be my guess. That's why he's suspended Parliament, so he doesn't have to ask their leave.'

'Persuaded . . . by whom?' Betsy asked. 'His ministers?'

'By King Louis, more like,' Mullin replied. 'Once the French come in with us, we'll have a real war on our hands — not a fiasco like we had back in sixty-seven!' He grimaced. The memory of England's humiliation four years ago, when the Dutch fleet had sailed boldly up the Medway and bombarded the towns, still rankled with all her subjects.

'But . . . I don't understand,' Betsy said, bewildered. 'Don't we have an alliance with the Dutch?'

'It's not worth a crock of spit,' the other said flatly. 'And de Witt and the other Dutch leaders are suspicious now — who could blame them? Even if those two crafty monarchs still bombard them with lies and promises. I speak of our dear Charles, and his good friend Louis Bourbon.'

'Then, what in heaven's name am I doing here, in all of this?' Betsy exclaimed. 'I don't understand that either.'

'Nor do I, just yet.' Gently, Mullin took her arm and tucked it under his. 'In the meantime, let's play a dull married couple and talk of trivia, shall we?'

'I thought you were certain no one could understand us,' she said drily.

'I'm as certain as I can be. But perhaps

we'll save the rest of our discourse for later. I need to ponder on what you've told me. Meanwhile . . . ' From the folds of his cloak, he produced a small silver flask and uncorked it. 'Will you take a sip, madam?' he enquired. 'It will help to settle your stomach.'

This time Betsy didn't hesitate. The brandy was coarse, but in the circumstances, very welcome.

★　★　★

That night, as Mullin foretold, the barque put ashore at a point halfway along their journey. It turned out to be the busy port of Flushing, about which even Betsy knew a little. Ships sailed often between here and England, which prompted her to wonder aloud why she'd arrived at Neiuwpoort.

'Vessels from home are closely watched,' was Mullin's answer. 'You'd stand out at once.'

The two were sharing a supper of spiced beef and onions, washed down with wine which even Mullin found acceptable. Also at the table, in a private room at an inn near the waterfront, were Peter Crabb and Eleanor. Away from scrutiny, their servant roles had been set aside.

'Do *you* not stand out here?' Peter Crabb

eyed his master across the table. 'An English captain?'

'Sometimes,' Mullin replied with his mouth full. 'But I not only speak the language, I carry a safe conduct to almost anywhere. There are some excellent forgers here, if you know where to look.' He turned to Betsy. 'Perhaps we should get a pass made out for you, too.'

But Betsy, who had been quiet during most of the meal, threw him a dark look. 'I don't intend to stay here long enough to need one,' she said. 'As soon as I have any intelligence to give to Mr Lee, I'm taking the first ship home.'

The others glanced at her. Soon after stepping ashore, Betsy had acquainted Crabb and Eleanor with Mullin's news, which they received calmly. In fact, they showed so little surprise that she'd begun to wonder if she were the only one who didn't know about an impending war. Now, she would wait no longer.

'I think it's time you told us what's going on in this country — *Captain*,' she said, pushing her plate aside. 'I don't like being kept in the dark.'

'Nor I,' Crabb murmured. 'I'd like to get a clearer picture of how things stand, here in the Provinces.' He raised his cup, drained it in one, then put it down with a thump.

'Well then — let me enlighten you.' With a sigh, Mullin took up his own goblet. 'You know of the treaty, I assume? The one our King signed with Louis of France at the end of last year?'

'Buckingham's treaty?' Crabb nodded. 'Louis has agreed to help the King — '

'May I continue?' Mullin interrupted, wearing his sardonic look. 'There's something even you don't know, Crabb. Indeed, it's known only to the King and two members of the cabal: Clifford, because he holds the purse-strings, and Lord Arlington, Master of Everything. Though naturally, Williamson has learned of it too. Not much slips past him.'

He took a drink, then glanced round the table. 'Before I tell you what it is,' he said, 'I want a solemn oath from each of you not to repeat it. If it became known that I'd told anyone, I'd end up in the Tower at best. At worst . . . ' He waved his hand, a gesture that was becoming familiar. Whereupon Betsy spoke up.

'You have my word.' She glanced at Eleanor, who flushed.

'I'm loyal, sir,' she told Mullin. 'I think you know that.'

The captain gave a nod, and turned to Peter Crabb. 'I know you'll swear,' he said.

'Men like us will swear to anything if we have to, won't we? So let me add a little codicil to our agreement, just to clarify matters.' Then after a theatrical pause, he added, 'If it *did* become known that I'd spilled this news, I would know who'd informed on me. In which case, by one means or another you would die, Crabb. Do you mark that?'

Silence fell. Through the wall, voices of other diners could be heard, while from outside sounds of the port drifted in. Betsy's eyes flew from Mullin to Crabb, and back to Mullin.

'I mark it well — sir.' Crabb met the other man's gaze without flinching. 'But I'll give my word, whether you think it worthless or not. If the matter touches on the safety of the King's realm, I'm as loyal as anyone here.' He paused, and matching Mullin's stare, spoke softly, 'You are truly His Majesty's loyal subject, are you not? I ask because, should it turn out otherwise, it's you who would die. And it may be that I'm the one who has to kill *you*.'

At that Mullin bristled — but before he could speak, Betsy broke in impatiently. 'Oh, flap-sauce, Wrestler!' she snapped. 'Haven't we enough to concern us, without your hectoring?' She frowned at Mullin. 'And you, sir: put aside your swagger and tell us what you know. Then we'll see if it was worth the theatrics.'

All eyes went to Mullin again. So, finally, after taking another fortifying drink, he made his revelation. 'What's known only to Arlington and Clifford — and to Williamson,' he said, 'is the existence of a secret treaty between our King and Louis, that was signed at Dover six months before the other one. It's almost identical to the one the Duke of Buckingham thought he'd secured — the fool believed it a triumph of his diplomatic skills. However, Royal Charles didn't tell him of the first treaty, which differs from it in vital respects. Some clauses are missing — especially the one in which Charles swears to convert. In short, our king will declare himself a Roman Catholic.'

Having delivered his little speech, Mullin poured himself more wine. He was about to refill Betsy's cup, but she waved the jug away; the news had stunned her, as it had the others. There had always been rumours of Charles's religious leanings, she knew; his brother the Duke of York was already believed to be a Catholic. But if the King were to convert too . . .

'Now you see, madam, why I wished to think over the intelligence you brought,' Mullin went on. 'Rumours of plots always abound, of course, and they seldom amount to anything. But there's been an odd atmosphere about London in the past year or two. Men speak of the Jesuits now seen in the capital, and the number of masses being said. It's almost as if the Papists knew something we didn't, wouldn't you agree?'

Now Betsy's mind was busy. 'Perhaps,' she allowed. 'In which case, I suppose those who are angry at the way things move might resort to desperate means. Hence — '

'Hence the need for us to investigate the doings of your friend the late Mr Venn, and his circle,' Mullin finished. 'This *Projection* of theirs, the chief mover in which appears to be a bogus priest . . . ' He frowned. 'It's real enough, I'd say, though its shape remains to be discovered. I don't imagine these hotheads would attempt a repeat of the Gunpowder Plot, and yet . . . ' He smiled faintly. 'Once in Delft, we must busy ourselves. This priest — '

'The *Papenhoek* — the Papists' Corner,' Crabb broke in, as if only now finding his voice. 'We should scour that first — '

'And scare him off?' Mullin snapped. 'The man will bolt at the first hint that anyone's looking for him. In any case, he may no longer be posing as a priest.'

'Then where would we begin?' Betsy put in. 'We don't even know what he looks like.'

'But that's why we're here,' Mullin said, somewhat impatiently. 'To move among the malcontents — the English, that is. You'll be surprised by how many of them there are in this country, madam. Scots and Irish too — the sweepings of Britain. Then, having charmed them and won their confidence — '

'I know — befriend and betray,' Betsy broke in drily. 'Isn't that what you were about to say?'

When Mullin didn't answer, Crabb spoke again. 'For myself, I've no orders apart from to protect Beatrice, and help in any way I can,' he said. 'Nor do I speak the language, save for *ja* and *nee*. The captain knows the terrain, so I must be ruled by him. Yet,' — he eyed Mullin again — 'I'm uneasy about this whole venture. So wherever Beatrice goes, I believe I should go too . . . with your approval, that is.'

'Of course, Crabb,' Mullin answered. 'Though I assume you're not referring to her bedchamber. That might excite suspicion, don't you think?' Turning pointedly to Betsy, he put on his most winning smile. 'I've engaged the best room for you, madam,' he said. 'Though I regret I won't be sharing it with you. I have a friend in Flushing, whom I'm eager to see.'

With that he stood up, dabbing a napkin to

93

his mouth. 'Until morning then,' he added. 'Let's hope the weather holds, eh?'

* * *

Mercifully it did hold, at least until the party arrived at Rotterdam the following afternoon. There, Betsy noticed, Mullin grew ill-at-ease. The port, he said, seemed busier than he had ever known it, and the reason was clear enough.

'The Hollanders are re-arming,' he told her. 'They smell the coming war.' He pointed out several large vessels, riding at anchor. 'Those are old merchant ships, but I'll wager a guinea they're being fitted out as men-of-war. May I suggest, once we're ashore, that if there's talking to be done, you allow me to do it?'

Betsy was tired, and numb from sitting on a hard seat for the best part of two days. All she wanted was food and a comfortable bed. Last night in Flushing she had had both and, as promised, Mullin had been out for the entire night. She hadn't asked him where he had been.

'You always do, don't you?' she muttered. 'Let's find an inn, or at least somewhere I can wash the salt off.'

But the captain was shaking his head.

'There's no time. We must conserve our funds — and besides, we've only a dozen miles left to travel. We'll take the road.'

And that was why, some two hours later, the party of four were sitting pressed together in a draughty coach, rattling along the highway between Rotterdam and Delft.

They were not the only passengers, which put them all on their guard. Crabb in particular, his huge frame squeezed into a corner, seemed tense. Mullin, by contrast, chatted amiably in Dutch with another traveller, a middle-aged burgher. Beside him sat his wife, her eyes closed. Betsy, huddled in her coat, feigned sleep, while Eleanor had no need to pretend. The girl was so tired, she was dozing within minutes of their departure.

'I've been having an interesting conversation, my dear — would you care to hear of it?'

Betsy opened her eyes to find Mullin smiling at her. Alert at once, she nodded.

'This gentleman is Meneer Katz,' he continued, raising his voice above the noise of the coach. 'He's the owner of a gin distillery in Delft, among other things. He has invited us to visit his home once we're settled.'

'Indeed?' Betsy turned to the gentleman,

who inclined his head. 'How kind. And does Meneer Katz understand English?'

'I regret he does not, madam, but I do.'

The speaker was the Dutchman's wife, a good-looking woman with pearls about her neck, who, it now seemed, had been awake all along. Mullin was startled, though he concealed it well.

'My dear Mevrouw Katz, I had no idea!' he exclaimed. 'Pray forgive my poor command of your language — I would have spoken English to you, with pleasure.'

'No apology is necessary,' the lady replied. 'I like to listen. Besides, you do yourself a disservice, sir. One seldom hears Dutch spoken well by an Englishman, even one who has spent as long in our country as you have — Captain Mullin.' And with that, she turned deliberately to Betsy.

'Your husband is not unknown to some of us, madam,' she went on. 'By reputation, at least. Though I confess I had not heard he was married — how fortuitous it is that we meet. We travel in our own coach as a rule, but it's being refurbished. You and the captain must be our guests in Delft. Then perhaps we may get to know each other — would that please you?'

'It would, madam,' Betsy replied. Then she met the cold blue eyes of Mistress Katz, and stiffened; this woman, she saw, was suspicious of her.

And moreover, instinct told her that she could prove a very dangerous enemy.

8

The house stood on a quiet street in the south-west quarter of Delft, near the large church known as the Oude Kierke. It had two floors, a small yard at the rear and a roof of red tiles. This was to be home to Betsy and the others for the present. It belonged to a family known to Captain Mullin, who it seemed had left the Dutch Provinces in a hurry.

That first day she slept late, awaking to sounds of movement from downstairs. Still stiff and sore from travelling, she roused herself and went down to find Eleanor in the kitchen.

'You should have woken me,' she said. 'Where are the others?'

'Crabb's gone to look around,' Eleanor answered. 'The captain hasn't come back yet.' Once again, it seemed Mullin had spent the night elsewhere. Yawning, Betsy sat down on a stool by the scrubbed table.

'Is there anything to eat?' she asked.

'There's a jug of whey. I bought it this morning, before you rose.' The girl seemed tense today, Betsy thought.

'Are you well, Eleanor?' she asked.

'I'm uneasy, madam.' Eleanor poured whey from the jug into a bowl, brought it over and sat down facing her. 'I don't really trust Captain Mullin.'

'For any particular reason?' Betsy enquired. 'Apart from his arrogance, of course, and disappearing whenever it suits him?'

The girl gave a shrug. 'Mr Lee doesn't like him. He's never said so, but I know him too well.'

'Well, as it happens I know Mullin too,' Betsy told her. 'Or of him, at least. He may be a cockscomb and other things too, but I'm sure he's loyal.'

'I'm sure of that too,' Eleanor said. 'Yet I'd advise you not to rely on him too much. Trust your own wits — you have them in abundance.'

She broke off at the sound of the house door, followed by heavy footsteps. Both women looked round to see Peter Crabb lumber in, stooping to avoid the low doorway. He carried a covered basket, which looked out of place in his huge hand.

'I found a market,' he said. 'I've got bread, a piece of mutton and some greens. As for Delft — it's like a maze. The town's a network of waterways, with alleys everywhere. A man could hide himself here for months.'

When Eleanor got up to take the basket, he lowered himself onto the stool she had vacated. 'I found out something else too,' he went on. 'There's an inn used by English exiles, called the *Bok* — it means 'goat', I think. It's one place to start, isn't it?'

'You have been busy, Wrestler,' Betsy remarked.

The young man eyed her. 'I hope our master has been busy, too,' he replied. 'And I don't just mean visiting whores.'

'You think that's where he goes?' she asked, whereupon the other's look was all the answer she needed. 'I see,' she went on. 'Well then, I don't intend to wait here like an obedient little wife. I suggest we use our own resources.'

The other two looked at her. 'What do you have in mind?' Crabb enquired.

'We'll take a stroll. An English gentlewoman, newly arrived, accompanied by her servants. What could be more natural?'

★ ★ ★

Delft, Betsy decided, was a pleasant town, even if the waterways smelled as badly as the Thames. It was surrounded by water and, as Peter Crabb had said, there was a network of canals. There were bridges, but many people

100

seemed to go about by small boat. The streets were cobbled, lined with houses of red brick. Beyond the walls the sails of windmills could be seen, and further off farmsteads surrounded by fields. Within its walls, the town was a thriving place of a hundred trades. Folk thronged the waterfronts: artisans in simple garb mingling with well-dressed merchants and their wives. And close to the main market-place stood the inn that Crabb had discovered: the *Bok*.

'I didn't go in,' he told Betsy. 'But I spoke to an Englishman who was passing. He was a Papist. Did you know a quarter of the population here are such?'

The three of them had spent an hour looking round the town, and now stood facing the inn: Betsy in a good cloak and hat, Eleanor in a plain linen hood. Crabb had on his everyday brown coat and a soft cap — not that it mattered what he wore: at each turning people stared at the young man, who was a head taller than anyone else.

'This Papist quarter,' Betsy said. 'Where is it?'

'The *Papenhoek*? I'm not certain, but I'll find out . . . ' and he would have gone off at once, had she not caught his sleeve.

'Not just yet.' She glanced round, feeling more conspicuous then she liked. 'Perhaps we'll take some dinner at the inn first.' She turned to Eleanor. 'Are you hungry?'

'I am, madam,' the girl replied, but her attention was distracted. 'Look there — it's the captain.'

The others turned sharply. Striding towards them with cloak flying was none other then Marcus Mullin himself; and he looked like an angry man.

'At last!' he growled, drawing close. 'God in heaven, madam, I've searched half of Delft for you! What do you think you're doing? I'm the one to guide you! You stick out like . . . well . . . '

'Like an Englishwoman?' Betsy said coolly. 'Why should that mark me out, since you say there are so many here already? Besides, you weren't at the house, and I didn't intend to sit and wait. Might I enquire where *you* were?'

'What does that matter?' Mullin retorted. 'I know this town — I have friends here. Had you been more patient this morning I'd have taken you sight-seeing — and perhaps made a few enquiries on the way. Instead, you go off at half-cock — '

'I'll ask you to hold your tongue!'

Mullin froze, then with deliberate slowness swung his gaze to Crabb. 'You'll ask *what?*'

'That you hold your tongue — sir,' the

other repeated, glaring down at him. 'How were we to know when you would return? We've neither the time nor funds to kick our heels in this place — nor to wait for you to take farewell of whatever trull you've spent the night with.'

At that, Mullin went white with anger. But before either could speak again Betsy gave a loud sniff — her King's Bench sniff.

'Come, Eleanor,' she said. 'You and I will take dinner, as I promised. As for these gentlemen' — she threw a withering look at Mullin — 'I suggest you find a low tavern where the ale's cheap, and you can drink yourselves into better humour. That, or have a fight — I care not!' And, grasping her skirts, she walked away across the cobbled street. With barely a glance behind Eleanor tripped after her, catching her up at the door of the inn. All Mullin and Peter Crab could do was stare as the two women disappeared.

But once inside they faltered. For one thing, the room was so full of tobacco smoke that they could barely see. For another it was crowded, and dirtier than Betsy had expected. Heads turned, and men regarded the pair curiously. There were women too, but one look at them was enough.

'This isn't the place for you,' Eleanor breathed.

Betsy was inclined to agree, even though the inn appeared no worse than some of those the actors used, back in London. It was the atmosphere that made them both uneasy: one of debauchery, even violence. But no one approached them, and the noisy hubbub, which had diminished, soon rose again. Betsy was pondering what to do, when the door opened behind her and Peter Crabb came in hurriedly.

'That was rash of you, madam,' he said. He gazed round, his fists clenching instinctively, and Betsy's heart sank: they could not have attracted more attention had they tried. People glanced warily at Crabb, then looked away.

'No more than it was of you and Mullin, to wrangle in the street,' she muttered. 'Where is he?'

Crabb shrugged to indicate that he neither knew nor cared. 'What do you wish to do?' he asked. 'Find somewhere — '

'More congenial?' Betsy shook her head. 'No, I think we should stay. Now that our protector's here we can't come to much harm, can we?' She looked round for a place to sit, whereupon someone hailed her in English.

'Welcome, madam! Newly come to Delft, are you?'

The speaker was a stout, florid-faced man in his forties, wearing a red coat and plumed hat. At once Crabb stiffened, for the fellow appeared the worse for drink. His bow was steady enough, however, and his manner friendly.

'Thomas Lacy,' he announced. 'Dealer in porcelain. Whom do I have the honour of addressing?' And when Betsy gave her name, his brows shot up. 'Indeed! Are you perhaps related to Captain Mullin?'

'His wife, sir,' Betsy murmured. Already, she realized, she resented the role almost as much as she was tiring of her bogus husband. 'And yes, I am newly arrived. My servants and I were taking a turn about the place — '

'Then please, permit me to be your host!' Turning aside, Lacy called something out in Dutch. There was an answering shout, whereupon he gestured towards the window. Betsy found herself guided to a table, which to her surprise several men quickly vacated. As she sat down she looked up at Crabb, who was hovering behind.

'You and Eleanor must take some repast,' she said, fumbling in her gown. Finding coins, she handed them to him. After a moment's pause, the young man inclined his head.

'I'll be close by, madam,' he said quietly.

'Just call if you have need.' And with a glance at Lacy, who was seating himself, he moved off to where Eleanor waited.

'You're most kind, sir,' Betsy began, but her new host was peering through the haze, gesturing to someone.

'You will find you're not alone here, Mistress Mullin,' he said, turning back to her. 'One encounters many Englishmen in the Low Countries — and women too, though regrettably they're fewer in number.' He beamed at her. 'How is the good captain?'

'He's well, sir,' Betsy replied, thinking fast. 'He has business here in Delft, so — '

'Of course!' Lacy broke in. He was holding a half-full goblet, which he almost spilled. 'You'll take a glass of sack with me?'

She was about to agree when a shadow appeared at her side, blocking the light. Standing over her was a very thin, ill-favoured man, his long hair falling over a soiled lace collar. And at once Betsy was on her guard: not because the fellow seemed threatening, but because the moment she looked up at his face she understood. Though he was unknown to her, his expression was all too familiar. She had seen that look on the faces of a hundred others, lounging about the yard of the King's Bench: this man, she knew, had been in prison.

'Here you are, Churston,' Thomas Lacy said. 'Permit me to present Mistress Mullin, wife to Captain Marcus Mullin. Madam, my friend Henry Churston: scholar and poet. Never knew a man whose head held so much!'

'Mistress Mullin.' Henry Churston bowed, then stood looking awkward until Lacy seized a stool and pushed it towards him.

'Seat yourself,' he said. 'The good lady's fresh off the packet-boat — she'll need a guide, I warrant.' He grinned at Betsy. 'Churston's been here for years,' he went on. 'Knows the place like he knows his home town — Oxford, isn't it?'

With a nod, the newcomer sat down and turned to Betsy with a bleak expression. 'How long do you mean to stay here, madam?' he asked in a reedy voice. Then he coughed . . . and she flinched. At once she was reminded of shrivelled Sarah, back in her cell at the prison. This man, she saw, was gravely ill.

'We are not certain, sir,' she replied. Her instinct was to recoil from him, but she managed a smile. 'Not for long, I fear . . . and Mr Lacy is mistaken. My husband knows Delft well enough, so I've no need of a guide.'

But Lacy broke in undaunted. 'Then at least visit my home before you leave,' he said.

'Surely you'll not disappoint a fellow countryman? It's near the Oost Poort — the east gate. There's much I would show you: Dutch tiles, fine crockery . . . and you'd not find the conversation lacking.'

'Very kind,' Betsy murmured. Just then a drawer appeared and placed a glass before her, and a jug before Lacy. The man looked at Churston, then moved off.

'As I thought, penniless again!' Lacy shook his head at his friend, then pushed his glass towards him. 'Drink this,' he urged. 'I'll refill it after.' With a smile at Betsy he picked up the jug and filled her glass. 'Your health, madam.'

'And yours, sir.' Betsy lifted it, took a sip and found the wine passable. Beside her, Churston seized his drink and gulped it down in one.

'I thank you,' he muttered, without looking up.

'So you are a poet, sir,' she said, with an effort. 'What brought you to make your home here, in the Provinces?'

Churston eyed her, then lowered his gaze. 'That's a long tale, madam,' he answered. 'And hardly worth the telling.'

'Even among friends?' Lacy gave him an odd look, which could have been one of encouragement — or even of mockery. Then abruptly he turned to Betsy and lowered his voice. 'You, too, are among friends, Mistress Mullin. Your husband's one of us. And I cannot believe that the woman he has married is of a different persuasion . . . you follow me?'

A warning sounded in Betsy's mind, as clear as a church bell. Again she was back in the King's Bench, this time looking into the face of a frightened man: a dead man named Venn. *Trust no one . . .*

'Perhaps, Mr Lacy,' she replied, lowering her voice too. 'Yet I seldom discuss matters of . . . belief, shall we say, with men I've just met. Do *you* follow?'

'Oh I do, madam, indeed I do.' Lacy's smile had faded, to be replaced by a look of some intensity. 'Yet I repeat, you're among friends here. Pray don't forget that.'

'I'm gratified,' was all she could say. She raised her glass, as deliberately as she would have done on the stage on the Duke's Theatre. She was acting, of course — why else was she here?

'Then I'm delighted.' Slowly Lacy's smile returned. 'And I repeat, you must come to my house. Mrs Lacy keeps a good table.'

'You have a wife, sir?' Betsy enquired.

'And sons too, madam, though they're in England. University men, like our friend here.'

Betsy favoured Churston with a nod and sipped her drink. Within a day of her arrival, she appeared to be surrounded by the kind of men she was supposed to spy on — and without any help from Marcus Mullin. Could it truly be so easy? she wondered. Emboldened, she ventured further.

'I was told the *Bok* was a favoured haunt of our countrymen,' she said. 'Exiles of one sort or another . . . is it so?'

The two men glanced at each other. 'Exiles?' Lacy echoed. 'I wouldn't describe myself as such. I hope to return to England one day, if God pleases.'

Churston coughed. 'I regret I must excuse myself, madam,' he said. 'I've an appointment.' He got to his feet.

'Of course, sir,' Betsy replied, but the scarecrow figure was already moving off. From across the room there came a crash as of something breaking, followed by a peal of laughter — female laughter. Lacy turned briefly to look, then faced Betsy with another smile.

'The *Bok* isn't the most salubrious of places,' he said. 'I only come here to catch the gossip. As do others, who at home might patronize more . . . fitting premises.' His smile appeared fixed now, Betsy thought. Taking up the jug again, he refilled his glass.

'Yet that can be something of a hindrance nowadays, don't you think?'

'I do, sir,' she answered in a level tone. 'As I understand why some of our countrymen have been forced to flee abroad — unjustly, perhaps. The King's reach is a long one, is it not?'

'The King? I don't think I follow you, madam.' Lacy raised his eyebrows, where-upon Betsy stiffened. Was the man as tipsy as she had assumed? Suddenly, she was unclear which of them was trying to draw out the other!

'I simply meant that His Majesty keeps a close eye on this country, Mr Lacy,' she said carefully. 'As he does on others . . . France in particular, of course. We can never forget how strong his ties are to King Louis.'

'Can't we?' Lacy was looking intently at her and now she understood. The man was trying to provoke her — daring her to state her position. This, she sensed, was an opportunity she must not miss.

'No, we can't,' she answered flatly and, leaning forward, she lowered her voice again. 'Moreover, unless I'm badly mistaken, sir, like me you wish both monarchs — one an unashamed Papist, and one who merely hides it — a speedy retribution for their sins. In short, that they be consigned to the Hell that's prepared for them.'

With heart thudding, she sat back and waited. But when Lacy's response came, it wasn't what she had expected. To her surprise, he threw back his head and shouted with laughter.

'Capital!' he cried, shaking his head. Betsy blinked, as several people nearby looked at them. But assuming some jest had tickled Lacy's humour, they soon lost interest. She breathed a sigh — then received a jolt.

'The fires of Hell are not enough!'

Lacy's voice was low, but the words were spat out with a venom that surprised her. He was leaning forward again, peering into her eyes, and there was something in his gaze she had not seen before: unfeigned anger. And so at last she understood: the man burned with the fire of the righteous, and of the dispossessed; those who feel shunned and unheard, and who yearn to take their revenge. Relief swept over her: her gamble had succeeded.

'Your words lift my heart,' he whispered. 'Charles Stuart's but a Papist devil! And if the Lord wills it, he may perish sooner than anyone thinks. So let's drink to it, madam — and death to all our enemies!'

9

In the afternoon Betsy, Peter Crabb and Eleanor returned to the house near the Oude Kierke, to find no sign of Mullin.

It didn't surprise Betsy; by now she had come to expect little of the man. She had been eager to tell of those she'd spoken to — particularly Thomas Lacy, who would surely be an introduction to republican circles in Delft. So when the captain had still not appeared by dusk she told Crabb and Eleanor, the three of them sitting in the candlelit kitchen.

'He's just another angry republican,' Crabb said, after she had related her conversation. 'Harks back to the days of the Good Old Cause, and swears damnation to the Stuarts. You'll find men like Lacy all over this country, drinking themselves senseless.' He shook his head. 'It doesn't make him a conspirator. Especially as he does good business exporting pots and tiles. From what I hear, he's a rich man.'

'What else do you hear?' Betsy enquired ruefully. 'I hope you're not going to tell me I've been wasting my time.'

'No — but Lacy wasn't the only Englishman in the *Bok*. Eleanor and I sat in the
chimney corner with a fellow from Essex.
Quite a gossip, wasn't he?'

The last remark was addressed to Eleanor,
who nodded. 'He was. Though most of what I
heard was mere bawdy talk. Some of it was
about that woman on the coach — Mistress
Katz.'

'What of her?' Betsy asked sharply.

'Seems she's a sly one,' Eleanor said. 'They
say she's bedded some of the most powerful
men in the land. Her husband's a weak fellow
— a cuckold, who isn't master in his own
home.'

'Our Essex friend heard this from an
Irishman,' Crabb put in. 'A papist, who lives
by the *Papenhoek*. The priest there is a rogue
and a lecher, they say.'

'Did you catch his name, Wrestler?' Betsy
asked. Crabb shook his head, then turned.
The street door had opened, and was slammed.
All three tensed as Mullin came striding in.

'Well, this is cosy,' he said, his sardonic
smile in place. 'I trust you've supped and
rested? Some of us, meanwhile, have been at
work,' And when no one spoke, he added,
'I've learned of a priest by the name of Father
de Smet . . . a newcomer. Worth tracking
down, I'd say.'

The others exchanged glances: it was as if Mullin had just overheard them. 'Do you mean the one in the *Papenhoek?*' Betsy enquired. 'The lecher? We heard of him too.'

A frown creased the captain's brow. 'Have you? How interesting. As it happens, this priest's as pious as they come. Not your man at all.'

After a moment Eleanor rose. 'I've got some ale, sir,' she said. 'And almond cakes.'

Mullin hesitated, then sat down. 'That would be welcome.' He glanced at Crabb, met his cool stare without comment, then faced Betsy. 'I, er . . . should ask your pardon, madam,' he said in a subdued tone. 'For my churlish behaviour today.'

'Most civil of you, sir,' Betsy said frostily.

'But then, I knew you'd be in safe hands,' the captain went on, ignoring her reply. 'I thought I'd visit one or two acquaintances . . . not the sort who frequent the *Bok* to drown their sorrows,' he added, with another glance at Crabb. 'I speak of others more discreet.' Seeing that he had everyone's attention, he risked a smile. 'One lives near the *Papenhoek* — it was she who told me of the new priest. Of course, it may be coincidence, but — '

'She?' Betsy echoed, arching her eyebrows, at which Mullin let out an elaborate sigh.

'Yes, madam,' he retorted. 'She's a widow, past sixty years — her husband was an old friend, from happier times. Does that excuse me?' He turned as Eleanor came up, and accepted a mug from her with a grateful smile. 'But that's enough gossip,' he went on. 'Let's share our findings, shall we?' Deliberately he faced Betsy again. 'With your approval of course, madam?'

And all she could do was nod. Mullin may have failed to charm them this time, but he had at least redeemed himself.

★　★　★

That night, in the chamber she occupied at the rear of the house, Betsy awoke from troubled dreams. She had thought herself in the King's Bench again, with Sarah coughing. She sat up and listened, but all seemed quiet. Delft slept peacefully, but for how long? she wondered. Was war really coming?

She shivered, hunched down beneath the covers, and thought of Marcus Mullin. The captain had been as good as his word and left her alone; this night too, even though for once he had not gone out. He and Crabb were sharing a room downstairs, while Eleanor had been given the front chamber, which was nearest the stair-head. The girl had been first to retire, after the group — Mr Lee's Family, as Mullin called them — had pooled their findings round the kitchen table. After all was said and sifted the intelligence was meagre, but there were paths to be followed. Mullin was intrigued by Betsy's account of Thomas Lacy, though it seemed he hardly knew him, and was far from the close acquaintance the other had claimed. But it was agreed that he and Betsy should take up the offer of the man's hospitality. As for Father de Smet: he would need to be approached with caution. This was difficult, for Mullin was known to some in Delft. And how Betsy might contrive to meet the priest had still to be determined.

Thinking on it now, she grew restless. She had taken on this venture for the best of reasons, she reminded herself. Yet she was at sea here — and had been from the start, in more ways than one. In spite of herself, the thought amused her. She sighed, yawned and turned over . . . only to jerk bolt upright.

For a second she thought she was mistaken — then she knew she wasn't. In a moment she was tumbling from the bed and groping in the dark for a night-gown. Dragging it on, she hurried to the door. As she ran out to the landing, she heard shouting.

'Who's there?' she cried. 'I heard a scream!'

She stopped: Mullin was hurrying up the stairs, half-dressed. 'It came from up here!' he snapped. 'The front — '

There was a crash from downstairs. Both of them started, hearing Crabb call out. More noise followed: running feet, a door banging. For a moment the two hesitated — then the same thought struck them both.

Eleanor . . .

Betsy whirled round and ran to the front chamber, finding the door ajar. Shoving it wide, she stepped inside. In the dark she stumbled over something, causing her to cry out. But a flame appeared, as Mullin came in bearing a tinder-box. He held it aloft — to reveal a sight which made both of them freeze. At the same time they heard a groan, and Betsy fell to her knees, her breath catching in her throat.

She had stumbled over Eleanor.

The girl lay in a heap beside the bed, as if she had fallen out in her sleep. But in the half-light, the room told a different tale, the most lurid sign of which was the blood. It streaked the bedclothes: a glistening stripe . . . and in horror Betsy followed it down the side of the bed, to where a pool was spreading across the floorboards. It came from Eleanor, whose shift was soaked with it from her chest downwards. And then came another shock:

the girl's eyes were open, and she was gazing up at Betsy.

With a curse Mullin dropped to one knee beside her. But even as they watched Eleanor gurgled, blood bubbling from her mouth. Then she moaned softly, and her head rolled aside.

Footsteps thudded, and Crabb came running in. 'He got away from me!' he panted — then he lurched to a halt, staring down at the sight: Betsy and Mullin, kneeling over Eleanor's body. Without a word the captain put his hand to the girl's bare neck, then sat back heavily.

'My God . . . why her?' Crabb muttered. But the next moment he flinched, as Mullin rounded on him in fury.

'Why her? Isn't it as plain as daylight?' And when Betsy looked at him, he turned his anger on her too. 'The front chamber!' he cried. 'Don't you see? We should never have put her in here . . . he got the wrong room!'

Bewildered, Betsy met his gaze, then gasped.

'What do you mean?' Crabb demanded. But Mullin didn't answer. Instead Betsy faced him, and her own words chilled her as she spoke.

'He means it was meant for me,' she said quietly. 'Eleanor's been murdered, because she was mistaken for me.'

★ ★ ★

In the grey dawn, she sat huddled by the kitchen fireplace in her gown. She had drunk brandy, which Mullin had pressed on her. Thereafter, she turned away from the house and all that went on. She was aware of the two men moving about, but felt it no longer concerned her. All she did was stare into the embers, remembering how Eleanor had banked the fire up the night before. It was the last thing she had done.

Betsy hadn't wept, not even for Eleanor's sake. Again it struck her how ill-suited the girl was for the task she had been given. Though she had been on secret ventures before, it was as a servant and an eavesdropper. Now she was dead, murdered by the hand of a man who believed her to be something more. Which begged a terrible question: who had wanted to kill Betsy?

The last few days, she realized, had left her disoriented. Now, she forced herself to think about the people she had encountered. First, the couple on the coach — Franz Katz and his wife, who appeared to be a woman of influence, if not notoriety. Then Thomas Lacy, the angry republican, and his unhappy friend Churston ... She frowned. The thought of any of them being involved in this desperate act seemed unlikely. Yet, someone wished her ill. And someone had managed to get into the house undetected, to commit cold-blooded murder.

'It's done.'

Emerging from her reverie, Betsy turned to see Mullin, hatless and dishevelled.

'What's done?' she asked in a dull voice.

'The body . . . we've got rid of it.'

'What do you mean?'

'What do you think I mean?' Finding a stool, Mullin slumped down on it. 'We can't let anyone know of this. The town fathers would ask questions, our mission would be spoiled — '

'Our mission?' Betsy stared at him. 'Is that all that matters to you? An innocent girl's been stabbed to death — '

'I know!' Mullin fixed her with bloodshot eyes. 'It's a risk we all take — Eleanor knew that as well as anyone. Our task here's too important. How many more might die, if we were to abandon it — have you not thought on that?'

'I don't care!' Suddenly Betsy exploded with anger. 'This is your doing, Mullin!' she cried. 'If you'd been alert, whoever killed Eleanor would never have gained entry here, let alone carried out the deed! On top of

121

which, he even got away . . . You should hang your head in shame!'

'We all should.'

Startled, she looked round to see Peter Crabb standing in the doorway in his shirt sleeves. The young man was sweaty and dirt-stained, and looked exhausted.

'What have you done with Eleanor?' she asked.

'We buried her, of course.'

It was Mullin who spoke, though less harshly. A brandy bottle was on the table, and he poured some into a mug. Getting up, he took it to Crabb, who drank deeply, then handed it back.

'The room's clear,' he said, wiping his mouth. 'Though I can't get the stain out . . . I'll cover it up.'

Mullin nodded and took a drink himself. 'We can't stay here,' he said. 'I'll go out soon, look for new lodgings. You'd better finish cleaning up — and burn everything she had.'

But at that Betsy gave a start. 'Is this how you work?' she demanded. 'Bury her like a dog, without ceremony, then wipe away every trace, as if she'd never existed?'

'That's exactly how, madam!' Mullin's patience was spent. 'What choice have we? Would you prefer a church funeral? One look at her body and there'd be a murder hunt. We'd be the talk of Delft, our faces known to all — we might even find ourselves under suspicion! Is that what you want?'

Lost for words, Betsy lowered her eyes. 'Perhaps not,' she said at last. 'Yet I want no further part in this.' She looked up. 'Let Williamson find another agent. London's awash with actresses — some less fastidious than me.'

For a moment both men gazed at her. Then without a word, Mullin slammed the mug down on the table and turned away. He waited for Peter Crabb to step aside, then went out. Soon the street door banged.

'He's right, mistress.' Crabb eyed her, grim-faced. 'It's our duty to continue. We owe it to our master, and to our King.' He moved heavily to the table, and eased his bulk on to a stool. There he sagged, eyes downcast.

'You should rest,' Betsy said, her anger evaporating.

But Crabb shook his head. 'I've got things to do. Then, when we're settled somewhere else, we can start in earnest.' He looked up at her. 'I speak of following every path until we flush out our quarry. For the one who killed Eleanor is among them — I'd swear to it. And when I find him . . . '

He trailed off. Their eyes met, and now

Betsy saw it: the young man too was grieving for Eleanor. After a moment, she moved to the table and sat facing him. 'You got a look at him, didn't you?' she asked quietly. 'The assassin. We heard noises . . . '

'I was too late — too slow.' Crabb sighed. 'I only saw his back. Though I know how he got in: Eleanor hadn't bolted the yard door. After he'd killed her he hid in here, then slipped out when the captain ran upstairs.' He hesitated. 'The way she screamed, she must have woken before he delivered the blow. She moved, or one stab to the heart would have despatched her. He had to take two or three thrusts. It was a broad blade: a short-sword rather than a dagger, I'd say. When it was done he flew, though by then we were awake. Another second, and I'd have grabbed him.'

He fell silent, whereupon Betsy reached out and put a hand on his arm. 'You mustn't shoulder the blame, Wrestler. There were two of you down there — '

'I'm the protector.' Crabb stared at her bleakly. 'Like in the prison yard, remember?'

'And you did well,' she said gently. 'You got me out of that place — I'll always be in your debt.'

'But what of Eleanor?'

'She shouldn't have been sent here,' Betsy replied. 'And you were right: I should hang my head too. If I hadn't wanted a chamber to myself — ' She broke off as Crabb withdrew his arm from her.

'This serves no purpose, mistress.' He dragged a hand across his brow, then frowned. 'Were you serious about abandoning us here?' he asked.

Betsy met his eye. 'I was.'

'But are you still? It would be a pity, for there's much you can do.'

'Do you truly believe so?' Betsy looked doubtful. 'Moreover, do you think Mullin really wants me here?'

'Of course he does,' Crabb answered. 'You're a lady of fashion, who knows how to converse — and better still, when to hold her tongue.' He gave a wan smile. 'You didn't know it, but I was watching you in the *Bok*. You had those men fawning over you.'

'That was naught,' Betsy said. 'With others, I might find myself in a quandary. I could even ruin the whole enterprise.'

'I think not,' Crabb replied. Picking up the mug that Mullin had left, he drank what was left. 'I'd better be about my work,' he said, and got to his feet. He looked disheartened, Betsy thought . . . whereupon a feeling stole over her: one of resignation, mixed with fear.

'Oh, cods,' she breathed. And when Crabb looked at her, she, too, stood up.

'I said I'm in your debt,' she told him. 'So if not for Mullin's sake, I'll stay and do what I can for yours. I, too, would like to see Eleanor's murderer found — and to know who thought I was such a threat, that I should die in my bed.'

'Then, that eases my burden,' Crabb said, after a moment. 'And whatever you may think of the captain, he will be relieved — I'd swear to it.' And with a more purposeful step, he went off to finish his grisly task.

Betsy, meanwhile, took a look around the kitchen before going upstairs to pack her belongings. She would have to manage without a lady's maid now, she thought.

And then, as she began sorting through her clothes, tears started from her eyes, and for some reason, she was glad of it.

10

By late afternoon, the three remaining members of Mr Lee's family had moved house.

In spite of herself, Betsy had to admire Marcus Mullin's ability to move swiftly when he needed to. In a matter of hours he'd paid a token rent on an old, tumbledown dwelling on the other side of the town, borrowed a boat and transported their baggage by canal to the new residence. It was less wholesome than the house near the Oude Kierke, and poorly furnished, but it had more rooms and boasted a cellar. Here Betsy established herself in a draughty upstairs chamber while the two men went out on business of their own. First to return was Mullin, accompanied by a round-faced girl in a yellow frock and a white hood, whose name he gave as Alida.

'She's our new maid-of-all-work,' he announced. 'We have to keep up appearances.' They stood in the kitchen, which looked as if it had been unused for months. Alida made a curtsy.

'Does she speak any English?' Betsy wanted to know.

'Not a word,' Mullin said. 'That's why I hired her.' He turned to the girl and spoke in Dutch, to which she nodded. 'She'll cook and keep house,' he went on. 'And accompany you outdoors, if you want her to. She knows how to serve ladies. Tonight you and I will go visiting, so you'll need her to dress your hair.'

'Where are we going?' Betsy asked.

'To the house of Franz Katz and his wife — you'll remember them from the coach journey. It isn't far away, I've discovered. They're having what she terms a small gathering — she was keen that we attend. And it might prove useful.'

'Indeed?' Betsy felt a pang of unease. 'What makes you think so? Aren't they merely members of the local gentry?'

'More than that, I think,' Mullin said. 'Mevrouw Katz is well connected. I've a suspicion she's something of a trepanner herself — for the Dutch Government, perhaps.'

'Then why didn't you tell me of this sooner?' Betsy demanded, taken aback.

'One thing at a time. It's months since I was here — things change.' Mullin shrugged. 'And you should be careful who you align yourself with. Yesterday in the *Bok* you were lucky: you took a risk showing your hand, though it seems to have borne fruit. But in

128

future, tread cautiously.'

'That isn't what you said last night,' Betsy objected — then seeing the look on the other's face, she tensed. 'You mean, in view of what happened afterwards?'

With the briefest of nods, Mullin turned to Alida again and spoke. The girl bobbed and answered him.

'She'll sleep in your chamber with you,' he said to Betsy. 'I've told her you don't speak Dutch. Also that we won't need supper tonight — ' He broke off as a loud squeal came from the passage, followed by a curse. Crabb appeared in the doorway.

'That door needs oiling,' he said. Then he caught Mullin's look, and stiffened. 'Or, perhaps not.'

For a moment Betsy was puzzled, then she too understood: if anyone tried to gain entry that way, they would give themselves away. 'You mean the assassin might return?' she asked in alarm. 'But who would know we're here? Unless . . . ' She caught her breath. 'Do you think we're being watched?'

Neither man answered.

★ ★ ★

Meneer Franz and Mevrouw Marieke Katz dwelt in a rather grand house facing one of

129

the larger canals. Though narrow-fronted, the place stretched back for a long distance, and had many rooms. Here after dark the Mullins arrived: the captain in a plumed hat and a black coat with lace cuffs showing, Betsy in her best blue gown with a dove-grey whisk. Alida had wound her hair into side-spirals, in the Dutch fashion. Thus attired, the two actors stepped forth arm-in-arm — and it wasn't long before they were performing.

'Welcome!' Madam Katz, wearing a splendid gold dress, greeted Betsy in the entrance hall. Beside her stood the smiling figure of her husband, in a loose suit of black silk. 'I'm glad we were able to meet again so soon. I trust you are settled comfortably in Delft?'

'Very comfortably, madam,' Betsy answered quickly. 'And the town is pleasant. I look forward to exploring it further.'

The lady smiled, but this time when those piercing blue eyes bored into hers, Betsy merely returned her gaze. Beside her, Mullin cleared his throat.

'*Goedenavond, Meneer en Mevrouw,*' he murmured, greeting both hosts. Switching to English, he added, 'We're honoured to be invited. Are there others from my country here?'

'There are indeed, Captain Mullin,' Madam Katz replied, and waved her hand towards the inner rooms. 'Please, let our home be yours.' And with a somewhat quizzical glance at them she turned to greet other guests, allowing the two to move away.

'Trivial talk only, remember.' Mullin spoke under his breath. 'And if anyone asks, we married in London, back in August. At St Botolph's by Aldgate.'

'Indeed?' Betsy maintained a broad smile. 'When did you decide that? No — never mind,' she added. 'Just tell me where we met, and anything else you think I ought to know.'

'I hadn't thought on it,' Mullin answered, somewhat testily. 'I'll leave it to your imagination.' He flinched, as Betsy squeezed his arm. 'What's the matter?'

She didn't reply immediately. Instead she allowed her gaze to sweep the candlelit room they were entering, which was quite crowded. Elegantly dressed men and women stood conversing, while servants moved among them with refreshments. In one corner a lutenist was playing a gentle air.

'It's Lacy,' she whispered. 'The man I met in the *Bok*.'

'Where?' Mullin's eyes scanned the assembly.

'By the chimneypiece, in the embroidered coat.'

'I see him. By God, the fellow's grown fat . . .'

Just then a servant arrived, bowed and proffered a tray. With a haughty air, the captain took a glass and sipped. 'As I thought — gin, mixed with some vile cordial.'

Betsy too accepted a glass, then waited until the serving-man had moved away. 'What's Lacy doing here?' she asked quietly. 'More, what will I say when he sees me?'

'You must improvise,' Mullin replied, with studied nonchalance. 'After all you're new here, and don't know anyone. Whereas I . . . ' He raised his glass and drained it. 'I think it best if I work my way round,' he added. And with that he placed the vessel in her free hand and turned away. But, as he moved off, he bent close and whispered, 'You're on, Brand — don't disappoint me.'

She was alone, but only for a moment. With growing unease she saw that Thomas Lacy had spied her, and was already moving in her direction.

'Dear Mistress Mullin — once again, this is an honour.'

'Mr Lacy.' Betsy smiled. 'What brings you here?'

'Perfidious curiosity, madam, nothing more.' The man smiled back. His eyes were very bright, Betsy saw, as she noticed a tautness in his voice. All at once, it struck her that it might be he who was at a disadvantage. How many others, she wondered, knew of Lacy's affiliations? In fact, the man looked very uncomfortable. Might he be regretting what he'd said in the inn the day before? He wasn't drinking, she noticed, and kept his hands at his sides.

'Does your wife accompany you this evening?' she enquired.

'I regret not,' the other replied at once. 'But where is your spouse? Didn't I see him a moment ago?'

'You did. He's gone off somewhere.' Ill at ease, Betsy looked away. The man was gazing at her intently — and his next words caught her off guard.

'Then, what's to prevent you and I doing the same?'

Slowly she turned to him. 'I don't think I follow you, sir,' she said, raising her eyebrows. But the other was unabashed.

'I have a coach outside,' he said, leaning close. 'Why not let me entertain you?'

'I'm well entertained already, Mr Lacy.' Betsy assumed her primmest voice. 'And I've no wish to step into a married man's coach, flattered though I am — '

'For pity's sake, madam!' Lacy was signalling with his eyes, though his meaning was unclear. Uneasily, Betsy gazed back.

'Did you think *that* was all I wanted?' He

kept his voice low, but irritation showed on his florid features. To collect her thoughts she took a drink, realizing she still had Mullin's glass in her other hand. In confusion she looked round and caught the eye of a servant, who hurried up. After disposing of the glass, she eyed Lacy.

'Your pardon, sir. I'm . . . well, I'm fearful,' she said under her breath. 'I may have spoken rashly at the inn. I was tired from travelling, and — '

'Evidently so.' Lacy glanced round to make sure no one was in earshot. 'I had a mind to cheer you, that was all,' he went on. 'But since you seem to think the worst of me, perhaps I should forgo your company.' And he would have turned away, had Betsy not stayed him.

'No, wait — I'm at a loss here,' she said quickly. 'I cannot tell friend from foe . . . ' Suddenly, she was gambling again. 'I . . . I even fear I'm being watched.'

Lacy hesitated. 'Why do you think so?'

'I'm uncertain.' Betsy was thinking fast. 'But it's the reason my husband and I left England. One of our acquaintance warned us — ' She broke off, as if regretting her words. 'See now, my tongue's run away with me again,' she added. Then she took another drink, and waited.

'One of your acquaintance?' Lacy echoed.

'Might I ask who that was?'

Whereupon throwing caution aside, she spoke the words that would either help her — or condemn her.

'His name is Venn,' she said softly. 'Or, it was: he's dead.'

All at once, the murmur of voices seemed to drop. Feigning mild interest Betsy looked round, but saw nothing amiss. In the corner the lutenist still played. Madame Katz was now in the room, the centre of a group of ladies as prosperous looking as she. But when Betsy turned back to Lacy, she was surprised to see him appear unconcerned.

'You knew Venn?' His voice was low, so she had to strain to hear. But her heart gave a flutter: once again, she thought, Lacy was sounding her out. She nodded.

'And do you know how he died?' he asked softly.

'He was murdered, in the King's Bench.' Betsy managed a frightened look. 'But perhaps you knew that already,' she went on. 'And if you knew it, then — '

'Please — no more.' Lacy's tongue appeared, and he wet his lips. 'You should have accepted my offer to get in the coach,' he went on tautly. 'We can't talk here.'

'Indeed not.' Betsy's pulse had quickened, and again she drank to cover it. 'But perhaps you have news to share with me?' she ventured. 'And with my husband, of course. He would be most interested.'

But an odd look came over Lacy's face. 'Would he?' he enquired. 'I confess I hadn't thought Captain Mullin was attached to any cause. Though he's no doubt one of us, I always saw him as . . . well, little more than an adventurer.'

'Perhaps he had that reputation once,' Betsy said, assuming a dry tone. 'But he is loyal, sir — and I mean to a cause dear to both you and me. Since we married I've confided my innermost thoughts to him. I believe he is coming round to my view of the world.'

Lacy seemed to relax a little. 'Then we will speak further,' he said after a moment. 'And you're correct that the *Bok* is not the place. I, too, spoke unwisely yesterday. I've fallen into the ways of some of our countrymen here — I drink to numb the bitterness of exile. When a newcomer appears from our homeland, I — '

'Please, no excuses are needed,' Betsy broke in. 'We are all impatient for change. And this time, Mr Lacy, it's you who have lifted my heart. Need I say more?'

'You need not, madam.' At last, the man smiled. 'Indeed, perhaps you and I have spent long enough together. Yet at my house we can converse freely — I'll send a message soon.'

'I look forward to it, sir.' She returned his smile. And with that, Lacy made a quick bow and left her. Soon he had returned to the chimneypiece where two or three gentlemen were conversing. He did not look at her again.

'At last . . . I thought he'd never go.' From nowhere Mullin appeared, another glass in his hand. 'Was any of that useful?'

'It might be,' Betsy answered, with a sigh of relief. Suddenly she realized how hungry she was. 'You spoke of a supper,' she added. 'Where might that be?'

'Upstairs, I think. Would you like to partake, my dear?'

'I would.' Betsy eyed him. 'And if I'm not mistaken, Mullin, you're looking very pleased with yourself. How so?'

'Perhaps I am,' the captain admitted. 'I've just had a most rewarding conversation — with a pastor.' But when Betsy gave a start, he shook his head. 'Not of *that* persuasion — remember the Calvinist company we're in. And yet, talking to him helped me hit upon a solution to our immediate difficulty.'

'Indeed? What's that?' Betsy asked suspiciously.

'Why, your next role. One that shouldn't tax you too heavily. You need only play it

137

briefly. I've even thought of a name for you: Mistress Cathleen O'Donnell.' And when Betsy stared at him, Mullin's smile widened. 'Yes, you'll be an Irishwoman. A devout Papist, passing through *en route* from a journey you've made ... a pilgrimage, perhaps. Naturally you'll be wanting confession, so you'll visit the *Papenhoek* in search of a priest ... Now, shall we take some supper?'

★　★　★

By the following morning it had been decided upon, but that didn't mean Betsy Brand was pleased with the arrangement; quite the opposite, in fact.

'I've never done an Irish accent,' she said. 'Someone might see through it.'

'Cods, madam,' Mullin replied amiably. They sat in the chilly back parlour of their new house, beside the fire Alida had lit. 'Priests here don't speak English,' he added. 'They wouldn't know an Irishwoman from a Margate cockle-girl.'

'But either way, we'll take no further risks.' Peter Crabb spoke up, from where he sat stolidly apart. 'Beatrice must not be alone again. Wherever she goes, I'll be with her.'

'I suppose it's best,' Mullin allowed.

138

'Though you stand out like a sore thumb. We'll need a reason for your proximity — '

'Forgive my intrusion,' Betsy broke in, 'but I'm not even sure of my disguise yet. I've already been seen about the town.'

'That had occurred to me,' the captain answered, looking somewhat smug. 'You must go in black, and wear a veil — I'll send Alida to the market for a cheap frock. Now I think upon it, you might say you're in mourning for a relative. If you can manage a few tears, all the better.'

Betsy considered the suggestion, which she had to admit seemed practical. And, from the look on Crabb's face, she saw that he approved of it too.

'I'd better stay back,' he said. 'I'll keep her in sight, but not know her. As far as anyone may observe, we're strangers.'

'Good!' Mullin nodded. 'Let's to business.' He eyed Betsy. 'We must first choose your strategy.'

'I'm glad you mentioned that — Husband,' she said drily. 'For I was awake half the night thinking on it. I don't believe I can walk into the Papist church and ask if they know of a priest who's really an English conspirator, can I?'

'Quite so,' the captain replied. 'I hope you'll say as little as possible. Though asking if there's a priest in Delft who speaks English wouldn't go amiss.'

'But we don't even know if the man we're seeking is English,' Betsy objected. 'Venn spoke of *our man*, who was still in Delft. How do we know the fellow isn't Dutch?'

At once Mullin shook his head. 'He's as English as the rest of them,' he said. 'I'd stake my life on it. From what Venn told you, it's clear this man means to travel to England to rendezvous with his friends. You don't think a Dutchman would go there now, do you?'

'Very well . . . ' Betsy thought for a moment. 'But what of your fear, that their man no longer passes himself off as a priest? This foray could be a mere waste of time, couldn't it?'

'Of course it could.' Mullin exchanged a bleak look with Crabb. 'I fear that's part of the intelligencer's life, madam. Weeks of futile, even foolish endeavour, spiced with an hour or two of danger — even terror. We can merely hope for a fair wind, and a pinch of luck. Now, have you any more questions?'

With a sigh, Betsy shook her head. Once suitably attired, she felt she could manage this role well enough. Though what to do if she found herself in the presence of a false priest who saw through her accent, she didn't like to think upon.

Nevertheless, some two hours later, a figure swathed in black could be seen walking through the streets of Delft towards the *Papenhoek*, the small Papist quarter. Once there, however, she encountered an unforeseen difficulty: there was no church, or at least no building that resembled one. Fortunately, her appearance allayed suspicions. And after making signs to passers-by, she was at last directed to the Jesuit church: an ordinary house on the Oude Langendijk.

There she knocked, and was soon announcing herself to a young and rather startled acolyte. She gave her name as Mistress Cathleen O'Donnell from County Limerick in Ireland, who wished for a priest to hear her confession.

11

The priest was not the pious Father de Smet
that Mullin had heard of; nor was he a
suspicious-looking Englishman. He was a
frail, elderly Dutchman, so stooped that Betsy
was taller than him by several inches. He gave
his name as Martins, or Brother Iohannes.
The surprise was that he did speak some
English, albeit haltingly.

'You are welcome, sister,' he said as he
greeted her. 'Our house is called the Hidden
Church by some — I hope you had not much
trouble to find her?'

'No, Father.' Betsy had lifted her veil, and
kept her hands clasped before her. The
disguise, she knew, would serve; how far her
Irish accent would take her remained to be
seen.

'And why came you to Delft?' the old priest
enquired, peering at her from beneath bushy
eyebrows. Then he frowned. 'I see you're
troubled — may I offer solace?'

'In truth, I do hope so,' Betsy answered
sadly. 'I have been travelling . . . I meant to
take ship from France, but a tragedy has
intervened. In brief, my poor brother died in

the Spanish Provinces. He is — he was, a soldier there.'

A sympathetic look appeared on Father Martins's face. 'You are grieving . . . please, come first to the confessional. Then after we are done there, we may talk a while.'

So Betsy followed the old man to a curtained recess. She had a list of minor sins to confess, which she hoped would sound convincing: this was something she had never imagined doing, in her entire life. And though she was as unhappy with the deception as she was with Mullin for concocting the idea, it went smoothly enough. A short time later, having been set prayers by her Father Confessor, she sat down beside him in the church. No one else was present. And soon, after the old priest had offered some words of comfort for her bereavement, she sought to change the subject. When she mentioned Father de Smet, however, Martins shook his head sadly.

'Poor Brother Willem,' he murmured. 'He came to us only recently. His trials are many, yet he bears them with great fortitude.'

'What trials do you speak of, Father?'

'He is very sick,' came the reply. 'And his sickness worsens . . . yet God has provided us with a way to help him. Willem will stay here for the remainder of his days, and teach in our school. He is an inspiration to our young folk.'

'You have a school here?' Betsy enquired.

'Close by,' the old man nodded. 'The faithful of Delft have always been generous in their support.' He sighed. 'I pray that will continue, yet I fear for the future. Our government seems bent on following the path to ruin.'

She murmured in agreement, but her mind was busy. Father de Smet, it seemed, was not someone she should concern herself with after all. 'And are there others among the faithful here, besides you and Brother Willem?' she asked. 'Aside from the young man who admitted me?'

The old man turned rheumy eyes upon her. 'There was another living in the *Papenhoek*,' he said after a moment. 'But I'll not speak of him. He's gone now, and we pray for him.'

'Why won't you speak of him?' Betsy asked, hoping she didn't sound too eager. But Father Martins's ear, it seemed, was poorly attuned to her speech.

'We pray for him,' he repeated. Then, just as she was wondering if he were deaf, he eyed her again. 'You ask a lot of questions, Sister. Curiosity is not a womanly virtue.' A look of disapproval crossed his features. 'Yet we'll pray for your brother too . . . What was his name?'

'Er . . . Michael,' Betsy answered, turning over what he had said. She wanted to pursue it, and his reluctance to say more merely increased her curiosity.

'And he was a soldier, you say.' Brother Iohannes sighed again. 'I hope he was blessed before he went into battle?'

'I know not, Father,' Betsy answered. Opportunity seemed to be slipping from her, which meant that once again she must be bold. 'This . . . the other person,' she went on casually. 'He wasn't English, by any chance?' And when the priest gave a start, she realized she had hit the target.

'Forgive my curious nature,' she added quickly. 'It's merely . . . Well, I heard a disturbing tale when I arrived in Delft. Of a man who dressed as a priest, yet was no priest . . . a most wicked deception.' She fell silent.

'I said I would not speak of him,' the other answered, frowning. 'Yet now I, too, am curious. Why do you ask about this person, Sister?'

Stuck for a reply, Betsy bowed her head. 'Your pardon, Father,' she said meekly. 'I shouldn't listen to idle gossip — it was always my downfall.'

'Indeed?' The old man paused. 'Well, we

145

are all but human. And it's no surprise that word has spread.' He shook his head. 'Let me say only that you heard truly: he was no priest, nor was he of our church. Grave sins were committed here . . . ' He sighed. 'Now, I must attend to my other duties. Perhaps we'll meet again when you attend mass. How long do you remain in Delft?'

And there, to Betsy's frustration, her enquiries ended.

A short time later she was back in the street, where she found Crabb waiting. He looked away at once and, adjusting her veil, she walked past him with head down.

She moved quickly, her thoughts racing. Along with the frustration, she felt excitement: her efforts had not been wasted, for it seemed there had indeed been someone here, who might be the one Venn referred to as *our man*. Though the news that he had gone was disappointing — she could imagine what Mullin would say. So preoccupied was she, that she scarcely knew where she walked until suddenly, she realized she was lost.

She sighed: she had taken a wrong turning. There was nothing for it but to retrace her steps, back to the *Papenhoek*. Impatiently she started off, but when she rounded the next corner, she stopped. Walking towards her was someone who looked familiar, though at first she couldn't place him. The man appeared ordinary enough, clad in a sober suit of clothes. Yet still, Betsy knew she had seen him before. She waited for his approach — whereupon he looked up, and at once recognition dawned.

'Why — it's you!' she blurted.

The fellow halted — then he recognized her too, and a look of dismay appeared. And he would have veered away had Betsy not covered the few yards between them at once. In disbelief, she stared into the round, pinkish face of a man she had never expected to see again: Dyer's dicing partner Gorton — her cellmate from the King's Bench!

'Your pardon, madam, are we acquainted?' He was gathering his wits, but Betsy wasn't about to let him go. Stepping so close that he flinched, she looked him in the eye.

'You know we are,' she answered. 'One jailbird will recognize another!' Whereupon the man gulped and, emboldened, she added, 'You're Gorton. We shared a stinking cell for a week — did you think I wouldn't know you?'

'Listen . . . ' The other swallowed, then quickly shoved a hand in his pocket. 'You need money? I have some . . . ' But at Betsy's look of contempt, he froze.

'All I want is some answers,' she retorted.

'And if you try cogging me I'll know it — do you doubt that?'

'No!' The man withdrew his hand quickly. 'But see, I'm not Gorton . . . not here — '

'Then who are you?' Betsy demanded. 'And if you're planning to run,' she added quickly, 'you're wasting your time. I know men in this town who'd track you down in an hour — and make you pay for wasting theirs!'

That was a bluff, but Gorton wasn't to know it. He was not only convinced by her air of outrage, he seemed frightened. 'I wasn't,' he said. 'God smite me if I lie . . . '

'I expect He will,' Betsy snapped. 'Meanwhile, I want to know what you're doing here — ' Then she gasped, as realization swept over her.

'It was you all along!' she cried. 'You were the trepanner in the cell! You were watching Venn. Which means you — '

Then she was struck.

She'd been about to accuse Gorton of being Venn's murderer; instead, a sickening blow to the side of her head sent her reeling. She found herself being pushed backwards, then she was falling, from what seemed a great height — and too late, she realized what that meant.

The water crashed about her, freezing her to the bone. One minute she'd been in daylight, the next she was floundering in icy darkness, her limbs like lead. Her clothes billowed about her as she sank. Down she went . . . Then there was mud in her face, and her arms were flapping feebly, while she kicked out like a drunken frog. And all the while the ice-cold water tightened its grip, slowing her movements, until at last a voice in her head pronounced her doom: she couldn't swim, and she would drown.

She struggled harder. Her clothes felt like swaddling, while her body seemed to have become one with the water. It filled her mouth, her ears and nose; wildly she thrashed about, seeing nothing.

Then there was something. One leg was grasped, and the sluggishness that had overwhelmed her gave way to violent movement. Now she was being dragged through the water — but she was choking! She tried to shout, but all that emerged was a gurgle. Then, with a great burst of sound and light, she was lifted from the canal like a child to be dumped onto hard stone. The next thing she knew, she was turned roughly on her side — whereupon the real torment began.

A moment ago Betsy had feared she would die, now she feared that she wouldn't. Such a coughing, retching and spluttering followed, the like of which she had never known. Limp as a cod on a fishmonger's slab, she lay on the quayside and vomited foul, slimy water, while her lungs heaved. Dimly, she realized someone was pummelling her. Then her ears emptied, and she could hear. Only now did she open her eyes, to glimpse through a tangle of wet hair a crowd gathered round her, chattering and pointing. Then a familiar face leaned close, filling her vision.

'Wrestler . . . ?'

'Thanks be to God!' Peter Crabb was pressing her body, forcing water from her lungs. 'Take deep breaths,' he urged.

Betsy coughed and retched again, then started shaking. Her clothes clung about her like wet sailcloth, and her teeth chattered — but despite it all there was a dizzying sensation: one of huge relief. Panting, she looked about. Crabb was kneeling by her side and he, too, was dripping with water. Meanwhile passers-by continued to gather, peering down at her. Some, it seemed, were offering advice, which he ignored.

'Stop, please . . . ' Weakly Betsy raised a hand and dragged hair from her eyes, whereupon Crabb stopped pushing. He was panting, his blond hair plastered to his face, as she had first seen it in the drizzle, back in the prison yard. But just now, she

150

could have kissed him.

'Wrestler,' she croaked, 'you've saved my life!'

'It's lucky I was near,' he breathed. 'There was some shouting, so I came over to look. I saw your black clothes . . . ' He frowned. 'How did you manage to fall in?'

'I didn't,' Betsy answered, and coughed again. 'Please . . . get me back to the house, for I've a tale to tell.'

But when she did tell it, more than an hour later by the fire in the back parlour, the reactions weren't what she had expected.

'By the Christ, madam, you try me to the limits!'

Marcus Mullin sat facing her, fuming. Crabb was there too, in fresh clothes, glum-faced and silent. For what had become clear, was that the consequences of Betsy's running into Gorton were graver than she'd realized: in short, she was now a danger to them all — and to their mission, too.

'You've been recognized,' the captain went on angrily. 'And whoever that fellow is, you're known. Which means that as an intelligencer, you're all but worthless!'

'Thank you for your frankness, sir,' Betsy answered. 'It's clear I should have stayed indoors. I assure you that the encounter wasn't planned. And as for getting hit on the

151

head and pushed into the canal — I'll admit that was most inconsiderate of me. If I'd drowned, of course, you could have disowned me and carried on as if nothing had happened. Or perhaps I should have stayed in London from the start — would that have been best?'

'Indeed it might!' Mullin retorted. 'As it is, you've thrown my plans awry.' Mastering his anger, he sighed. 'And how we move from here, I confess I don't know.'

Nobody spoke for a while. Betsy had on clean, dry clothes, though her hair was still damp. Alida was washing her linen, but the black gown she'd worn was ruined. Her ear still smarted from where Gorton had struck her, but no bruise would show. All in all, it appeared, she had been lucky.

'You should have waited for me,' Crabb said to her, for perhaps the third time. 'I wasn't far behind. You must never go off by yourself again — will you give me your word?'

'I will, Wrestler,' Betsy replied. 'And since I owe you my life I'll agree to anything else, within reason.'

'Now you make too much of it,' he said in some embarrassment. 'The water in that canal's only neck-deep. You could have stood up, had you not panicked.'

'I was dazed,' Betsy said indignantly. 'And

how was I to know — ?'

'For pity's sake!' Mullin broke in. 'You're wasting time . . . we have to form a new strategy.'

Betsy met his gaze. 'Well, since I'm now surplus to needs,' she said drily, 'I suppose my strategy is to get myself back to Rotterdam, or somewhere else I can take ship for home.'

'Oh, don't play the martyr,' the captain retorted, putting on his sardonic look. 'I had a mind to keep you out of sight for a while, at least until I think what to do . . . ' He faced Crabb. 'Yet my other fear is that you, too, are known to this man Gorton, from your time in the King's Bench. Which makes our task all the more difficult.'

'I know that,' Crabb admitted unhappily. 'But one mystery at least is solved: I'd swear it was he who killed Venn. He must have been set to watch him . . . by his own friends, perhaps?'

Mullin nodded. 'As I've said before, such men are more afraid of each other than anyone else.' He eyed Betsy. 'And now I'm drawn to another conclusion: that this man knows our purpose here. It could even be that he's the one who came to kill you — and killed Eleanor instead.'

At that, Betsy was dismayed. 'Can it be so?'

she murmured. 'I can't think Gorton would have the nerve for such an act. He was frightened when he saw me. He's a foppish fellow.'

'If he's killed once, he may do so again,' Mullin countered. 'More, we don't know what drives him. Perhaps they have a hold over him that forces him to such deeds . . . ' He trailed off, and a wary look came over his face. He was looking at Crabb — and when Betsy followed his gaze, she too stiffened.

'There's one thing you forget,' the young man said softly. 'I, too, have a memory of the man — enough to pick him out in a crowd, I think. So, who is in more danger — him or us?'

'Now listen, Crabb,' Mullin said, after a moment. 'Whether that cove killed Eleanor or not, this is no time for taking revenge. We need to puzzle out who his associates are.' He let out a sigh. 'If they haven't flown the coop already, of course.'

'Yet, if we did find Gorton . . . ' Suddenly, Betsy was hopeful. 'Aside from Mr Crabb, he's the only one who can identify me from the prison. With him out of the way, I'd be just someone who was assaulted in the street. If asked, I could merely say I was robbed.'

'Perhaps,' Mullin conceded. 'But if he's revealed your presence here to others, we're

154

still tied. We can only — '

'Captain.'

Startled, Mullin turned to see Crabb on his feet, towering over them both; one look at him was enough.

'You said we were wasting time,' the young man said. 'And so we are — for whatever scheme you may think up next, our first task seems clear: to find Gorton before he flees, by whatever means we can. And I for one won't rest until I've found him, even if I have to scour the whole of Delft!'

In silence Betsy gazed at him. Mullin opened his mouth to speak, then thought better of it.

'Very well,' he said finally. 'But we go together, after dark, and you follow my orders. I know the town and you don't. Though short of entering every house, I can't see how we'll winkle him out.'

He gave another sigh, and got to his feet. 'Now, I need a glass of strong water,' he added. 'And I don't mean the sort that comes from a canal!'

12

The task was impossible, of course. Mullin and Betsy knew it, even if Crabb refused to face it. But having no better plan, the captain was as good as his word. After dark the two men left the house, leaving Betsy in a state of some unease.

For a while she sat in the parlour with Alida, until the girl made signs that she would go and prepare a posset. Whereupon, relieved to be alone, Betsy lay down upon a worn-out couch and tried to think. But her thoughts were so jumbled, she found it hard to unravel them — apart from one sobering notion: that her foray as Joseph Williamson's only female intelligencer had not, thus far, been a success. In fact, she thought ruefully, she had come close to ruining everything.

After a while she rose and walked the bare room restlessly. Outside a breeze had got up, and the windows began to rattle. She was about to fetch a shawl, when she was startled by the sound of loud knocking. She hurried out to the hallway to see Alida unbolting the front door.

'Don't answer it!' she called. But she was

too late, and in any case the girl didn't understand. With a screech the door swung inwards to reveal a skinny young boy on the step, holding a flaming torch. A rapid exchange of Dutch followed, whereupon Alida turned and beckoned.

'What is it?' Warily, Betsy came to the door and gazed at the boy, who made a clumsy bow, fished in his pocket and produced a folded sheet of paper.

'Meneer Lacy,' he mumbled, and held it out. After a moment Betsy took it, whereupon the boy jerked his head, pointing up the street. As she unfolded the letter, he lifted his torch for her to read. The paper bore a single, scrawled sentence:

If you come to my house now, this boy will light your way.
    T.L.

At first taken aback, she was now both uneasy and intrigued. Her choice was stark: accept Lacy's invitation, which might reveal important intelligence; or play safe, and remain here as she'd been instructed. To go might mean danger, of course. Whereas staying indoors meant . . . what?

Standing in the hallway, she tried to weigh the risks. She didn't trust Lacy; indeed, she feared him. Was he inviting her and Mullin, or her alone? Surely he couldn't have known she was on her own in the house . . . She frowned. Her instinct was to send the boy away, and berate Alida for answering the door. But soon her adventurous side began to assert itself and, as usual, it was more persuasive.

She had no way of knowing how long Mullin and Crabb would be out; perhaps all night. It was likely they were on a wild goose-chase in any case — whereas she might be the one who learned something to their advantage. Though she could imagine what Mullin would say, once he learned of her rashness . . .

'Well, cods!' she said aloud. 'Let him rant all he likes. I'm not his servant, nor even his wife!' And with that she turned to the link-boy, who was growing impatient.

'I'll come,' she said. She pointed to the letter and nodded. 'Let me get a cloak.' She mimed it to Alida, pointing out to the street. After a moment the girl nodded and went off, whereupon Betsy nodded again to the boy, who nodded back to show that he had understood . . . Then she remembered something else: she would be leaving Alida alone. No, that would not do. What's more, she reasoned, if the girl accompanied her the two of them would be safer together. So, when she returned bearing Betsy's cloak and hat, another exchange of signs took place. The outcome was that a few minutes later three people left the house: two cloaked women and a boy with a torch.

The journey didn't take long. Once he had turned the corner the boy broke into a steady trot, forcing Betsy and Alida to hurry. They skirted the canal into which she had fallen only that morning, prompting a shudder which had little to do with the chilly wind. Then they crossed a footbridge and followed another street. The canal here was wider and bent in an arc, and now there were lights, and people on foot. Boats moved on the water, their stern lanterns aglow. Soon they were passing large houses with private frontages on the waterside, and here at last the link-boy stopped. Turning to Betsy, he gestured to a pillared portico, then without further ado climbed the steps and banged on the double doors. They were opened by a stolid-looking manservant, who was quickly joined by another figure, his portly frame blocking the light.

'Mistress Mullin, welcome to my house!'

'You're most kind, sir.' Betsy picked up her skirts and ascended the steps. As she did so, she indicated Alida. 'I've brought my servant.

She'll wait, then accompany me home.'

Thomas Lacy, dressed in a flowered suit and yellow silk stockings, had stood aside to admit her, but when both women came in his broad smile faded.

'Of course . . . Jacob can take her to the kitchen.' Turning to his own servant he spoke rapidly in Dutch, whereupon the man regarded Alida with some interest. Then, indicating that she should follow him, he made a rapid retreat.

'Your link-boy, Mr Lacy,' Betsy said, 'will he light our way home?' But when she looked round, the lad had vanished.

'Never fear, madam, there are dozens like him!' Lacy's smile was back. After closing the front door he gestured to a doorway at the rear, from where candlelight flooded.

'Please come in,' he said in a hearty voice. 'I've been so looking forward to this conversation.' So Betsy entered the room — only to stop in her tracks.

She had heard that Lacy was wealthy, but she had not expected the sight which greeted her. Her first thought was that this was a treasure hoard, then she realized it was a showroom. Three walls were hung with maps and portraits, while shelves of fine blue-and-white china lined the fourth. There were tables covered with Turkey carpets, on which lacquered boxes and silverware lay. Faced with such riches, it took an effort not to look subdued.

'Oh, how charming!' she gushed. 'I guessed you were a man of taste, sir, but this array robs me of speech.'

Lacy inclined his head. 'I'm but a humble collector.'

'And how is your friend, Mr Churston?' Betsy enquired, by way of gathering her wits. She had just caught sight of herself in a gilded mirror, and was alarmed to see how tense she looked.

'He's unwell, madam, as I think you perceived,' came the reply. 'But please, shed your cloak and be seated. Have you dined?'

'I have, sir,' Betsy replied; though her supper had consisted of a stew and stale bread, while Mullin and Crabb had eaten virtually nothing. 'And your wife, Mr Lacy?' she continued. 'Will I have the pleasure of meeting her?' But when she glanced round, the man was closing the door. Suddenly she was on her guard: any moment now they would drop the formalities, and she must dissemble to the last.

'Alas, she is indisposed,' her host replied, turning to face her. 'She seldom keeps company.'

'I'm sorry to hear it,' Betsy said. Then,

seizing the moment, she added, 'Yet it may be that our discourse is best kept secret, unless I mistake your reasons for inviting me after dark, without my husband.' She raised her eyebrows — but the next moment, her heart gave a jolt.

'I don't think you mistake anything, madam.'

Lacy had stopped smiling. In fact, he had discarded all pretence at courtesy so abruptly, Betsy almost shrank from him. His cheeks were flushed, as she had seen him first in the *Bok*, but his eyes were blazing. Pulse quickening, she struggled for some reply when another sound startled her: the click of a key turning in the lock. Her eyes flew to the door, then back to Lacy, and now she knew what a fool she had been. Her instinct was to shout, until she saw how useless that was.

'You may scream if you like.' Lacy stood with his hands at his sides. 'The house is very solid, and my neighbours are absent. As for your servant, I expect she has other things to concern her just now.'

Betsy caught her breath. 'What have you done with her?' she cried. 'If you dare to — '

'Sit down, Mistress Mullin — or whatever your name is!'

The order came like a whipcrack; but Betsy remained on her feet. Lacy, however, was unperturbed. With a shrug he sat himself in an armchair, folded his arms and fixed her with a look of near contempt.

'You're not married to him, are you?' he said drily. 'Nor are you devoted to any cause. Do you think I believed that tale? Men like Mullin don't change, any more than women like you appreciate fine objects such as those that surround you. Where did he find you, in some bawdy-house in St Giles? Or are you one of his friend's cast-offs?'

Stung, Betsy didn't answer.

'Well, no matter . . . ' He gave another shrug. 'Silence won't serve either. Soon you're going to tell me who sent you and why — and don't try my patience with more lies. If I have to call Jacob in to question you, I will, but you'd be most unwise to force me to it. He has skills learned in the Dutch Army, that even I prefer not to dwell upon.'

Heart pounding, Betsy kept her eyes on his face. She had already seen that there was no other exit from the room, and she imagined the windows, which were heavily curtained, would be secured too. There was no one to help her, nor did Mullin or Crabb know where she was. For the second time that day she was in trouble, and she had no one to blame but herself. Trickery was her only

163

weapon, she knew — whereupon something else occurred too.

'There's no Mrs Lacy, is there,' she said quietly.

At that, her host — or rather the one who was now her captor — grew impatient. 'Much as I adore gossip,' he snapped, 'I have no inclination for it now. I want to know who sent you here . . . ' Then he stiffened. 'Why, you're one of Downing's flock, aren't you?'

Downing? In an instant, Betsy recalled Mullin's account of the new ambassador. 'I don't know what you mean,' she said.

'Don't lie!' Suddenly Lacy was on his feet. 'You came to this town to snoop, woman! So answer me!'

'Did I?' Thinking fast, Betsy tried to judge the man's strength. His girth meant that he would be slower on his feet than she, yet he was nearer to the door. She glanced about for a likely weapon.

'We'll speak of Venn first,' Lacy said, taking a step towards her. 'How did you learn of his death?'

'What does it matter?' Betsy countered quickly. 'More important to my mind, is who killed him — '

'Precisely!' Lacy glared at her. 'So — who did?'

'I think you know that,' she replied. And

now she did take a step back, which merely brought her up against a table's edge.

'Let's say that I don't,' the other threw back. 'And more, let's say that if you want to remain alive, you tell me all you know — now!' And with that, he stepped closer.

'It was Gorton,' Betsy said quickly. 'And I think that name is known to you!' But a puzzled frown crossed Lacy's features.

'Who's Gorton?' he snapped. 'And what's he to you? Tell me!' And he would have seized her, had Betsy not moved.

Her hands were at her back, feeling along the table-top, and now her right hand closed on something cold and solid. Without thinking she grabbed it and swung her arm round, driving the object against Lacy's head. Then she ducked aside and looked: she was holding an ornate silver tray. Without pause she raised it again, and slammed its edge into his face.

There was a moment, which seemed to last a long time. Panting, Betsy looked into the face of her interrogator . . . then blinked. A livid streak had appeared on Lacy's forehead, while at the same time blood spouted from his nose. With a look of amazement, he staggered backwards and sat down on the floor. There followed a clang, as Betsy dropped the tray. Then, stumbling over her gown, she ran to the door and banged on it.

'Come quick!' she shouted. 'Your master's sick!' Nothing happened, so she banged again, then bent and put her mouth to the keyhole. 'Jacob!' she cried. 'Come here!'

She straightened up, and risked a look round, but to her relief Lacy hadn't moved. Blood ran from his nose and down his flowered coat. Stupidly he stared up at her . . . Then the dazed look on his face changed to one of fury.

'*Jacob!*' he shouted. '*Kom! Haast u!*' Clumsily he put out a hand and tried to raise himself, whereupon again Betsy acted on impulse. The tray was lying where she had dropped it, so she ran and picked it up. But even as she lifted it there came the sound of a key turning. The door opened to reveal Jacob, looking startled.

'Please, Mr Lacy is hurt!' Thinking rapidly, Betsy pointed to her chest and made gestures to indicate a seizure. The tray she thrust behind her back, but luckily Jacob hadn't noticed it. With an oath he hurried to his master, only to stop short when Lacy shouted out in Dutch. At once the servant whirled round, but Betsy was ahead of him. In a moment she had covered the short distance to the door, got herself through and slammed it behind her. Then she turned the key in the lock, and leaned breathlessly against it.

'*Mevrouw* . . . ?'

With a gasp she looked round. Alida was standing in the hallway, an odd look on her face. At first Betsy read it as one of alarm — then caught her breath: the girl was embarrassed! And at once she saw why: she was not only uncloaked: the top buttons of her bodice were loose.

'Cods!' she cried. 'I thought . . . ' Then she sighed. 'Never mind, let's get out of here!'

Alida's face had reddened. Quickly she began to button her bodice, but the next moment such a thudding and banging began that she flinched.

'We're going — now!' For once, Betsy's meaning was clear enough. With a swift glance at the closed door, which was shaking alarmingly, the girl followed her across the hallway. Mercifully the front door was unbolted, and the key was in the lock. In seconds Betsy had opened it and the two of them were flying down the steps. From the house there came a crash of splintering wood, followed by a shout.

'Come on!' she cried, grabbing Alida by the arm. Whereupon the two women began stumbling along the street. A man who was walking past stopped and stared.

'A boat . . . we need a boat!' Heart

thudding, Betsy halted and looked down at the canal. To her relief, there were two or three small craft moored by the landing steps. She called out, and was rewarded to see the man in the nearest boat look up. But at the same time, there came a cry from the doorway of Lacy's house. Both looked round to see Jacob on the top step — and in a moment he had spotted them. Still holding on to Alida, Betsy lurched down the steps.

'Help us!' she cried, grasping the gunwale. 'We need to get away . . . ' She made rapid signs to the boatman, who was gaping — whereupon she realized she still had the tray in her hand. Stifling an oath, she thrust it at him. 'Take it!' she shouted. But still the man stared. Then his eyes went to Alida, who spoke in Dutch. Without a word he reached out and helped Betsy clamber into the boat. Alida got in too, and the small craft lurched, but in a moment the man had pushed them out on to the water. And even as Jacob appeared on the steps above them, Betsy knew they were safe. Breathless, she turned to Alida — and almost laughed with relief.

Her face averted, the girl was buttoning the top of her bodice. And she did not lift her head until they had left the boat and were on foot again.

* ★ ★

The house was still in darkness when they arrived home. Having found coins to pay the boatman, Betsy ordered the man to stop some distance away, below the footbridge. The two women then walked, doubling back until Betsy was satisfied they were not followed. Only then did she turn down the familiar street, unlock the door and usher Alida inside. With a last look about, she went in, drawing the bolt firmly.

In the darkness she stumbled, but soon there came a spurt of flame, which revealed Alida holding a tinder-box. By its flickering light the two made their way into the back parlour, where the girl lit candles. The fire was still aglow and at once Betsy went to it. She was trembling, she realized, then she looked at Alida, and received a surprise: the girl was in tears.

'*Goede hemel, Mevrouw!*' she sobbed, while her shoulders shook. Thereafter she spoke rapidly in Dutch, not a word of which Betsy understood. The meaning, however, she guessed.

'Cods, she thinks I'll dismiss her,' she muttered. 'Because she let that servant fumble her . . . ' Quickly she shook her head. 'It's all right!' she said, making signs, but they

169

were of no use. The girl howled, shook her head from side to side and continued to plead.

'Stop this!' Betsy went towards her. 'You're quite safe. No harm will come.' She struggled to form a word or two of Dutch. '*Meneer Mullin*,' she said. 'Not send you away!'

Suddenly the girl stopped sobbing. '*Nee?*' she asked.

Betsy nodded, then spun round. Both of them were alert in a second: someone was rattling the front door.

'Wait!' She shook her head, and for once Alida understood. The two women waited — then flinched as there came more knocking, followed by further rattling of the handle — but the next moment both let out exclamations of relief, as a familiar voice shouted through the keyhole.

'Where the devil are you? Open this door, or I'll break it! Do you hear me?'

More knocking followed, but now Betsy drew the bolt. At once the door flew inwards, prompting her to step back in surprise. Behind her Alida let out a shriek.

For it wasn't only Mullin who entered, looking angry and flustered; nor merely Peter Crabb, who loomed up behind. To the surprise of the women there was a third man, red-faced and terrified, who was now thrust forward into the dim light, hands behind his back. As Betsy watched he fell to his knees, grunting with pain, while Crabb turned swiftly to close the door. The hinges squealed and the bolt was drawn, whereupon the young giant stood with his back to it. In shocked silence, Betsy stared down at the man whom she had confronted not a dozen hours ago, and who had almost ended her life.

Slowly she lifted her gaze and found Mullin's eyes upon her.

'Well?' he snapped. 'Is this fellow Gorton, or isn't he?'

13

The questioning began the following morning.

At first Mullin had not wanted Betsy present, but he was persuaded otherwise. She knew Gorton, but moreover she had a right to be there, if only in view of her sojourn in the canal. Or so she insisted, despite what Williamson's letter had said about leaving Mullin to conduct interrogations.

The household had taken food and rested, except for Peter Crabb, who had kept a watch on Gorton all night. Not that the prisoner had any chance of escape, confined as he was in the windowless cellar with hands bound and his gaoler seated by the door. There Mullin would question the man until he was satisfied that he had told all he knew.

'Whatever he says, assume first that it's false,' he said to Betsy. 'Moreover, don't speak unless I ask you to — this is my task. Do you understand?'

'I do, but if you mean to use harsh methods, you must give me time to go out,' she answered. 'I'm not afraid of blood, but I prefer not to see it spilled.'

They were standing in the hallway. A murky greyness showed at the windows: rain had started in the night. Betsy had slept for some hours, having been too exhausted not to. That was after she had given Mullin a full account of her experience at the hands of Thomas Lacy. But to her relief the captain was too elated by the capture of Gorton to be annoyed with her for her rashness; or with Alida, who had kept well out of sight ever since. And it turned out that, by contrast to Betsy's, his night's work had been almost mundane.

'We went first to places I knew,' he had told her. 'I tracked down a few unsavoury fellows, the sort who'd inform on their own mothers for a guilder. But nobody knew anything about your friend, or if they did they weren't talking. In the end I would have given up the search, if not for Crabb. It was he who suggested the *Bok*, where the landlord's been known to hide men for a price. Sure enough, there we found our quarry, cowering in an attic. When he saw Crabb, he almost soiled his breeches. If he's a paid assassin, he's the feeblest one I've ever encountered — skulduggery's not his *forte* at all.'

Now, as the two of them descended the stairs to the cellar, Mullin brought the matter up again.

'He won't have slept much, he'll be afraid and weak from hunger,' he said. 'Remember, we've told him nothing. He knows you and Crabb from the prison of course, but he doesn't know me from Adam. So whatever cock-and-bull tale I spin, mark it well — you may need to use it yourself.'

Betsy murmured assent, yet her thoughts were elsewhere. And when they both entered the store-cellar, which was lit by a single lantern, her first reaction was one of pity. Gorton was sitting in a corner, and he was a sorry sight. He looked haggard and dishevelled, his clothes dirty, his stockings torn. Crabb had removed his shoes and loosened his bonds so that he could drink, though on Mullin's orders the man had been given no food. When they came in Betsy's one-time cellmate stiffened, and spoke immediately.

'Thank God you're safe!' Wide-eyed, he gazed at her. 'I wished only to escape, when I — ' He swallowed. 'See, I was confounded. God smite me if I meant you any harm — '

'Stop that babble!'

At Mullin's snapped instruction, the man fell silent. He watched as the captain put down the stool he had brought in, and sat down facing him. There was nothing else in the cellar apart from another stool, on which Crabb sat without expression. Betsy preferred to remain standing.

'So, I understand your name isn't Gorton, while you're here,' Mullin said, sounding amiable all of a sudden. 'But I'll use it anyway, or perhaps I'll dispense with formalities. What is your first name?'

Nervously, Gorton lifted his hands and rubbed his forehead. Though the cellar was cold, he was sweating. 'It's James, sir,' he answered.

'Well, James . . . ' Mullin frowned, as if perplexed. 'Tell me, how on earth did you get yourself clapped up in the King's Bench?'

'A gambling debt,' the other replied quickly. 'A man may easily over-reach himself at the cock-pit.' He attempted a glassy smile, which didn't work. 'I see you're a man of the town, sir, you know how things are.'

'Do I?' Mullin exchanged glances with Crabb, who remained expressionless. 'Well, even if you speak the truth, that too matters little. What interests me more is why you killed a man called Venn. Slit his throat with his own pocket-knife, I heard. Most unpleasant.'

At that, Gorton gulped audibly. 'Please hear me, sir,' he said. 'I'll not lie — I know I'm at your mercy, as I know what the wrestler here could do to me. Though quite what this is about, and how this . . . this lady

175

comes to be a part of it, I swear I'm at a loss to know. So ask what you will, I — '

'Now you're starting to bore me, James,' Mullin broke in. He gave a long yawn, which fooled everyone except Betsy. 'As for lying, I'll judge whether you do or not. I'll ask you again, and this time I want an answer: why did you kill Venn?'

But Gorton coughed, and his eyes went to a mug which stood by Crabb's feet. 'For the Lord's sake, let me have water,' he breathed.

'Later, perhaps . . . ' Mullin waved a hand. 'It depends on the answers I get. Indeed . . . ' He leaned forward, making the other flinch. 'Did I forget to mention that your very life depends on that too, James? Pardon me if it slipped my mind.'

Gorton's eyes flew from Mullin to Crabb, then finally settled on Betsy. There was a pleading look in them, as if he believed his hopes rested on her.

'Mistress, you'll heed me, won't you?' he said. 'You know I'm not a murderer! Those dreadful hours we spent in that stinking prison, sharing our last morsel, our last drop of water . . . You know me! I'm just a man who fell foul of the law, as you did.'

He flinched, as Mullin raised a hand quickly. It appeared as if he meant to lash out at the prisoner, but instead he scratched idly at his scalp. 'That's better,' he sighed, adjusting his periwig. 'I'm not a man who likes to repeat himself, James,' he went on. 'So I advise you to cease prating and tell me something that interests me. This woman' — he pointed over his shoulder — 'I'm afraid she can't help you, but I can.' He paused dramatically. 'So answer truthfully, and you may not only live, you may even leave here unharmed. Do you see?' Then deliberately, he threw a glance at Crabb. A look passed between the two men which Betsy realized was a signal. On cue, the young giant spoke up.

'I don't think we can promise that,' he said with a shake of his head. 'Not if he's the one who killed Eleanor too . . . ' He eyed the prisoner. 'It was you who got in and stabbed her, at the house near the Oude Kierke — wasn't it?'

Slowly the colour drained from Gorton's face while his fingers worked nervously at his bonds . . . and suddenly, the wretched man was in tears.

'Good God, will you believe naught I say?' he whimpered. 'Whoever — whatever you think I am, you're sorely mistaken. I know nothing of a house near the Oude Kierke. I know nobody here from anywhere but the prison, which is why I was so confounded when I ran into her!' He pointed at Betsy. 'So you may break me and burn me, and do what you will, but I can't tell what I don't know! God-a-mercy, sir, won't you listen?'

The last part was directed at Mullin. Though he and Crabb remained impassive, Betsy was torn. She had felt anger against Gorton a moment ago; now he looked so forlorn, that she was suddenly filled with doubt. Either he was a better actor than she had imagined, or he spoke the truth.

'Dear me, what a speech!' Mullin let out a sigh, of mingled weariness and disdain. 'Do you think I care a jot for your weasel words? I simply want answers, James, which you seem determined not to give. Now, shall I try again, or must I ask your old friend the wrestler to break a finger or two?'

'He's no friend of mine,' Crabb put in casually. 'I'll gladly break all his fingers — and his wrists too, if you like.'

A tense silence fell. It was turning serious, as Betsy had expected, and all at once, she saw both Crabb and Mullin in a different light. She thought she knew them, yet she had not seen them at this most brutal of tasks. It was a side of their work that wasn't to her liking.

'I'll go back upstairs,' she said.

There was a stir, and for a moment she

thought Mullin was angry; she had disobeyed his order to keep silent. But when he swung his gaze to her, she was surprised to see him smile.

'Perhaps it's best,' he said. 'A woman shouldn't witness this.' Abruptly he turned back to Gorton, who was a picture of terror. Sweat ran down his face, while his hands shook.

'Please, won't you speak for me?' he begged, staring at Betsy. 'I'm a sick man — I swear it. I cannot bear this! God smite me if I lie to you — '

'I'm afraid God isn't here, James,' Mullin said. 'And sick or not, you'll soon feel a deal worse. Now, if you won't speak of Eleanor's death, or of Venn's, I've no choice but to — '

'Damn you then — I killed him! I killed Venn!'

It was almost a shriek, and it took even Mullin by surprise. He and Crabb gazed at the snivelling figure. Betsy was shaken, but suddenly, now the words were out, memories rushed back.

'So you *were* the trepanner — the cross-biter in our cell!' she cried. 'I said so before you struck me!' And ignoring Mullin, who turned in irritation, she went on, 'He told me he knew someone was watching him. I didn't think you had the nerve, but I was wrong. You're one of them — you and Thomas Prynn and — '

'Be quiet!'

In a trice Mullin was on his feet. 'Or be gone,' he added. 'This man's in my charge, and I'll choose how to proceed. Now, will you go, or will you hold your tongue?'

Breathing hard, Betsy mastered herself. 'Your pardon,' she said finally. 'I'll stay.'

'Very well!' Impatiently Mullin turned back to his prisoner, but remained standing. 'Well, at last we come to the nub of it, James,' he said, gazing down at the man. 'Not that the matter was in doubt. Now I want to know *why* you killed Venn, or rather, on whose orders. And don't waste any more of my time!'

But another expression had come over Gorton's face. He was still shaking, especially as Crabb looked angry enough to fly at him, but there was something else too: a look almost of resignation.

'Nobody ordered me,' he said, wiping his face with the back of a hand; his tears had ceased as quickly as they had begun. 'I loathed the fellow. I saw him talking close with Beatrice — if that's her name.' He threw a dark look at Betsy. 'I . . . we all believed her to be a whore, yet she did nothing but taunt us. I caught Venn alone, and he scorned me.'

180

He gave a shrug. 'I was jealous, that's all.'

'And you expect me to believe that?' Before the other could reply, Mullin raised a hand and pointed at him. 'You drive me too far!' he shouted. 'You're a damned conspirator — one of a piss-hatch group of traitors who are up to mischief. And in case you hadn't guessed, I'm here to unpick it! Now, my patience is gone. I want the names of your fellows, though we know those of Prynn and Phelps already — and the late Mr Venn, of course. So if you want to save yourself a deal of pain, I advise you to begin talking. Mr Wrestler . . . ?'

He eyed Crabb, who also stood up, whereupon Betsy decided it was time to leave after all. But, as she started for the doorway, there came a yelp and as always, her curiosity overruled her. She looked round to see Gorton also struggling to his feet, his back against the wall.

'You'll get nothing more from me!' he cried. 'I've admitted I killed Venn, so hand me over to whomever you will. The gallows will be a blessing, believe me . . . ' he made a choking sound, between a cough and a sob. 'Press me all you like, you'll find I've never heard of Prynn or Phelps, whoever they are. As for being part of a conspiracy . . . ' He shook his head, as if the idea was too ridiculous for words.

'What about Eleanor?!'

Crabb towered over Gorton, his fists clenched. But when Mullin looked at him sharply, he raised a warning hand.

'Back off, Captain,' he said gently. 'It's my turn.'

'Wait . . . ' Mullin read the look in the young man's eyes. 'Rein your anger in,' he ordered. 'We want intelligence, not a corpse on our hands.'

'Why not have both?' Crabb replied — and without warning he lurched forward and seized Gorton by the throat. The man gave a strangled cry and grabbed his wrist, but to no avail. Though he wriggled like an eel he was held fast, and would remain held until Crabb had had his way.

'You killed Eleanor,' he muttered, bending so that his face was close to his victim's. 'You thought it was her mistress' — he jerked his head to indicate Betsy — 'but you went to the wrong room. In the dark you found a woman in the bed, and you stabbed her — three times, by my reckoning. You think I'm going to let you hang, without wringing every word out of you first?'

Once again the room fell silent. Mullin said nothing, and Betsy, standing by the doorway with heart thudding, guessed why. She knew Crabb's action was spontaneous, but she saw too that it might bring results. As if to confirm it the captain stepped back, caught up his stool and moved it away. Sitting down beside Betsy, he folded his arms and waited.

Gorton's face, meanwhile, had turned an alarming shade of red. Still he gripped Crabb's wrist, panting and struggling. But he was weakening visibly, as the young giant's fingers remained clamped about his throat. A hissing came from his mouth, he kicked out wildly, but the blow to Crabb's shin was as nothing.

'Eleanor was an innocent girl,' the giant said, through his teeth. 'Admit you killed her, and I'll let you breathe. Then tell us why you came to kill her mistress!'

'I can't . . . ' Gorton was purple now, his eyes popping. Sweat dripped on to his collar, and suddenly he sagged. His eyes rolled, his arms fell, and he went as limp as a rag. With a muffled oath, Crabb let him fall. Whereupon with an oath of his own, Mullin stood up.

'Water!' he snapped.

Breathing heavily, Crabb stooped, picked up the mug from the floor and dashed its contents into Gorton's face. The result was instantaneous: a gasp, and the man's eyes flew open.

Mullin stepped forward and dropped to his haunches. 'You know this can all end, James,' he said, calm again. 'You must excuse the wrestler: the girl who died was his friend. But tell me why you came to kill, and I'll yet be lenient.'

'God help me, I cannot!'

The prisoner gazed into his inquisitor's eyes, and shook his head slowly. 'I never went to any house,' he said hoarsely, 'and I didn't kill this girl you speak of, nor had I any wish to kill anyone here. Do what you will, you cannot alter that. For pity's sake, have me committed or kill me . . . my game's over in any case!'

After a moment Mullin turned to Crabb, who had resumed his stolid look. Then he glanced at Betsy; and now there was doubt on his face. She nodded, for she too had come to a conclusion that surprised her: she believed Gorton.

'We'll leave him a while.'

The captain had made a decision, and the look that he now gave Crabb brooked no argument. 'Give him water and a morsel of food, then lock him in,' he added.

The younger man hesitated, but his anger was gone. With a curt nod, he ambled across the room and went out. Betsy followed, but in the doorway she stopped. Hearing a sound, she snapped round, and saw that Mullin had heard it too. Then she looked at Gorton and gave a start.

The man was no longer red-faced: he was as pale as linen. His hands were pressed to his chest, which was heaving. He tried to rise, then groaned and sank back, trembling. And slowly, the fear in his eyes gave way to a look of surprising calm.

'Tell . . . I didn't squeal,' he mumbled, though his words were slurred. 'And tell her . . . I always loved her . . . '

Then his body twitched, and the life slipped out of it.

Betsy's hand went to her mouth, while Mullin stared. Then with a curse, he dropped to one knee and lifted the man's hand. After letting it fall he stood and faced Betsy, his face taut.

'Perhaps he really was sick,' he murmured. 'Or perhaps I begin to find it hard to tell truth from fables . . . ' He sighed. 'Now we'll never know, either way. It's but — '

'One of the hazards?' Betsy broke in. 'For the children of Judas?'

But her only answer was a shrug. Whereupon she turned and walked back upstairs to the hallway. There she stopped, her eyes fixed on nothing, as a new and alarming truth dawned.

If Gorton was truly innocent of Eleanor's murder, then who had come to kill Betsy? And how long might it be before they tried again?

14

Early that afternoon a meeting took place in the back parlour, and from the outset tempers were frayed. For once it wasn't Marcus Mullin who was the angriest, however, but Peter Crabb.

'I'll tidy up — again,' he muttered. 'Gorton's body will be found floating in a canal . . . Folk will assume he fell in, and his heart gave out.' He glowered at Mullin. 'Yet we're no nearer to breaking this conspiracy — if we ever were close. Now the one who killed Venn is dead too, I fear the whole pack of them will panic and flee. I'm tempted to throw the game up here and now, and return to England . . . what do *you* say?'

His question was addressed to Betsy, who had remained silent. Rain lashed the windows. Mullin, who had been pacing the room, stopped and faced her.

'You believed Gorton, didn't you?' he said abruptly. 'You don't think he was one of these plotters — despite what he said about not squealing. Am I correct?'

'I don't believe he killed Eleanor,' Betsy replied, after a moment. 'Or that he killed

Venn out of jealousy. I saw no sign, when we shared that cell, that he had any interest in me. There's something more, that he kept back to the very end. Perhaps his last words offer a clue — tell *her*. Even Gorton had someone he loved — could it be for her that he took such risks?'

'Well whoever the woman may be, we'll learn no more of her now,' Mullin said. In irritation, he turned on Crabb. 'If you decide to abandon me and go back to Williamson, then I can't stop you,' he snapped. 'Even though there's some damned murky business in train here, that's brought about the deaths of three people already. It strikes me as worth taking trouble over — doesn't it you?'

'It does,' Crabb retorted. 'But you're the prize cockerel hereabouts — sir. If you'd taken a firm grip on the matter from the start, instead of strutting about like — '

'Wrestler, this won't help.' Betsy met Crabb's eye. 'None of us knew what we faced when we came here. All we had was Venn's testimony, and Mr Lee's suspicions. But we've learned there was a false priest, of some sort. And since Gorton, too, turned up in Delft . . . ' She shrugged. 'It can't be coincidence, can it?'

'I think it most unlikely,' Mullin put in. 'What's more, our portly friend Lacy needs investigating.' He faced Crabb again. 'There are trails to be followed, and I mean to pursue them. That's what Williamson pays me for — when he remembers. So, whether I must work alone or not — ' He broke off, frowning. 'But there's another thing: the attempt on your life,' he added, eyeing Betsy. 'Perhaps Crabb's right, and you should return to London. I can't watch you all the time — '

'Cods, Mullin!' Betsy's anger was roused. 'You haven't watched me at all! It's Wrestler who saved me from drowning, while I got myself out of Lacy's clutches. As for Eleanor's murder: it was sheer luck saved me from that fate. So cease your posturing, and let us form some strategy!'

And with that she sat down again, fanning herself with the edge of her whisk. Mullin seemed rather relieved, she thought, but covered it with his sardonic look. Wearing a look of some amusement, Crabb spoke up.

'Those are brave words,' he said. 'You shame me, mistress — indeed I shame myself, since it was I who swore to discover Eleanor's killer.' He turned to Mullin. 'So it seems we're in your service still. Do you have a strategy, or do you not?'

'In truth, not much of one,' the other replied, after a moment. 'And there's no escaping the fact that you're a risk,' he said to Betsy. 'You've drawn too much attention to yourself. I see but two choices: either you return home and give our esteemed master such intelligence as we have, or you remain here out of sight. In other words — '

'What, keep to the house?' Betsy broke in indignantly. 'I will not, sir! In case you forget, I'm supposed to be your wife. Besides, the only undue attention I've attracted so far has been through getting pushed into the canal. As for Lacy . . . ' She paused. 'There I'll agree with you. He's hiding something — and more, he regards me as a threat. Though why he should accuse of me being in Downing's pay, I cannot know. It would be useful to find out, would it not?'

'It would.' Crabb was nodding. 'But more important, to my mind, is finding this fellow who was about the *Papenhoek*. Whoever he is, he's at the heart of it — I'd swear to that.'

All three fell silent. Betsy, though shaken by Gorton's death, realized that she was now more determined than ever to solve this riddle. Plots hatched on foreign soil — and by Englishmen — alarmed her more than she liked to admit.

'Would anyone care for some wine?'

Mullin's question broke her train of thought. She looked round to see him opening the door. He called Alida's name, added a few words in Dutch, then turned back to the others.

'Thirsty work, all this cogitation,' he muttered. 'I find a cup of something strong focuses my mind.' He sat down heavily. 'Then, since I seem to be over-ruled at every turn, let's lay out our stall, shall we?' He eyed Crabb. 'I suppose you could try and track down the false priest, but you don't speak Dutch. I, on the other hand, could contrive to run into Lacy, get him drunk and see what he spills, while — '

'I don't speak Dutch either,' Betsy broke in. 'But Alida does. After our experience yesternight, I believe she'll be willing to go with me and do what I ask.'

After a moment, Mullin nodded. 'Then why not go to the *Papenhoek* again and make more enquiries? I don't believe the old priest will tell more, but you might poke about a bit.'

'I might,' Betsy agreed, 'but I've thought of a better idea.' And so she had, though for the present she had a mind to keep it to herself. 'As a gentlewoman with a servant at my disposal, I don't believe I'll come to any further harm in daylight,' she added. 'So, with your leave, sir, may I pursue it?' She smiled at Mullin, to let him know that she cared little whether he gave leave or not.

'Why of course, my dear.' The captain threw her a wry look. 'In which case, I'd better blunder into Lacy.' But it was clear that his customary spirit was returning. When the door opened and Alida appeared with a tray, he brightened visibly. 'However, you, too, have become rather a familiar sight in Delft, Crabb,' he observed. 'Where do you propose to venture?'

'I said I'd go where Beatrice goes,' the young man answered. Though there was unease on his face.

'It's all right, Wrestler,' Betsy said. 'I'll be safe — please go where you will. If I don't return by nightfall, you might come looking for me at the *Bok*.' And with that she turned to Mullin, and waited for him to pour the wine.

Having got her way, she couldn't help feeling elated. But less than an hour later she was on tenterhooks again, as she stepped out of the rain and entered the inn where she had first met Thomas Lacy.

To her relief he wasn't there — but someone else was, who knew her at once. Seated at the same table where she had sat before was Lacy's friend, the down-at-heel poet Henry Churston — and the moment he saw Betsy, he started like a nervous rabbit.

'Mistress Mullin . . . ' The man got to his feet as Betsy drew near. Alida was behind her.

'Mr Churston.' Betsy smiled brightly. 'An unexpected pleasure . . . May I buy you a glass of something?' Whereupon the fellow blinked, and sat down again. Beside him was a ragged young woman, the sorriest-looking slattern Betsy had ever seen. At once she scowled, but when she looked past Betsy, her mouth fell open.

'Alida!' she exclaimed, getting to her feet. Betsy looked round to see her servant looking uncomfortable — and realization dawned. Here was an explanation for how Mullin had managed to hire her so quickly: from among the sort of women best known to him.

'I see my maid and your friend are acquainted, Mr Churston,' Betsy said drily. 'Here's a half-guilder . . . why not tell them to go and share a mug?'

Churston hesitated, then muttered some words in Dutch. Betsy, meanwhile, met Alida's eye and nodded. Without a word the girl jerked her head to Churston's friend, who moved off with a final glare. Ignoring her, Betsy took the vacant stool and seated herself. When the drawer appeared, she pointed to a glass. But when she turned to Churston, she saw him eyeing her suspiciously.

'If you seek Lacy, he's not here,' he said hoarsely. 'I haven't seen him all day.'

'That's no matter, sir,' she answered: it was not Lacy she had sought at all. 'I'm merely eager for the company of my compatriots. Indeed, I've a weakness for poets — and playmakers too,' she added, smiling. 'Are you acquainted with Mr Shadwell, or Mr Wycherley? They're friends of mine.'

'Oh?' Churston frowned. 'How is that?'

'Why, I've seen them at the theatre,' Betsy answered. 'We've often conversed together after a performance.' Whereupon she gazed into the distance, and recited:

'*Poets, like cudgelled bullies, never do*
At first or second blow submit to you;
But will provoke you still, and ne'er
    have done
Till you are weary first with laying on.

'Are the lines familiar to you, sir?'

'Perhaps.' The man coughed, then turning away, spat heavily. Betsy blanched, but kept her smile.

'It's generous of you to pay for my drink,' he resumed, without much warmth. 'Yet I fear I'll be poor company. I've lost touch with England. As for London's literary men . . . ' He gave a weary sigh. 'They would scorn you for spending time with me — if any of them remembered me at all.'

'Come sir,' — Betsy put on a reproachful look — 'you an Oxford man? Why, Mr Lacy himself said he's never known such a learned one as you.'

'Lacy says a lot of things.' There was an odd look in Churston's eye. 'And with your leave, madam, I don't care to discuss him.'

Betsy nodded, then decided to strike. 'Then there are other things you and I might speak of, sir,' she said, lowering her voice. 'One of them being the prison you were unfortunate enough to get yourself into. Which one was it? My own brief holiday was spent at the King's Bench.'

Churston stiffened, but made no answer.

'Forgive my boldness, but I recognized the look,' Betsy went on. 'I saw it on the faces of many, not knowing if they would eat that day, or the next . . . ' She paused. 'A friend of mine was even killed while I was there. A man called Venn, found in the jakes with his throat cut . . . '

She looked up as the drawer appeared with a jug and cups. After he had gone, she looked deliberately at Churston again. The man was staring at her, and now there was no mistaking the fear in his eyes. Seizing the jug he slopped wine into a cup, spilling some on the table, then picked it up and drank greedily.

'Your pardon,' Betsy sighed, and filled her own cup. 'I've stirred bad memories. I meant only — '

'Who are you?'

The question startled her. But taking a sip of the strong red wine, she faced the other calmly. 'I'm the wife of Captain Mullin, sir,' she began — then flinched. Churston's hand had shot out to seize her arm.

'No, you're another of them! Come to get me soused, then play me like a bagpipe, have you? Well you're wasting your time. I know nothing about anything, and I care even less!'

Carefully, Betsy put down her drink and glanced about the smoky room. Then, when no one seemed to be looking, she leaned close to Churston's unwashed face. 'I've a poniard strapped to my thigh,' she said gently. 'If you don't let go of my arm, I'll stick you with it.'

But the other did not let go. 'I don't believe you,' he breathed. 'Any more than I think you're a gentlewoman who's married to that rakehell Mullin.' He stifled a cough, and it was all Betsy could do not to gag at his sour breath. 'So I ask again: who are you, and what do you want with me?'

'Very well!' With an effort, Betsy met his

eye. 'I'll speak plain if you will,' she said. 'But I know you've been in prison as I have. And let's leave Mullin out of it — he's nothing to me. I want to hear what you know about Thomas Lacy — a man you despise even as you let him pay for your drinks.' Then she frowned. 'And what did you mean, *you're another of them* — another of what?'

A moment passed before, to her relief, Churston let go of her arm. Taking up his drink again, he drained what was left and banged it down. 'I thank you for the wine, madam.' He placed both hands on the table and leaned forward. In a moment he would be gone and this chance lost. So, on impulse, Betsy placed her hand firmly on top of his.

'If you go,' she murmured, 'I'll tell Mullin you put your hand up my skirts. I think a man of your sensibilities may imagine what he will do.'

Without looking at her, Churston swore profanely. But when he tried to withdraw his hand, Betsy pressed on it harder.

'What do you want of me?' he spat. 'I'm nobody — I have nothing you want! You're not the first rummager to come here from England — the Provinces are riddled with them. Now, let me be!' And with that he gripped her hand and thrust it away — but at that moment something caught her eye. It was only a brief flash of silver at the man's neck, but it was enough.

'In fact there's another man I seek,' she said. 'He dressed as a priest once — yet he was no priest, but a rogue. He hid himself in the *Papenhoek* for a while — an area I think you know well, Mr Churston. Who's your confessor, Father Martins?'

But at that Churston jerked back, gazing at her wildly. 'You can't know what you speak of,' he said, with a sudden twitch of his face. 'You're angling in the dark . . . and if you value your life, you'll get out of this country — take ship for England, today! Now go away and leave me be!'

He lurched to his feet, sending his stool flying. 'I may live in the gutter here, mistress,' he cried, 'but I'm a free man! So do your worst and — ' Then suddenly he doubled up, coughing uncontrollably. People stirred and, as Betsy stared in alarm, the drawer appeared, a frown on his face. When he spoke to her in Dutch, she spread her hands. Churston coughed and coughed, leaning on the table. Finally he retched and sank to the floor, wheezing.

'*Wat gebeurt hier?*' the drawer said sharply. Betsy shook her head, looking round. One man was getting to his feet. Uneasily she scanned the room — whereupon there was a shout. To her alarm, a figure came hurrying out of the tobacco smoke: the ragged-looking woman who had been with Churston. The next moment she was in Betsy's face, shrieking at her like a fishwife.

'Oh, cods . . . ' With sinking heart, Betsy backed away. But then Alida was at her side, tugging at her gown. She too spoke rapidly, though her words needed no translation. Together, the two women moved to the entrance. Men pointed at them, and there were dark looks, but mercifully no one tried to stop them. Finally they were through the door, and safely outside.

But, as they hurried away through the rain, sounds still carried from inside the inn, and followed them along the street: the screeching of Churston's woman-friend, and the noise of his cough. It sounded like a death-rattle.

15

'Angels of Mercy preserve me — what must I do with you?' In exasperation, Marcus Mullin stared at Betsy. She was sitting at the kitchen table drinking a posset, while he stood across from her. Both women had returned wet from their foray to the *Bok*, but Alida had stoked the fire, and the room was warm. Outside dusk was falling, and the girl was preparing supper. The captain had only just returned — in a poor humour — and what Betsy had told him merely worsened it.

'That was rash in the extreme,' he went on. 'You were lucky not to get into a fight with Churston's whore — in which case she'd likely have torn your eyes out! You should have taken Crabb instead of Alida. She's not — '

'I know what she is, Mullin,' Betsy broke in. 'And she did well enough. Where is Wrestler, by the way?'

'How should I know?' came the terse reply. 'And please oblige me by not changing the subject! If you'd told me what you were going to do, I might have been able to assist. As it is you've simply put Churston on his guard.

Though from what I hear the fellow's just a hanger-on anyway, a ne'er-do-well Lacy amuses himself with. You've learned nothing new, apart from the fact that he's a Papist. So are many in this town — it matters not a jot.'

But Betsy shook her head. 'The man knows something, I'm certain. When he told me I was in danger and I should leave, he was in earnest. Which makes me wonder — '

'Don't tell me you think he's a part of this damned conspiracy,' Mullin interrupted. 'The man's too sick to climb a staircase!'

'Indeed, I don't know what to think,' Betsy said, thinking of the sorry figure Churston cut. 'May we talk of something else? Did you find Lacy and get him drunk, as you intended?'

'I did not.'

With a sigh, the captain sat down. 'It seems he's gone from Delft, but will return tonight. I thought . . . ' He hesitated. 'No, I've a better idea. I think you and I should pay the man a visit and confront him — put the fear of God into him!'

Betsy showed her surprise. 'Aren't you the one who's being rash now?' she enquired.

'Perhaps. But in truth, I'm tired of walking on eggshells — I want some answers.' In sudden irritation Mullin banged his fist on the table, causing Alida to look round.

'We need answers, Brand,' he repeated, lowering his voice. 'And the one who seems likely to have them is Lacy. Apart from this phantom priest, of course . . . ' He frowned. 'The Papists are a close community. Surely we ought to be able to trace the man — especially as he seems to have left the *Papenhoek* in a hurry. What mischief did he get up to, I wonder? Try to ravish a nun — or a novice?'

Betsy shrugged — then, as Mullin's words sank in she gave a start. 'Perhaps that's exactly what he did!' she exclaimed. All at once she had a memory of the nervous young acolyte who had admitted her to the Jesuit church. 'Martins spoke of grave sins — perhaps too grave for his confessional. In which case, you should ask among the gossips yourself. After all, in your eyes I'm merely a blunderer. I'm surprised you want me there when you confront Lacy. At sight of me, he'll throw a fit.'

'But it's precisely *because* your presence will unsettle him that I want you there,' Mullin retorted, with a gleam in his eye. 'Shock tactics, madam. I wasn't an officer of horse for nothing.' He sighed again, and began to relax. 'For now, I confess I'm mighty hungry . . . what's holding up our supper?'

★   ★   ★

But that night, the peace of the household was shattered.

It happened not in the small hours, but soon after midnight. Betsy had retired to her chamber, though she couldn't sleep. Alida slept on a pallet by the window, and her snores filled the room. Mullin, who had the small chamber nearest the stairs, was not yet abed. Betsy had left him and Crabb talking in the parlour, the younger man having returned after dark with nothing to report. Outside the rain had ceased, but a wind had got up, and the old house creaked.

Wrapped in a bertha against the draughts, Betsy found herself frowning. The events of the past few days ebbed and flowed in her mind, as she tried to make sense of them. She was intrigued by the way things moved, but her thoughts were clouded by unease. Her inescapable conclusion, as Crabb had said, was that Mr Lee's family were no nearer to breaking the plot she had stumbled upon, back in the King's Bench prison. The thought was almost enough to make her lose heart.

Across the room, Alida turned on her pallet and muttered in her sleep. Betsy turned too, and tried to empty her mind. Usually, she only lay awake when she had speeches to memorize . . . and now her thoughts drifted to the Duke's Theatre. She fancied she stood on its stage, in a part she didn't know well: that of Lady Waspish, whom she had not played after all. She saw the footlight candles before her, and heard the crowd. At last her eyes closed, and she began to drift into sleep ... until a loud crash shook her awake.

It was followed by a scream. For a moment Betsy thought of Eleanor, back in the house near the Oude Kierke — then she realized it had come from inside her room. She was about to call to Alida, when, in the half-light, she saw the girl sitting up, apparently unharmed.

'*Mevrouw!*' Alida clambered out of bed. But from downstairs came shouting — and Betsy's heart jumped. Some dreadful repetition seemed to be taking place, of that night in the other house!

'Stay there!' She was up, the bare floorboards cold under her feet. Then as more noises came from below, she turned to the door.

'*Mevrouw — nee!*' Alida cried, but Betsy ignored her: she knew something terrible had happened. She found the door, unlocked it and threw it open and, as she stepped out, Mullin's voice flew up from downstairs.

'Down here!' he shouted. 'Crabb's wounded!'

Betsy froze. Behind her Alida stumbled from their room, whimpering. But she heard

Mullin's voice again — then another's, low but unmistakable. Turning to the girl, she took hold of her by the shoulders.

'Listen, Wrestler's hurt,' she said. 'We have to help him!' With that she hurried down the stairs. But, as she gained the ground floor, her spirits almost failed her.

Peter Crabb was lying sprawled on his back. Beside him in his shirt-sleeves knelt Mullin, swearing roundly. He was pressing downwards, apparently on Crabb's upper arm. Light came from a lantern in the parlour doorway, where someone had seemingly left it.

'Stir yourself! Find cloths, and tell the girl to fetch water!' The captain turned on Betsy, his face livid — whereupon a grunt came from the prostrate figure.

'Tie it,' Crabb muttered. 'Staunch the flow . . . '

'Don't talk — I know what to do.' Mullin bent to him again, keeping pressure on his arm, while over his shoulder he proceeded to call out in Dutch. Hearing footfalls, Betsy looked up to see Alida descending, and quickly mastered herself. Leaving Mullin, she flew up the stairs, brushing past the girl. In her bedchamber she began ransacking her portmanteau for linen. Clutching an armful, she ran out again and got herself downstairs.

'Tie his arm with this,' she breathed, thrusting a silk stocking at Mullin. 'Where is he hurt?'

'Where do you think?' He snatched the garment from her and jerked his head at Crabb — and only now did she see the blood soaking his shirt-sleeve. The captain was twisting the stocking into a cord. From the floor, Crabb spoke up again.

'It was a short-sword again,' he muttered. 'I'd swear it . . . Italian, I think. I nearly got it off him . . . the same man . . .'

'Quiet!' Mullin ordered. He fumbled with the stocking, whereupon Betsy lost patience.

'Give that to me,' she snapped. 'You tear his shirt open. Keep the pressure on while I fashion the tourniquet — you'll have to lift him up so I can tie it.' She thought the other would rail again, but instead he thrust the garment at her, his hands covered in blood.

'Very well . . . give me a cloth.' And, when she handed him a shift, he took it, balled it and pressed it to Crabb's shoulder. From the kitchen came the sound of water pouring.

'*Alida — haast u!*' Calling over his shoulder, Mullin moved aside. 'When I take my hands away, swab the wound,' he ordered. 'Then I'll lift his arm while you slip the tourniquet under. Bind it tight, close to the shoulder. When I put my finger there, knot it again — can you do that?'

Breathing steadily, Betsy nodded. Side by side the two of them worked to save the life of the young man who had saved hers — and suddenly she found herself talking. 'Don't move, Wrestler,' she said, as she fashioned the cord. 'We'll patch you up . . . though you won't be jumping into canals again. Likely you'll be excused duties . . . lie on a couch like the Grand Turk, while Alida feeds you. I'll even feed you myself — how would you like that?'

'I'd like it . . . well . . . ' Crabb's voice came between breaths. Now Alida appeared carrying a basin, and Mullin issued instructions. The girl put it down and stepped away. Taking the blood-soaked shift from Mullin, Betsy dunked it in the water. When he tore Crabb's shirt she leaned forward, trying not to look too closely at the ugly wound, and wiped the worst of the blood away. Crabb twitched, then groaned as Mullin raised him, but Betsy moved quickly. It was only a moment's work to thrust the tourniquet under Crabb's arm and draw it tight. The captain lowered him to the floor and pressed his finger to the knot so she could tie it again. Then she sat back, breathing hard — but immediately Mullin got to his feet.

'Stay with him,' he ordered, moving off.

'Give him brandy, and make him comfortable until I get back.'

'Where are you going?' Betsy asked, but he had disappeared into the parlour. Soon he reappeared, pulling on his coat.

'To fetch a surgeon, of course.'

'But . . . won't he ask questions?'

'He can ask whatever he likes,' Mullin threw back. 'It matters not, because Crabb won't be here much longer. As soon as he can walk I'm sending him home. Now, lock up when I've gone!' With that he unlocked the door, opened it with its bone-jarring squeal and went out.

Betsy turned back to Peter Crabb, to see him regarding her with a strained smile. 'I like that . . . about home,' he murmured. 'For once I won't argue . . . ' Then he closed his eyes and sank into unconsciousness.

★ ★ ★

It was dawn before the surgeon finished his work. Methodically he packed his bag, talking in Dutch to Mullin. He was an old man, grey-haired and bespectacled. Mullin answered him mechanically, his face drawn in the light from the parlour windows. Meanwhile Peter Crabb lay asleep on the broken couch, his legs draped over its end. His left arm was bound in a sling. Betsy sat beside him on a stool, where she had been for much of the night.

'The surgeon says he'll sleep for a day,' Mullin said, turning to her. 'He's sewn the wound and given him a draught.'

He looked away and spoke again. After a moment the surgeon bent his head to Betsy and moved to the door. Mullin followed him out. When he returned he found her on her feet, gazing at the sleeping figure.

'So — to business,' he said briskly. When she didn't reply, he cleared his throat. 'Alida will look after him,' he went on. 'You and I have work to do . . . and early morning's the best time to do it.'

'Work?' Betsy faced him. 'What do you mean?'

'I mean confronting Lacy!' There was an angry gleam in Mullin's eyes. 'By the time I've finished with him, he'll have told me everything — that's a promise.' Then his face clouded. 'Or, perhaps you wish me to go alone,' he said uncertainly. 'I would understand, if — '

'Would you, indeed?' Betsy broke in. But when the captain braced himself for the expected onslaught, she flagged. She had been about to give rein to her anger; now it seemed pointless. 'I still don't know what happened,' she said finally. 'How the man got in, I mean . . . ' She shook her head. 'Can we be sure it was the one who killed Eleanor — and who came to kill me?'

After a moment Mullin nodded. 'I think we can. Crabb will tell us more when he wakes. I saw nothing — I'd fallen asleep. The first thing I heard was the sound of a struggle.' He grimaced. 'The fellow got in through a window in the kitchen, that much I know. The frame's rotten . . . any fool could force it. Crabb must have heard him. They grappled . . . I suppose the fellow bolted after he'd drawn blood. Our friend's lucky to be alive.'

'Lucky?' Betsy glanced at Crabb's face and sighed. 'Well then, how soon will it be before he can take ship?'

'I don't know.' Mullin sounded impatient. 'And there's nothing more we can do for him now, except follow our course. But if you need to rest — '

'No.' Betsy met his eye, for her mind was suddenly clear. 'I'm coming with you. Though if you go barging into Lacy's house, you'll have his servant to deal with — which may be no easy matter.'

But a grim smile appeared on the other's face. 'That's not quite what I had in mind,' he said. 'Now, would you care to get dressed? We have some walking to do.'

In the early morning light Thomas Lacy's house stood silent, its windows shuttered. The canal was quiet, boats swaying gently at their moorings. The streets too were empty, though smoke rose from nearby chimneys. Some distance away, on a corner, Betsy and Mullin stood gazing at the entrance from which she and Alida had fled, but two days ago.

'You have your speech?' The captain murmured.

'I do,' she answered. 'But you'd better not take too long . . . my wits aren't up to improvising at this hour.'

'Remember, count to fifty before you move. And don't — '

'There's no need to direct me, Mullin,' Betsy broke in. 'Just don't disappoint me, either.' Whereupon her companion gave a nod, turned and slipped away down the alley behind them.

Feeling somewhat foolish, Betsy began to count. Meanwhile her eyes swept the street, the canal and houses. To her relief nobody appeared, and when at last she reached fifty, she gathered her skirts and walked quietly to Lacy's front door. Mounting the steps, she knocked, waited, then knocked again.

A minute passed, and there was no response. Anxiously she scanned her surroundings, starting as a whirring came from overhead. But it was only a flock of pigeons, that wheeled and flew off. Then the sound of a bolt alerted her and, as soon as the door opened, she went into action.

'*Jacob! Jacob, alstublieft* . . . ' Gasping, she lurched forward and groaned. Ignoring the look of astonishment that appeared on the face of Lacy's manservant, she fell weakly against the door. 'Please help me,' she muttered in English. 'I must see your master . . . Meneer Lacy . . . ' She sank to her knees, while to Jacob's alarm her hands clawed at his clothing.

'*Wat gebeurt* . . . ?' Clumsily, the man caught Betsy's arms. He was in his stockings, a loose gown over his nightshirt. When she let out another groan, the man muttered under his breath. But to her relief, instead of pushing her out of the door as she had feared, he dragged her in across the threshold. Then she slumped on the polished floor of Lacy's hallway, seemingly in a faint. Above her, Jacob cursed, but hearing a footfall, he stiffened. Even as he turned, however, Betsy threw her arms tightly about his legs — which was all the time Mullin needed. There came a sickening thud, then another. Still Betsy held on — then just in time, she slid aside to let the manservant crumple to the floor. Mullin was bending over him, holding a short black cudgel.

Panting, she got to her knees. When the captain offered a hand, she took it and allowed him to help her up. Then she looked down at the prone figure, while Mullin stepped over him and closed the door. There was little doubt that Jacob was unconscious. Blood showed on his head, where Mullin's blows had fallen.

'Ebony,' he said, gripping the truncheon. 'Hard as iron — I needed it, for a thick skull like that.' He was slightly out of breath. 'It's lucky I haven't lost my touch as a picklock too. Are you sure nobody saw you?'

'I don't think so — though I couldn't very well look back, could I?' Betsy glanced round at the door to the room in which she had locked Lacy. She recalled the noise of splintering wood as she and Alida fled, but there was no sign of damage. 'He must have had it repaired,' she mused — then flinched.

Her eyes flew upwards, while Mullin sprang to the stairs. The portly figure of Thomas Lacy had appeared above, staring down in alarm, but before he could speak, the captain was upon him.

'Mullin . . . Great God!'

But those were the only words the man got out before the other grabbed him. 'My dear Lacy!' he cried, taking him by the edge of his nightgown. 'Forgive the intrusion . . . ' And with that he stuck his truncheon in the other's face. 'Our business wouldn't wait, you see.' He grinned wickedly. 'I refer of course to myself and Mistress Mullin — she's been so impatient to see you again. Now, shall we go downstairs?'

16

It was the second interrogation Betsy had seen Mullin conduct, but it bore little resemblance to the first. Instead of a dank cellar, they were surrounded by the splendour of Lacy's showroom. And there was no Peter Crabb to threaten their captive: Mullin himself looked capable of that. With a determined air, he seated himself on a hard chair while his host, now his prisoner, sat opposite. Lacy was still in his ornate night-gown, and without his periwig appeared a diminished figure, his greying hair cropped short. The man knew there would be no help: Jacob, though now conscious, was securely bound and locked in his own kitchen. Yet despite his predicament, Lacy had not lost his powers of speech — far from it.

'This is intolerable!' he cried. 'I could have you hanged, Mullin — do you doubt that? I have the ear of the Grand Pensionary himself — '

'Indeed? How is de Witt these days?' Mullin asked. 'None too popular, I'd say. I incline to the Orange faction myself. I'm surprised you don't, as a man who knows how the wind blows.'

'You're a rogue, sir!' Lacy threw back. 'You've broken into my house like a common thief — and you' — his eyes flew to Betsy, who sat beside her fellow-actor — 'I knew you for a harlot, the moment I saw you.'

'Enough!' The captain leaned forward. He had his truncheon, which he levelled at Lacy. 'We're not here to trade insults,' he snapped. 'I dislike the way you treated my wife — in this very room, I believe. I've a mind to give you a thrashing before I come to my questions. That should ease the wheels of discourse, shouldn't it?'

'Your wife?' Lacy sounded scornful, but there was fear in his eyes. 'She's no more married to you than I am. And were I to swear a warrant, who would be believed? This is how she served me!' He pointed, and now Betsy noticed the bruise: a dark stripe above the bridge of his nose. The nose too was red and swollen.

'Dear me, did I do that?' she said. 'Your pardon, sir, but you were threatening me. A woman must defend her honour.'

'From your lips, madam, that word's an insult!' Lacy retorted. But he was blustering, and he knew it. 'This cannot continue,' he said, eyeing Mullin. 'You know I'm not without friends in Delft. I advise you to cease this foolishness and go while you can.'

'Believe me, I'd like nothing more.' Mullin sighed; but Betsy was growing impatient.

'Haven't we spent long enough on banter?' she said. 'Ask him about Prynn and the others — and Gorton, too.' She threw Lacy a disdainful look. 'Then we can leave. The air's stale here — is it your perfume? In London, men have long since put aside that fragrance.' Stifling a yawn, she looked away.

'How dare you!' Lacy shouted. 'And as for Gorton — you spoke the name before, and I said I know nothing of any such man.'

'Well, he's dead anyway,' Mullin said, in a conversational tone. 'He killed Venn, I assume because his friends deemed him a threat to their enterprise. His friends being a man named Thomas Prynn, and another called Phelps . . . shall I go on?'

Lacy was reddening. 'These names are but chaff to me,' he snapped. 'As for this enterprise you speak of, it sounds pure fancy. You should go upon the stage!'

Mullin and Betsy couldn't help exchanging glances. Whereupon as if sensing advantage, Lacy swung his gaze towards her.

'See now — I know you're bent on some trepanning,' he said, with an effort. 'Whether it's for Downing or for someone else, is no business of mine. We're English, and our loyalties are the same, are they not? Hence, why question me? I'm not — ' But he broke off, as with sudden force Mullin banged the truncheon on the arm of his chair.

'Loyalties?' He echoed. 'Then what's a loyal Englishman doing, here in Delft? Moreover, when Mistress Mullin spoke to you of Venn, she believed the name was known to you — is it not so, madam?'

'It is,' Betsy answered. And when Mullin raised an eyebrow, she sensed he was urging her to press further. 'And now I think on it, perhaps Mr Lacy had good reason to leave England,' she added. 'As others have done, to save their necks — like the Regicides did, a decade back.' She eyed Lacy. 'I haven't forgotten your words, when we first met in the *Bok* — and nothing you've said since has changed my opinion. A man can't pretend such hatred of Popery — and hatred of our King too . . . ' but she fell silent, struck by a change in Lacy's manner. A moment ago he had been angry and afraid; now a knowing look appeared.

'Ah . . . I begin to understand,' he said.

'Understand what?' Mullin snapped.

'But of course — I should have known.'

To their surprise, the man seemed to be relaxing. 'What pains you must have been put to, to winkle all this out,' he went on. 'And I

217

take back what I said — you're not Downing's creature, after all.'

That part was addressed to Betsy. 'Am I not?' she asked, after a moment. 'Then whose creature am I?'

'Why, his!' Lacy indicated Mullin. 'And married or not, you make a fine couple.' He managed a thin smile. 'You should have got down to bargaining sooner,' he added. 'Not that I admit to any of this nonsense, but I admire your persistence. So ... ' He shrugged. 'Would you care to name your price?'

Silence fell. Outside, Betsy heard the shouts of watermen from the canal. The people of Delft were up and doing business, and that was what was in hand now, in this darkened room. She glanced at Mullin, and saw him put on a smile to match Lacy's.

'My price?' The captain hesitated. 'Well now, my price, sir, would depend on what I'm selling. If you mean my silence, concerning your connection to the men I spoke of — men, I should add, whose mischief we've uncovered — then we may perhaps agree upon a sum. If on the other hand, you're asking me for further assistance in some way ... '

'I'm asking no such thing.' Lacy's smile faded — and suddenly there was doubt in his eyes. 'This . . . mischief you speak of,' he went on, 'what is it, precisely?'

Betsy stiffened: despite the plight he was in, the man was turning the tables on them, calling Mullin's bluff! For of course, they didn't know what Prynn and Phelps and their circle were planning, and Lacy suspected as much. When the captain hesitated again, she spoke up.

'Need we spell it out?' she asked, adopting her brazen look. 'Surely you're in enough danger already? Venn's dead, Gorton too . . . For all I know, since we left England the rest of your little band have been caught. All men will break under questioning, sooner or later — will they not?'

Lacy frowned. 'Gorton again? I've said I don't know this man,' he said quickly. 'Were I even put to torture, I could tell you naught of him, nor the others you name. Now, can't we bring this distasteful business to an end?' He eyed Mullin. 'You might have stumbled on rumours,' he went on, 'tavern talk . . . the sort of rant one can hear in certain quarters, on any day of the week. I care not what you know — or think you know — yet I'll buy your silence anyway. And in that you are very fortunate.' Whereupon the other two stiffened, as his voice dropped.

'Mark it, sir — and madam,' he went on,

'for quite soon, no one will care. Your intelligence will be yesterday's news, as stale as the Great Fire. So let's waste no more time, but strike a bargain so you may go. And when I say go,' he added, looking at each of them, 'I don't only mean from my house: I mean leave Delft, for somewhere far away. Not England.' He shook his head. 'That would be unwise. And you've been most fortunate of all, madam — I mean, by your very presence here. Do you follow?' His eyes glinting, he gazed at Betsy — and in an instant she understood.

'You sent him!' she cried, sitting bolt upright. 'It was you who tried to have me killed — '

'Of course he did!'

Mullin had jumped to his feet, wearing a look of grim triumph. Taking a step towards Lacy he lifted his truncheon, and involuntarily the man's hand flew up.

'Don't!' he cried. 'I've said we'll do business! If you leave the country, I'll call off — ' He stopped, but too late.

'Call off whom?' Mullin stood menacingly over him. 'Your hired assassin, who climbs through windows?' He grimaced. 'It's I who should have guessed sooner,' he went on, half-turning to Betsy. 'Our friend here is the purser — their treasurer! He stays abroad out of harm's way, handling disbursements, while the ones in England take the risks. Though if anyone comes prying, he has a mastiff to call upon.' He glowered at Lacy. 'Who is he?' he demanded. 'Some ex-seaman you've bought, who can handle a short-sword? Or an old soldier, one of those embittered souls who drift about Europe?'

'No, he's more than that.' Now Betsy too was on her feet: it was all falling into place. 'He's the false priest,' she said.

A look flickered across Lacy's features. It was gone in an instant, but she knew she had hit the mark. Her heart was pounding, whether from anger or triumph, she didn't know. 'He's the one who didn't scruple to kill Eleanor,' she went on, 'any more than he'd scruple to kill me! It was he Churston warned me about, when he said I should leave the country if I valued my life! He's the one Venn spoke of, who was still in the Provinces, but would return in November.'

'You're too late — he's already left!'

Betsy started, and so did Mullin, but at once Lacy sprang from his chair. Neither of them had expected it, and the captain was caught off guard. He swung his truncheon, but with surprising agility the other man ducked under it. Then he leaped for the door — but Betsy was quicker. With a rapid movement, she kicked out: a step that would have pleased the dancing master at the Duke's Theatre. With a cry Lacy stumbled over her leg and fell headlong to the floor — and at once Mullin had him.

'Get up!' Gripping the neck of the man's gown, he yanked him to his feet. Lacy writhed, swinging a fist, but it missed by a mile. The next moment he found himself thrust back into the chair he had just vacated, where he sat red-faced and breathless.

'Now I've truly had enough.' Mullin's voice was icy. 'I want to know who it is who's already left and what he means to do. And as you suspect, sir, I'm no gentleman. Either I get answers or you die here among your treasures.' He waved a hand at the room. And to show that it was no idle threat he dropped his cudgel, reached inside his coat and pulled out a small dagger. Lacy gulped.

'This will avail you nothing!' he cried. 'Matters are set in motion. I couldn't stop them if I tried! Leave me, and get out while you may, or there'll be a price on your head!'

But with a snort of derision Mullin gripped Lacy about the throat, forced his head backwards and put the dagger to his neck. 'First, the name of the killer,' he said. 'The one who went as a priest.'

A sheen of sweat stood on the other's brow,

but with a rapid movement, he shook his head.

'His name!' Mullin repeated. 'Then I want to know what he intends to do, and when. The projection — what is it?'

Still there was no answer. Lacy's hands shook, and his eyes swivelled towards Betsy. 'You'll listen, won't you?' he said. 'It's too late: the die is cast. Take my offer — a hundred gold guineas! More may follow . . . Don't you understand? You'll be rewarded — you could live as I do, once it's all over — ' Then he yelped. And even Betsy flinched, as blood appeared: Mullin had pricked his ear.

'The projection!' He pressed the dagger to the man's neck again. 'The Roman Plate — wasn't that it?' His question was snapped at Betsy, who nodded, recalling Venn's hurried testimony — then her heart gave a jolt.

'Oh, cods!' she cried.

With a frown, Mullin turned.

'The horse races . . . the location changed from N to D.' Betsy stared at him. 'The Roman Plate must be a trophy. The King goes to Newmarket in early November, then to Datchet for the last race.' She swallowed. 'They're planning to kill the King!'

Mullin froze. Then, slowly, he faced his

victim again. Lacy's face had a ghastly pallor now. Blood dripped on to his collar, while he eyed his interrogator.

'Name your price!' he hissed. 'Whatever you wish for, it can be arranged. In God's name, use your heads! There's nothing you can do to stop it. Get away while you can!'

But neither of the others spoke. Betsy stared in horror, half-hoping she'd been wrong, but she knew she wasn't. The truth was out. Financed by this zealot, a group of desperate Republicans had hatched the boldest plot of all: to rid themselves of their hated king. They would do it when he was most exposed: at the races, where he mingled freely with jockeys and friends alike. The audacity of the scheme stunned her. Small wonder Venn had been killed if they thought him a risk . . . and no wonder Lacy had tried to have her killed too!

'You suspected me from the first day, didn't you?' she asked. 'You sent your assassin to find me, and an innocent girl was murdered instead! That's why you were shaken when you saw me at the Katz house: you thought me dead!'

'So he had his tame mastiff try again, and this time another almost died.'

Mullin had found his voice at last. Thrusting his face closer to Lacy's he breathed heavily, his hand shaky as it held the dagger. Fearing what he would do, Betsy was about to speak, but a cry rang out.

'Don't kill me!' Lacy yelled. 'I promise you money — more than you've ever dreamed of! You know I can do it . . . ' He swallowed, talking rapidly between breaths. 'Or I can help you in other ways. I have friends in many countries — dukes, even princes — you'll want for nothing! Let me go, and I — '

'Let you go?' Mullin swore, an oath of contempt mixed with disbelief. 'Do you think me mad? I've done some questionable things in my time, Lacy, I won't deny it. But you . . . ' He shook his head, almost in admiration. 'I spit on your pleading, as I do on your promises — and on your politics! God knows I've no love of Papists either, but nor do I wish for an England run by men like you!'

He stepped back, as if in disgust. 'No, I won't let you go,' he went on. 'And though you say we're too late, I throw that back at you too!' He turned to Betsy and, at the wild look in his eye, she gave a start.

'We're taking ship for England — immediately,' he said. 'We'll spill our tale too, and see how fast our friend Mr Lee can move. Meanwhile we give chase: I'll ride to Datchet myself. I'm as good a horseman as any in the King's service!'

Her heart thudding, Betsy met his eye. 'Then at least we'll have tried,' she said, nodding. 'And this one and his friends will pay the price.' She looked at Lacy who misunderstood. In terror, he shrank back.

'No, not in cold blood . . . ' he began, then faltered. To his surprise, Mullin was putting his dagger back into his coat. With a casual movement, he picked up his truncheon and gestured with it. 'There's no need to wet yourself, sir,' he grunted. 'I'm no murderer. When I said we're taking ship, I meant all of us. You're coming too — to face English justice. Now, on your feet, before I spike you again!'

17

By nightfall, the old house had become a hive of activity. Peter Crabb was awake, sooner than expected; clearly his colossal frame needed a stronger draught than the one the surgeon had provided, though Betsy insisted that the big man eat supper and rest while she packed. The plan was to take a coach to Rotterdam at once — that night, if possible. Mullin had been out all afternoon trying to arrange it. Meanwhile Thomas Lacy, dressed in travelling clothes, was locked in the cellar, having endured a forced march through the streets with Mullin's dagger pressed to his side. Crabb would take charge of the prisoner on the journey to England. Indeed, now that events had forced a rapid return, the young man was in better spirits than Betsy had seen for days, despite the terrible plot that had been uncovered. As far as the false priest was concerned, it merely made him more eager to pursue the man. His wound wasn't serious, he claimed; a few days, and the sling would be off.

'And when we find that murdering devil, I want to be the one who grabs him,' he'd announced. 'He won't slip by me again if I die in the attempt!'

Now he stood in the hallway, his bandaged arm under his loose coat. His pack was ready, along with Mullin's. When Betsy and Alida came downstairs with the last of her bags, he lifted it with his free hand and stowed it beside the others.

'What about her?' he asked. 'She's not coming, is she?'

Betsy glanced at Alida, who had been very quiet since their return. 'I can't see how she can,' she answered. 'But Mullin will have to tell her.'

The two of them went into the parlour. Crabb had been told of events at Lacy's house, and now he spoke of them again, remarking how it was Betsy who had pieced everything together. 'If you hadn't insisted on going into the *Bok* that first day,' he said, 'we'd still be groping in the dark. Now, see what a snake-pit we've uncovered!'

Since the morning, Betsy had barely had time to ponder the matter. 'And if I'd known Lacy would set a murderer on me, within hours of meeting him . . . ' She shook her head. 'What kind of man is it he uses — one who dressed as a priest, yet would stab a woman to death in cold blood?'

Crabb's face darkened. 'If the captain

allowed me half an hour with Lacy in the cellar, I'd find out everything there is to know,' he muttered. 'Instead, he means to dump the fellow on Mr Lee for questioning, then charge off to Datchet.' He sighed. 'Why did nobody think of the race-track? For an assassin, it's an ideal spot. The King sometimes takes to the saddle and races himself . . . a real sitting target.'

Betsy said nothing. The notion of an attempt on the King's life still took her breath away. But a moment later there came noise from the street, and she gave a start.

'Hoofs — he's found a coach!'

It was true. Soon they were at the front door, to greet a sweating but triumphant Marcus Mullin. Outside stood a rather fine coach, drawn by a team of four black horses. Betsy gaped.

'You haven't hired this, surely? We've no money!'

'I know that,' Mullin said. 'It's being loaned to us — can you guess by whom?' And before she could reply, he supplied the answer.

'Meneer Katz?' She echoed. 'How on earth — ?'

'Not him, *Mevrouw* Katz,' Mullin corrected. 'It was her idea. Her husband didn't like it, but the poor fellow wasn't allowed to get a word in. In fact she insisted, as soon as I arrived. She'd heard I'd been around the town trying to borrow a coach, but no one seems to trust me.' He gave a wry smile. 'No matter, we have our conveyance, we even have a coachman: the Katz's own. Generous, eh?'

'Generous indeed . . . ' Betsy was frowning. She had hardly thought of Madam Katz in recent days; now she was uneasy. 'Why did she agree so readily?' she went on. 'What reason did you give for needing a coach urgently?'

'Simple enough,' Mullin replied. 'I said you'd received urgent news from England — a relative lies close to death. It's your grandmother, if anyone asks.'

'Cods, Mullin!' Betsy eyed him. 'Must you always fashion such tales? Why not say . . . well, Wrestler's had an accident, or — ' But Crabb interrupted her.

'The less people know the better,' he said. 'Though from what I hear, I wouldn't trust Madam Katz an inch.'

'Nor do I,' Mullin said impatiently. 'But we're in no position to refuse the offer. I've promised a payment for the coachman. Once we're at Rotterdam, he'll set us down and return to Delft. So let's cease prating and get aboard!' With that he turned and shouted in

Dutch. Betsy's eyes went to the man seated on the driver's box, who raised his whip in reply. So, thrusting doubts aside, she went indoors — and at last, relief swept over her. They were going home, though not quite in the way she had imagined. Whereupon a different anxiety surfaced: the thought of another sea crossing.

But some hours later, even that was forgotten. For, despite all that had happened since Betsy first arrived on the windy quay at Nieuwpoort, the events on the journey to Rotterdam would throw everything into a new light.

★　★　★

They were five in the coach, for to Betsy's surprise Alida was with them. Mullin insisted on it, though in the haste of embarking he hadn't explained why. And once they'd clattered through the East Gate of Delft and turned south, neither Betsy nor Crabb pursued the matter. She was busy with her thoughts, while the other had enough to occupy him. In a corner sat Thomas Lacy, sullen and silent in his cloak. Crabb was on his left, an end of rope in his right hand. The other end was tied to Lacy's wrists, which were bound. Opposite the prisoner sat a bemused Alida, with Betsy between her and Mullin.

'She's here for appearance's sake,' Mullin murmured, nodding to indicate the girl. 'A gentlewoman needs a maid . . . Besides, I've another use for her when we arrive.'

The coach swayed, picking up speed, while above the rumble of wheels the driver's whip could be heard. 'What sort of use?' Betsy enquired, then frowned. 'This payment for the coachman,' she began. 'You don't mean . . . ' She glared at him. 'You wouldn't!'

'What, act as her pander? Of course not,' the captain replied. 'She's never ridden in a coach before. When I told her she could travel back to Delft alone in high style, I couldn't have stopped her if I'd tried. But if she wants to do business with the coachman on the way, who am I to interfere?'

'Flap-sauce, Mullin!' Betsy sighed, then gave up. She glanced at Crabb. His wound clearly pained him, but he would bear it stolidly as always. Her eyes slid to Lacy, huddled like a black presence in the corner. The man's hat was pulled low and he appeared to sleep. So she sat back and looked through the coach window, as another mile of open countryside went by. The leather flaps were down, although chinks of moonlight showed. She glimpsed fields, and the occasional light of a distant farmstead. Beneath her, the floor shook . . .

Then the unexpected happened.

The first thing they knew there was a shout, followed by a startled neigh from one of the horses. The coach lurched, slowing abruptly. Betsy, Alida and Mullin were thrown backwards, while Crabb and Lacy shot forward into their laps. Instinctively Crabb righted himself and jerked the rope, pulling his prisoner back. Everyone looked about, even Lacy, for something was going on outside: shouting, and hoofs stamping. And all the while the coach slowed, until with much jangling of harness it drew to a halt. Mullin reached out for the window flap — then froze.

'All of you, come out!'

The flap was thrust aside and a face appeared: that of a heavy-set man, glaring at those within. The next moment the barrel of a horse-pistol was thrust through the opening. Alida let out a squeak and put her hand to her mouth.

'Come — now!' The man opened the coach door and threw it wide. There were voices, and Betsy glimpsed the silhouettes of figures on horseback. Then, with Mullin's hand on her arm, she was clambering from the coach and stepping out into the chill night air. The others followed, to stand in a ragged line beside the vehicle, whereupon the captain spoke up.

'If you want money, you'll be disappointed,' he said, facing what they assumed were highway thieves. 'We're humble English travellers, going home — '

'Silence!' The man who had ordered them out waved his pistol menacingly. Beside Mullin, Peter Crabb stood as rigid as a tree. Heart pounding, Betsy saw three other men on horseback, watching them closely. There was more movement: the coachman, climbing down from his box. For a moment the fellow stood there, regarding the highwaymen, then he thrust out a hand, and clasped that of the leader. An exchange in Dutch followed — and Mullin groaned.

'What's going on?' Betsy began, whereupon all became clear.

'You people!' The man with the pistol spoke with a heavy Dutch accent. 'You charged with stealing this coach, the property of Meneer Franz Katz of Delft. You will come back with me, to face justice!'

For a moment, the only sound was that of horses blowing and stamping. In disbelief, Betsy glanced at her fellows. Mullin was tense with anger, while Crabb had assumed his stolid look. Alida's eyes were everywhere, while Lacy . . .

Lacy was smiling. Lifting his hand, he showed the rope which tied him to Crabb, and called out in Dutch. Mullin groaned again. 'He says we've kidnapped him,' he muttered.

'Stop talking!' The Dutch leader pointed his firearm, then called over his shoulder. A second man dismounted and came forward, and he too carried a pistol. Approaching Crabb, he motioned to him to release Lacy. But Crabb simply shook his head, as if he didn't understand.

'Let go of the rope!' the leader cried. It seemed he was the only one who spoke English. 'You had no right to take this man: he's a Dutch citizen!'

'No, he's an English traitor.' To the others' alarm, Mullin took a pace forward. Then he went into a stream of Dutch, which apparently confused their captors. The two on foot looked at each other, then at the coachman, who shrugged. But Lacy spoke again, his voice rising in indignation.

Switching to English, Mullin half-turned to Peter Crabb. 'Better do what they say and let him go,' he said. 'I'm not sure who they are, but they're not constables — ' He broke off, as once again the leader brandished his pistol.

'Release this man now,' he ordered. 'Then we go back to Delft. You walk in front, we ride behind. The coach will follow.' He turned and gave orders to the others. Betsy glanced at Mullin, her hopes crumbling. Already, in England, the King's life might hang by a thread . . . She flinched, as the leader turned back to them.

Then mayhem broke out.

The first to move was Crabb who, without warning, slammed his bandaged shoulder into the Dutch leader, throwing him off balance. But as the man fell, he fired his pistol wildly. There was a spurt of flame, a deafening report and then everyone jumped at once. Another pistol went off, causing someone to scream in agony, whereupon in seconds the roadside became a battlefield. All Betsy could do was grab Alida and pull her to the ground. Then both women were scrambling under the coach while the fight surged about them.

And what a fight it was! The two remaining Dutchmen had jumped from their horses and were closing in. Mullin, outnumbered as he was, pulled out his ebony truncheon and began laying about him. Blows fell, men grunted and cursed. Then Betsy's eyes flew to Crabb.

The big man was transformed: not into a wrestler but a knuckle-fighter, worthy of any Bankside contest. He had dropped the rope, and with his free right hand he struck out. With a single blow he downed the nearest man to him, then half-crouching, turned to meet the next. But as the fourth man darted forward there was a glint of steel. Betsy shouted, then saw that it didn't matter. Barely glancing at the dagger his assailant wielded, Crabb seized the man's arm and bent it savagely. There was a crack of bone, a screech and the fellow dropped, clutching himself in agony. Crabb stooped, wrenched his dagger from his hand and whirled about . . . barely in time.

Weakened but still struggling, Mullin was about to fall. His assailants were not only the Dutch leader, now on his feet again, but the last man too. Locked in a bizarre embrace, the three lurched about the moonlit roadside, arms working. But even as Mullin's knees buckled, blows slamming into his body, Crabb lunged. The dagger pierced the nearest man, who gave a cry and staggered away. The leader scarcely had time to look round before Crabb's fist thudded into his face. Without a sound he keeled over and lay still.

And suddenly, it was over. Panting, the two agents stared at each other: Mullin on his knees, his face bloody in the moonlight, Crabb wincing with pain. His sling had come loose and his wounded arm dangled.

Grunting, he tried to lift it . . . then sat down heavily. It had taken little more than a minute.

Shakily, Betsy got herself out from under the coach and stood staring round at the sight. Aside from Crabb, four men were on the ground: two lying dazed, two sitting. One whimpered as he clutched his broken arm, while the one Crabb had stabbed sat very still, gasping. Then with a start she remembered Lacy — whereupon Mullin spoke.

'He was hit . . . the second pistol shot.'

She turned to the captain, still on his knees. He nodded towards the coach . . . and there was Lacy, slumped against a wheel. His chest rose slowly, his bound hands upon it. Even in the semi-darkness Betsy could see the blood . . . a trickle that seeped from his cloak, staining the ground beside him.

There was a thud of boots, and all of them looked round sharply to see the coachman take to his heels, sprinting away up the deserted road. In seconds, the gloom swallowed him up.

With a groan Mullin tried to rise, then flagged. So Betsy stepped up close and helped him. His periwig had fallen off, there was blood at his mouth and bruises on his cheeks, but to her relief he didn't seem to have taken grievous hurt. Meeting her eye, he jerked his head towards Crabb.

'Go to him. I'll see if our friend's alive.'

Slowly he walked over to Lacy. There was a rustle of skirts, and Betsy found Alida by her side. Wide-eyed, the girl seemed to be taking in the situation. When she gestured to Crabb Betsy nodded, and the two hurried over to the big man.

'If you'll tie the sling again, I'll be fit enough,' he said, looking up. 'Though I fear I've undone the surgeon's good work.'

'Don't fret, Wrestler.' Hitching her skirts, Betsy knelt beside him. 'There are other surgeons — or failing that I'll sew you up again myself. I'm no slouch with a needle.' She glanced round. The captain was standing over Lacy . . . and slowly he shook his head.

'I fear our friend won't be able to enlighten us further,' he said. The others looked, and saw for themselves: Lacy was dead.

'But what troubles me now is, well . . . ' looking at each of them in turn, Mullin gestured to the horses.

'Who's going to drive the damned coach?'

18

In the end nobody drove. Instead the party travelled the rest of the way to Rotterdam on horseback.

For Betsy, the ride was almost a relief after the turmoil they had been through. At least she wasn't cooped up inside a stuffy, bone-shaking coach, or being threatened with pistols. It was a long time since she had sat on a horse, but when their predicament became clear she agreed. The coach, Mullin said, was now a hindrance: driving it through the narrow streets of Rotterdam required skills even he didn't possess. Crabb had only one usable hand, and the coachman had fled — so the solution was obvious. The party would take their assailants' horses, and leave them to their own devices.

'What other choice have we?' the captain demanded. 'We'll unhitch the coach-horses and drive them away. Then we'll release these men so they can walk back to Delft — as they would have made us do.'

He indicated the Dutchmen. Two — the party's leader, and the one who had ended Lacy's life — were now conscious, disarmed and sitting with hands bound. The others — one wounded by a dagger thrust, another with a broken arm — looked in no condition to travel.

'He's the one who shot Lacy,' Mullin said, pointing. 'Let him explain it all — I care not to whom. By the time they reach the town, we'll be in Rotterdam. When they return to help their friends, we'll be aboard ship — and I for one can't put to sea quick enough!'

So it was decided. In a short time, Betsy and Mullin transferred their baggage to three of the small, nimble horses their captors had ridden: Spanish jennets, Mullin said. Crabb meanwhile, his good hand doing the work of two, unhitched the coach-horses. With much shouting and slapping of rumps, he then drove them off into the night, sending the fourth riderless horse after them. So it only remained for the party to get mounted — apart from Alida.

The girl had watched the preparations in silence. But once they were ready she grew agitated. Mullin took her aside and coins were produced, yet though the girl took them she was unhappy. She stood shaking her head mournfully, until at last Betsy went to embrace her.

'Tell her she's been a true friend — a

treasure,' she said. Then, as Mullin inter-
preted for her, she turned and walked to the
horses. To her surprise there was a lump in
her throat, as she and her fellow-intelligencers
at last rode away from the scene of the
débâcle. Their would-be captors, now on
their feet, watched them depart with baleful
looks. But Alida did not wait. When Betsy
looked round, she saw the girl walking up the
road without looking back.

Now, riding by moonlight, the three broke
into a trot along the highway, Betsy and
Crabb working hard to manage their skittish
mounts. They went at the best pace Crabb
could manage, for the big man was not only
in pain: he was as unused to riding as the
horse was to bearing a man of his size.
Mullin, of course, though bruised and
battered, sat easily in the saddle, reining in
impatiently to let the others catch up.
Eventually they settled on a steady pace,
stirrup to stirrup, which allowed them to talk
— and to wonder at last why they had been
tricked by Madam Katz. For a cruel trick was
what it appeared to be, until Mullin told a
different tale.

Before leaving their assailants behind he
had taken a minute to question the leader,
using his own pistol to threaten him. And
since, after all that had happened, the man

didn't doubt he would use it, he had spoken readily enough. Now, the captain relayed his account to the others.

'She sent them — our charming friend Marieke Katz!' he said grimly. 'The one who spoke English works for her husband; the others are ruffians he rounded up at short notice. They were told to follow us, waylay us in open country and bring us back — and there's more.' He shook his head. 'Can you countenance this? They were also supposed to let Lacy escape!'

Crabb took in the information in puzzled silence, but Betsy's mind was busy. Holding tightly to the reins, she faced Mullin. 'Do you mean that Madam Katz is somehow part this conspiracy?' she asked incredulously.

'I confess I don't know.' Mullin kept his eyes on the road. 'I suspected she might be an agent for de Witt, or someone else at the Hague . . . though what she wished to gain by these measures I can't fathom. Yet it explains why she was so eager to lend me the coach.' He put on a wry look. 'It pains me to admit it, madam, but you were right to be suspicious.'

'Then, let's turn it about,' Betsy said thoughtfully. 'If what your informant says is true, it looks not only as if the woman knows what we were doing in Delft, it also appears that she wanted Lacy's plans to succeed. Why so?'

'Why indeed?' Mullin shrugged. 'This game may be somewhat deeper than you or I thought, Crabb,' he said, with a glance at the younger man. 'Or perhaps there are things known to men higher up than your master — things they chose not to tell him.'

Crabb looked troubled. 'I'd swear Mr Lee knows naught of any circle here, apart from his own agents,' he said. 'In the same way that I knew nothing of Gorton, though he was under my nose in the King's Bench all the while, watching Venn.' He frowned at Mullin. 'If someone else has a stake in seeing the King murdered,' he went on, 'I can't guess who it could be, apart from fanatics like Lacy.'

Betsy gave a start. 'The words Gorton spoke, before he died,' she murmured. '*Tell her I didn't squeal*', and '*I always loved her . . .* ''

But at that Mullin snorted. 'Now who's fashioning tales?' he demanded. 'You don't think Gorton was speaking of Madam Katz? That's preposterous!'

'Then what was he doing in Delft?' Betsy countered. 'And how did he come to be released from the King's Bench, so soon after I was? I never believed his tale about being jealous of Venn. Someone ordered Gorton to kill the man after he was seen talking to me.' She lowered her eyes. 'Yet I did believe him, when he claimed he knew nothing of Prynn and the others. And why would he, if he was working for someone else entirely — someone who had such power over him, that he would do murder? The man had little stomach for killing — you said it yourself.'

Now Mullin too fell silent. Both men gazed at Betsy, but while the captain's face showed disbelief, Crabb's was filled with admiration. 'Why, I believe she has something!' he exclaimed. 'Gorton, that foppish fellow who never looked as if he belonged in prison . . . ' He eyed Mullin. 'As for Madam Katz — if she's up to her neck in some mischief, it's a pity you didn't dig further when you went to her house. If we'd known — '

'Known what?' Mullin broke in irritably. 'Even if this were true, you think such a woman would give herself away — especially to an Englishman?' He frowned at Betsy. 'Not that I agree with your fanciful theories — though I won't dismiss them entirely. Once at sea, we might speculate further — our task now is to get to England. Then you two should report to Williamson, while I ride on to Datchet. Lay the whole murky business before him, and let him tease it out.'

'Oh no you don't!' Betsy snapped. 'I know you, Mullin. You picture yourself galloping to the racecourse to save the King's life. You'll give a fine performance, then drop to your knee to receive His Majesty's thanks while we kick our heels in London! No doubt you'll expect a handsome reward — well, flap-sauce, sir! Once we're on English soil, I'm coming to Datchet with you. I've earned the right, have I not?'

And with that, she dug her heels into her horse's flanks and shook the reins. The animal snorted and leaped forward, and in a moment she had outdistanced the two men. Then she drew rein and, readying herself for a verbal tussle, turned in the saddle; but when Mullin came up, he was wearing a thin smile.

'As you wish, madam,' he said coolly. 'But first, you'd better pray that the sea is calm, for once we reach Dover, the last thing you may wish to do is ride another horse. Now, would you care to look at those lights ahead? For if I'm not mistaken, that's Rotterdam!'

⋆　⋆　⋆

Once they were at the port however, both luck and the wind were on Betsy's side. For by dawn, when she, Crabb and the captain had spent their last guilders and finally boarded a packet boat, she was too exhausted to care whether she got seasick or not. Instead she slept through the entire voyage, waking to the cries of seagulls. And when she looked, the cliffs of Dover were ahead, gleaming in bright sunshine.

She was home.

19

It was the ride of Betsy's life and, long before it was over, she had made herself two promises. The first was that she would never sit on a horse again as long as she lived; the second that she would cease being a crown intelligencer at the first opportunity. But for the present, her chief concern was how to keep pace with Marcus Mullin.

'From Dover to Datchet is more than ninety miles, by my reckoning,' he said. 'That's two days' hard riding, at the least. And if you fall behind, madam, you must look to yourself, for I will not stop!'

And that was why, within an hour of arriving back in England, Betsy found herself standing beside the stirrup of one of the two spirited horses the captain had hired. Since they were both almost penniless, Peter Crabb paid for the mounts with sterling he had kept in reserve. Still weak from his wound, the young man accepted the impossibility of his riding to Berkshire. Taking most of the baggage, he would make his way to London by other means and report to Joseph Williamson. Betsy and Mullin, meanwhile, would travel fast and light. How things might move in the coming days, neither of them knew; their fear was that they were already too late to stop the assassin from doing his terrible work. So on a windy morning the three of them parted, in the drab surroundings of a stable yard in Dover. For Betsy it was a sad moment.

'Take care of yourself, Wrestler,' she said brightly. 'And get a surgeon to tend your arm.' Then she startled the young man by kissing him on the lips. Mullin, already mounted, was holding the reins of her horse. Betsy looked about for a mounting block, then found herself lifted high into the air. Peter Crabb sat her in the saddle and stood back, assuming his stolid look . . . but now, she knew him better. Taking the reins, she smiled and urged her mount forward. The young man raised his good hand as they turned into the street, then was lost to sight.

And so it began: the most desperate and exhausting journey she had ever undertaken. Luckily the weather was fair and the road passable. They took the highway westwards through Kent, making at first for Ashford. Here, after many hours of riding, Mullin allowed a short halt, but only to feed and water the horses. Betsy's plea for a rest, let alone food, met with a blank expression. Not until the late afternoon, when they had skirted the southern edge of the North Downs as far as Lenham, did he finally draw rein. Already, dusk was falling.

'I'd hoped to reach Maidstone by dark,' he said. 'But the way grows dim . . . ' He glanced at Betsy. She was so tired, so dusty, stiff and sore, that she had ceased to wish for anything but to stop and rest. When she raised her eyes, she expected little mercy — so the other's words came as a welcome relief.

'There's an inn here,' he said, waving his hand at the tiny village square. 'But as we've no money, we'll have to use our wits. Are you game for a little rough work?'

Wearily she nodded. 'I don't care if I lie in a stable,' she replied.

Bedding down in a stable, however, was not what Mullin had intended. Instead Betsy found herself in the inn's best chamber, eating a supper of good soup followed by a roasted pullet. Aching in every muscle, she then lay down upon the wide bed while Mullin paced the room, frowning to himself.

'You've done well — better than I expected,' he allowed. 'But we must make better time tomorrow. I've no idea if our quarry has reached Datchet yet . . . I'm certain he took ship at least a day before us. But he doesn't know we're on his tail, so we have the advantage of surprise.' He stopped pacing. 'Will you be ready to ride, when I wake you?'

She signalled her assent, though she was uneasy about Mullin's escape plan. His idea was to leave the inn in the small hours, without paying. 'And if someone wakes?' she queried. 'What will you do, wield your truncheon?'

'I doubt it will come to that. Our only danger is the ostler: he sleeps in the hayloft. However, I sense he's a man who enjoys a mug, so . . . ' The captain leered at her.

Betsy lay back. In spite of herself, she had grown to think very differently of Marcus Mullin since their first meeting at another inn, in Nieuwpoort. It seemed a lifetime ago . . . With a yawn, she turned to him.

'You must sleep too,' she murmured. 'And I don't mean on the floor. If you promise to be a perfect gallant and forbear to maul me, you may share this bed. It's certainly big enough.'

'Why, dear madam!' Mullin's eyebrows rose. 'I'd thought to offer the courtesy of a bolster, placed between us. But if you prefer another body to warm you, then I must oblige. Indeed, should you find . . . ' Then he trailed off. Betsy's eyes had closed, and already she slept.

But minutes later she was awake; or at least, it felt like only minutes. She sat up — and flinched as a hand was placed over her mouth. 'Not a sound, remember.' Mullin's voice came softly out of the dark. 'Carry your shoes with you. The way's clear, but be ready to run if I call out. Understand?'

When Betsy nodded, he removed his hand. And, moments later, wrapped in her cloak, she was following him out of their chamber and down a creaking staircase. Mercifully they were not challenged, even when Mullin unbolted the inn's door. Then they were out in the night air, with nothing but the distant bark of a dog to disturb the stillness.

'We must lead the horses,' he whispered. 'Once we clear the village, I'll saddle them. You can put your shoes on then.'

'What about the ostler?'

'Sleeping like an infant, courtesy of strong ale laced with brandy. Come, we've a long ride ahead. By the way, here's breakfast.' Mullin pressed something into her hand, wrapped in a cloth. So, without further delay, she followed him into the stable in her stockinged feet. The horses recognized their riders, and it was but the work of a minute to loose them and get them outside. Then, weighed down with trappings, the two led the animals along the quiet moonlit street, until the last cottage was passed. There by the roadside they made ready, while behind them Lenham still slept.

'Captain Fly-by-night, I should call you,' Betsy said, as she put on her shoes. 'Not that I've much experience of fleeing from inns without paying — but it was smoothly done.'

Having saddled her horse, Mullin was busy saddling his. 'My conscience is clear, madam,' he said. 'The safety of the King's at stake. When all this is over, let His Majesty pay the reckoning — provided he's still alive, that is.'

Betsy straightened up. 'Don't jest about that, Mullin,' she muttered.

'Do you truly think I do?'

'No,' she admitted, after a moment. 'And if I were a devout woman, I'd pray that we get there in time to act. As it is . . . '

'As it is we must trust to Dame Fortune, and the horses,' her companion replied. 'Now, if you'd care to put your foot into my hands, I'll hoist you up.'

★ ★ ★

For another long day, the countryside swept past. By the time the sun rose Betsy and Mullin had reached Maidstone, crossed the River Medway and pressed on to Malling, where they halted. Here she unwrapped her

253

breakfast and discovered that it consisted of a hunk of rye bread. But even that was welcome, washed down with weak beer from a horseman's flask Mullin had somehow acquired. Then they were back in the saddle, moving ever westward. In Reigate they halted briefly for the horses' sake, before crossing the River Mole and bearing north-west. Then at last, with darkness closing around them, they reached Chertsey by the Thames. By Mullin's calculations, they had ridden more than fifty miles.

'Splendid progress,' he said approvingly, as the two walked their tired animals through the town. 'Just a little further and we'll be in Egham, where comfort awaits us. Does that cheer you?'

Bleary-eyed, Betsy faced him. Yesterday's ride had been an ordeal; today's was pure torture. She and the horse had become one creature, to the extent that she didn't think she would ever be able to dismount. In fact, sleeping in the saddle seemed a blissful prospect.

'Why Egham?' she asked. 'Can we not stop here?'

Mullin shook his head. 'The inns are larger and busier. To attempt the strategy I employed in Lenham would be too great a risk, whereas in Egham we have no need. I've a regular haunt there — and an old friend, who will offer us hospitality.'

Despite his own tiredness, the captain was looking somewhat smug, Betsy thought. 'Would this old friend be of the female sex?' she enquired wryly.

'Indeed, yes.' Mullin eyed her. 'As are all those who lodge with her. She keeps a bawdy-house — but there may be a bed free. Do you have objections?'

But all Betsy could do was bend to the reins again. Just now, she thought, even a hard floor would feel like a feather-bed.

★　★　★

The captain's old friend, however, was something of a surprise. Instead of the ageing bawd Betsy had expected, Mother Curll was a pleasant enough woman of middle years, still attractive despite her large girth. And the moment she opened her door to the travellers, holding up a lantern to view them, she broke into a smile.

'Danny, my duck!' She grabbed Mullin and drew his face down to kiss. 'It's a while since you paid us a visit . . . what have you been about?'

Mullin returned her kiss and, holding the woman by the shoulders, favoured her with a grin. 'Too long and tedious a tale, Mother,' he said breezily. 'Yet I'm here now . . . could you spare a corner or two, where a couple of weary travellers may rest for the night?' Stepping aside, he indicated Betsy. 'This is Beatrice — my cousin. She's had a very taxing ride.' Then he half-turned and whispered in Betsy's ear. 'Here I'm Daniel Dark, cavalry officer — don't forget.'

Mother Curll looked Betsy up and down. 'You look ready to drop, my dear,' she said. 'Come inside, and I'll call one of the girls . . . ' She peered past Mullin. 'Are those your horses? Take them to the stable. I've a new man working for me, who will look to them.'

'Mother, you're a saviour.' The captain was already moving off. 'I'll see them bestowed and be back,' he called. Then he was gone, leaving Betsy in the hands of their new host. Walking stiffly, portmanteau in hand, she entered the house.

'It's most kind of you . . . ' she began, then paused; Mother Curll was eyeing her shrewdly. 'Cousin, eh?' she said.

'Er . . . I assure you,' Betsy stammered. 'The captain . . . Daniel and I are not — '

'Save your breath, my duck,' the bawd broke in. 'It matters naught to me . . . ' She sighed. 'I never knew a man who lives by the seat of his breeches as does Danny Dark — then you know it too, I'd wager.'

Wearily, Betsy nodded. And ignoring the sounds of revelry coming from other parts of the house, she was soon content. Having undressed and washed herself, combed the dust from her hair and eaten a bowl of curds, she was given a tiny attic chamber at the top of the house. There she fell into an exhausted sleep that lasted until morning.

She was woken by loud knocking. Blinking, she looked round to see Mullin enter, stooping under the low ceiling. He, too, had cleaned himself and rested — in fact, he looked like a different man, Betsy thought. With a groan, she sat up.

'Please don't tell me I must get up and ride,' she begged. 'For I swear I cannot!'

But Mullin shook his head. 'No, I think you should stay here for the present. I'll ride to Datchet and see what's what — it's barely three miles. This will make a good base for us, if only for a short time.'

At that Betsy fell back on her pillow in relief — then she saw the look on Mullin's face. 'What's wrong?' she asked.

'Nothing, I hope . . . ' The captain was thoughtful. 'It's Mother Curll's new servant — the man who looks after the stable, and other things. He's the one who throws out troublemakers and minds the door — her Cerberus, you might say.'

'What of him?'

'I've seen him before.' He frowned, glancing through the tiny window. 'My difficulty is, I can't remember where. I've a mind it was in London . . . but perhaps not. He calls himself Blunt, but I think it's no more his true name than mine's Daniel Dark. Keep an eye on him for me, will you?'

'How am I to do that?' Betsy countered. 'And when you say you're going to find out what's what — '

'Your pardon, did I omit to mention my news?' Suddenly Mullin was smiling. 'It seems we're not too late to save the King: in fact, we're too early.'

'What?' Abruptly, Betsy sat up. 'Explain, Mullin — and stop looking so pleased with yourself!'

'The races,' the other replied. 'Mother says they haven't begun yet. The King arrives tomorrow, I'm told, and will stay at the Manor House at Datchet. So we can draw breath, and thank Dame Fortune for her bounty.'

Betsy stared at him . . . and felt a great weight lift from her shoulders. Their ride had not been in vain: the King was safe. Indeed, he was still in London.

'Then, what should we do now?' she asked.

'Wait,' came the reply. 'I'll ask around Datchet — it's a tiny place. Any strangers hereabouts will stick out like tulips in a midden.'

'As will we, won't we?' Betsy said. 'What disguise will serve us best?'

'Well now . . . ' Mullin was smiling again. 'When he comes to the races, His Majesty makes merry. I hear he often takes a house in Datchet for one of his mistresses. I thought, now we're here . . . '

'Now we're here, what?'

'Why, we join the party. How else will we get close to the royal personage?' For the first time, Mullin looked positively cheerful. 'Our clothes are travelstained and unfit, of course, but it's likely I can get my hands on something suitable, while the trulls here will be delighted to dress you, I'm sure. They seldom have a gentlewoman in their midst — shall we be Sir Girvan and Lady Mullin this time?' As he warmed to his idea, his smile broadened. 'We're keen race-goers, who have come down from the North Country. Not a bad little scheme, wouldn't you agree?' And before Betsy could answer he stepped to the door, pausing with a hand upon the latch. 'Do you think you could mimic Williamson's ghastly accent?' he asked, and was gone.

Whereupon all she could do was groan again, and pull the bedcovers over her head; but it didn't help.

20

In the mid-morning, Betsy rose and took a dish of porridge in Mother Curll's kitchen. Apart from a taciturn servant, nobody seemed to be up yet and the house was quiet. Not wishing to stay indoors, she ventured outside to look around.

The house, she now saw, stood on the edge of the little country village of Egham. There was a stable at one side, and a pathway leading off through some trees. Betsy took it, finding herself at last by the Thames, which flowed gently eastward. There were small boats upon the water, and men fishing on the far bank, while in the fields beyond sheep and cattle grazed. The place was tranquil, yet she was uneasy. Slowly she began walking by the riverside, pondering the bizarre set of events that had led her here. She was still deep in thought when hoof-beats behind startled her. Looking round, she saw Marcus Mullin riding towards her.

'Here you are!' he called, as he reined in. 'I thought I'd find you indoors.' He dismounted, then dropped the halter. The horse dipped its head and fell to cropping grass.

'Indeed?' Betsy said. 'And how long would it be before someone assumed I was for hire, like the other occupants?'

'Nonsense,' the captain retorted. 'It's a perfect hiding-place . . . ' His gaze wandered to the river. 'Anyway, I have tidings. Let's take a stroll, shall we?' So the two of them began walking, while Betsy listened to his news.

'Windsor is abuzz with those here for the racing, at Datchet Mead,' Mullin told her. 'Across the water in Datchet village it's the same. Plenty of trade for the locals — especially the ferryman, who takes people back and forth. I was glad to find him a talkative fellow. Like everyone else, he can't wait for the King's arrival. So I ventured to ask him if he knew of any odd-looking group who may have rented a house nearby — and I was lucky. In short, I believe Prynn and his fellows are here already!'

Betsy started. 'Won't they be using false names?'

'No doubt they are,' Mullin replied. 'But they stand out from the usual sporting men. A party of three or four strangers, the ferryman says, have taken over a near-derelict cottage opposite Black Potts — that's an island in the river, where the King sometimes goes fishing. They've been here for days, yet they don't fish — and one of them sounds to me as if he might be Thomas Prynn.'

'Then why delay?' Betsy was anxious now. 'Surely you must inform the nearest authority — '

'What, some dim-witted constable?' Mullin gave a snort. 'That could ruin everything! We have to be sure of our ground — which means waiting until they show their hand. Only when the scheme is laid bare can I make a move and spoil their game, otherwise where's the evidence?'

'You mean, wait until the assassin breaks cover?' Betsy said, aghast. 'But that would mean putting the King's life in danger. Anything might happen!'

'It might.' Mullin looked behind to where his horse was quietly grazing. 'But I see no other way. Once I've managed to get a look at Prynn's little 'family' as Venn called them, I don't intend to let them out of my sight. All through the races I'll be close by the King — and the moment one of them tries to get near him, I'll be ready.'

'Mullin, listen.' Betsy faced him. 'You can't do this alone. Even if Wrestler's told Mr Lee everything by now, he may not be able to help us. The King will be on his way here already — '

'Yes, yes . . . ' The captain sighed. 'But

come what may, I have to stop the assassin.' He hesitated, then, 'Let's say it's become a matter of pride.'

'Well . . . then what about our disguise?' she asked, seeing there was no persuading him. 'Are we still to be Sir Girvan and Lady Mullin?'

'Ah — I've had thoughts about that. It would mean moving to Windsor or Datchet, where either of us might meet people who know us — especially you. Supposing the King has Nelly with him? She'd soon recognize you. She may be as coarse as a heifer, but she's no fool.'

At that Betsy fell silent. There was no doubt that, as a woman of the stage, she was recognizable — as she and Nell Gwyn, the former actress and now one of His Majesty's mistresses, were acquainted. Moreover, among the collection of noblemen, gallants and hangers-on who followed the King about, there would likely be others who knew her. She tried to think of some solution, when suddenly Mullin brightened.

'By God, I have it: I'll become a jockey!'

'Well, that might serve,' she replied, in some surprise. 'You're a good horseman, if somewhat tall for the role.'

'No matter — it's perfect!' Quickly Mullin warmed to his idea. 'That way I can be in the thick of things without attracting attention — and for that matter, so can you.'

'Me? How do I fit in?'

'You can be the horse's owner — or rather, his wife. Fashion a tale about your husband being too ill to attend . . . You've come in his place, to cheer your horse on. Think of a new name — wear a lot of paint and powder, perhaps. I don't need to advise you on your appearance, do I?'

'Not if, as it would appear, you've decided upon it,' Betsy said drily. 'Perhaps you'd better find me a large hat, whereby I can keep my face hidden — '

'And I've another idea,' Mullin broke in, without listening. 'You should lodge in Windsor or Datchet after all. A jockey can stay anywhere, but a gentlewoman needs a good room, and a maid to attend her. Provided you remain discreet and stay clear of people you recognize, you should fare well enough.'

'And how do we pay for that?' Betsy enquired. 'I'll need new clothes.'

'That's my idea!' The captain wore a look of triumph. 'My horse isn't a true racer, of course, but he's the better of the two. Your mare, on the other hand, we can sell!'

'But . . . she isn't ours to sell,' Betsy faltered. 'What if — ?'

'Oh, the devil with that!' Mullin waved a hand. 'Once it's all over, Williamson can pay.' He gave a shout of laughter. 'Just to see the look on that skinflint's face, would be worth any risk! Now, I'd better go back to Mother's stable and get your horse. Are you coming?'

Back at Mother Curll's house, however, Betsy was unwilling to go inside. She couldn't help but think she would be in the way — and perhaps take up a chamber that was needed for other purposes. She waited while Mullin tethered his mount, then accompanied him into the stable . . . where both of them stopped.

A man in shirtsleeves stood with his back to them, grooming a sleek, dappled-grey horse. Hearing footsteps he turned round and Betsy stiffened. She realized this was the person Mullin had meant, who seemed familiar to him. She saw a slim, well-proportioned man in his thirties, who peered at her from a pleasant, if weatherbeaten, face. When she put on a faint smile, he spoke up.

'You didn't mention that your companion was such a beauty, Mr Dark,' he said, raising his eyebrows. 'Your cousin, I understand. Is that not so, madam?' And he returned Betsy's smile, while with his eyes he let her know that, like Mother Curll, he didn't believe that tale for a moment.

'We're here to fetch the mare, Blunt.' Mullin addressed the other man haughtily. 'Don't let us detain you.' He stepped past him to the furthest stall, and busied himself saddling Betsy's horse. But the man who used the name Blunt continued to pay attention to her.

'What brings you to this spot, madam?' he enquired.

'I'm merely passing through,' Betsy answered. She, too, was suspicious; as whorehouse bullies went, this man looked an unlikely sort for such a job.

'To the races?' Blunt went on. 'Indeed, it's the best time to be here. I'm trying my luck with this one — Silverfoot, I call him.' He patted the grey horse affectionately, at which the animal tossed its head.

'You mean, you're a jockey?' Betsy was taken aback. Over by the stall, she knew Mullin was listening.

'Of a kind,' Blunt answered. 'There's to be a race at the end of the first day, open to all comers. It's a new event — The Roman Plate. The King himself will reward the winner with a silver platter. Worth a try, eh?'

With that he grinned, turned away and resumed brushing the horse. But Betsy's heart had jumped, and when she glanced towards Mullin she caught his eye: The Roman Plate.

Once again, she saw Venn's haggard face in the prison yard, as he spilled his testimony. Williamson had not understood that part, but now, the intelligencers knew better. The Roman Plate was a horse-race, open to anyone — and the King would present the prize. That was when the assassin would strike.

She turned quickly and went out. A moment later Mullin appeared, leading her horse. They looked at each other, but no words were needed. And very soon, after the captain had helped her into the saddle, the two of them were riding the short distance upriver to Windsor. After a while they spoke of Blunt and what he had said, and were in agreement.

But though he racked his brains for a memory, Mullin still couldn't remember where he had seen the man before.

★ ★ ★

By the end of the afternoon, all domestic matters had been settled.

Once again, Betsy had to give credit to Mullin for his speedy work. In a matter of hours he had sold her hired horse to a dealer

268

in Windsor, who, by good fortune, was too near-sighted to notice the brand on its flank. He had then brought her baggage from Mother Curll's and, newly in funds, hurried about purchasing second-hand clothes for the two of them. So it was that, by evening, Betsy was established in the last available chamber at the Five Bells Inn in Datchet. Though she had talked Mullin out of hiring a servant: even if one could be found at short notice, that was an extravagance too far.

Instead, she made the best of the frocks and petticoats, relieved to find that he had bought garments of about the right size. There was also a hat, and a good outdoor gown. For his part, Mullin had obtained tight breeches and a close-fitting blouse of the kind jockeys wore, along with a new coat, stockings and shoes. Thus attired, the two of them felt equipped for their roles — even if the difficulties they faced seemed as stark as ever.

'Remember: you're the wife of George Smith, a gentleman farmer from Yorkshire,' the captain reminded her. 'I'm merely your husband's jockey, so treat me like one. And don't pretend to know about horses. You're merely here — '

'To see ours run,' Betsy finished wryly. 'I'm

hardly likely to forget, am I? Now, to borrow your phrase, shall we cease this prating? I want to know what you've found out about the men up at . . . where is it? Back Potts.'

The two of them were in her chamber overlooking the street, finishing a hasty supper. Mullin had come in half an hour ago, having been out on a foray. From outside came sounds of activity: Datchet, a village scarcely any bigger than Egham, was already swollen to twice its size with visitors. Here, at the nearby manor house, the King would stay. Betsy meanwhile, must play yet another part: again, a role for which she would receive no credit.

'*Black* Potts, yes . . . ' Mullin dabbed his mouth with a napkin and got up from the table. He was restless, as nervous of the morrow as Betsy. Moving to a window seat, he sat down.

'I rode by there, without getting too close,' he told her. 'The cottage is easy to find, though shaded by trees. The island's wooded — and there's a rowing boat moored nearby.' He grimaced. 'Too easy to escape, for my liking — they could cross the river before anyone reached the ferry. As for the occupants . . . ' He paused. 'Now, here's a curious thing: there appear to be but two men there.'

'I thought the ferryman said there were more,' Betsy said.

'He did. Perhaps the others have gone — I know not. But the important part is, one of them is indeed a white-haired fellow who fits our picture of Thomas Prynn. The other's a younger man . . . ' A frown creased his brow. 'I didn't get a proper look, but something troubles me. For, try as I might, I can't see him as our assassin.'

'How can you be sure?' Betsy asked sharply. 'Neither of us has ever seen him. Only Wrestler could identify him — '

'I know that.' Mullin glanced outside where lights showed at the houses opposite. 'But this man was too portly; he doesn't look the part. Our quarry's as agile as a cat — and far more dangerous. Which is why I think he's not with them — indeed, he may not even be here yet. Their plans could have changed in the time we were still in the Provinces — or more likely, the fellow stays apart, so the three won't be seen together. Yet they haven't called the scheme off, or they wouldn't be here.' Turning from the window, he faced her. 'I see only one solution: to confront them and get at the truth.'

'What?' Betsy was aghast. 'You said we must let them show their hand — catch the assassin in the act!'

'But think of our position now,' Mullin countered. 'I don't know where the killer is; he could be under our very noses, in some disguise. I can't watch everyone. By the time he made his move I could be too late — and we have but a day left.' He sighed. 'I know what you'll say,' he went on, 'that I should tell the constables, or hire some other help.'

'No, I won't say such.' Betsy, too, dabbed her mouth, and sat back. 'Perhaps there's a way for me to get close to the King, while you move about . . . ' She frowned. 'You aren't really intending to race your horse, are you?'

'Of course I am!' Mullin retorted. 'I'll enter for The Roman Plate. If I don't, yet go about dressed as a jockey, I'll stick out like a fool. Don't you see — one sniff of a trap, and our man will be away!'

'I do see,' Betsy replied. 'And I also see that a jockey might find it difficult to get close to the King. You'll be on horseback — by the time you dismount, it could be too late. And what if you fell off, or — ?'

'Thank you, Brand!' Irritably, Mullin got to his feet. 'I can stay on a horse, I assure you. And despite your low opinion of me, I might even win the race — had that not occurred to you? In which case I'd be in a good position to protect His Majesty when he presents the prize, don't you think?'

'Oh, flap-sauce!' Betsy, too, stood up. 'That's hoping for a little too much, isn't it? Not only is your horse unfit for making such speed, so are you! Could you outrun that slippery fellow in Egham — Mother Curll's flirtatious servant?'

'Blunt?' Mullin glared at her. 'He's full of bombast. What's a fellow like him doing working in a run-down trugging-house? For all we know, that grey horse isn't his — he might even have stolen it! Whoever he is, he's no Cerberus, I'd swear that. In fact I wouldn't be surprised if — '

With a sharp breath, he broke off, while Betsy sat down abruptly. From outside there came shouting, but they scarcely heard it. Instead they stared at each other, dumb-founded.

'Not him, surely . . . ?' Slowly, Mullin sat on the window seat again. 'I mean, he's sly, and no doubt a fighter — else he could hardly do his work — but could he be the one we've chased all the way from Delft — the one who killed Eleanor, and almost killed Crabb?' He gulped. 'No — I can't believe it!'

'Mother Curll said he was new,' Betsy said, thinking fast. 'He was ahead of us: he could have made better speed. The other men might have prepared the ground, even arranged the door-keeper's job for him. And what better guise for attending the races than that of a jockey? You chose it too! Whether the man wins or loses, he could get close enough to the King . . . ' She caught her breath. 'Then what's to stop him galloping off? By the time anyone saw what had happened, he could be a mile away!'

She stopped, while Mullin stared, his mind also busy. Then he frowned. 'And if we're wrong? What if we found ourselves watching the wrong man?'

Betsy hesitated, yet instinct told her she was right. From outside meanwhile, came not only shouts but cheering too. Absently she stepped to the window, whereupon Mullin, who had turned to look out, uttered an oath.

'By the Christ, he's here already!'

He stood up and flung the window open, letting a burst of shouting and cheering into the room. Lights blazed below in the street; there was a sound of clopping hoofs, a rumble of wheels . . . and now there was no mistaking the cause. Betsy put her hand upon Mullin's shoulder and leaned out — to see Charles Stuart arrive in Datchet, amid a host of followers.

The King was here, earlier than expected. And though he had no way of knowing it, his life was in grave danger — from a man nobody knew.

21

The races began soon after midday. And in bright autumn sunshine, Betsy Brand walked through Datchet in her new hat and gown, eyes peeled for the first sign of anything amiss. Though very soon after she had taken the ferry across the Thames, her task began to look impossible.

Datchet Mead lay just below Windsor Castle, a grassy level beside the river. Here a course had been marked out, and a winning post set up. Facing it was the royal box, a makeshift affair of boards hung with carpets and flags. Steps led up one side, to a raised platform where the King and his party would stand. From the castle high above, the Royal Standard fluttered. By late morning a crowd had already gathered, consisting largely of sporting men and hangers-on. Betsy soon found that she was more conspicuous than she liked, though she managed to avoid conversation. She was relieved when she saw Mullin in his jockey's clothes, leading his horse through the onlookers. Casually she wandered over to the riders' enclosure, where the captain made a bow to her and touched his forehead.

'Don't overdo it,' she muttered, drawing close. 'I'm not Lady Castlemaine.'

'She isn't here, and neither is Nelly. The King's brought his French mistress instead.' Mullin spoke low, holding the reins of his mount tightly. The animal was skittish, sensing the excitement.

Betsy glanced about. Other jockeys were assembling, readying for the race. 'Have you seen any sign of Prynn?' she asked, but Mullin shook his head.

'The crowd's bigger than I expected. You must circulate . . . I'll have to stay with the horse. There are coursers aplenty here — priggers, too. I daren't let go of him for a minute.'

'That's all we'd need, you getting him stolen,' Betsy said in dismay. 'If the assassin does make his play, how do you hope to waylay him?' She sighed. 'I still say you'll need help . . . ' She trailed off. There was a noise of hoofs, and heads turned as a party of about a dozen horsemen rode up. They wore the royal livery and carried short halberds: the King's bodyguard. The crowd parted as they made their way across the course, where they reined in to form a line, backs to the riverside.

'Well, they might be of some help,' Mullin said drily. But when Betsy turned, she saw no trace of a smile. 'I mean after the event,' he added. 'If I'm too late to foil a regicide, it's good to know Royal Charles's servants will hunt down the culprit.'

'This is no time for comedy, Mullin,' she snapped. 'You'd best watch the course while I walk . . . and I have a feeling it's going to be a long day.'

With that she gave the horse an encouraging pat on the rump, and left the two of them. And a short time later, with much cheering, shouting and ballyhoo, the King himself arrived to watch the races.

It was some time since Betsy had set eyes on Charles Stuart, and that was at the theatre, where he had fallen asleep. He was now forty-one years old, still handsome enough, though he appeared ever more languid as the years passed. When his coach and six drew up, he stepped out to cheers and waving of scarves, smiling indulgently and flapping a hand. Other lords and gentlemen accompanied him, splendidly dressed in long coats, lace cravats and plumed hats. Still more were riding up and dismounting, while grooms and servants fussed about them. There were ladies too — a pair of them. Betsy saw Louise de Kéroualle, the King's striking

Breton mistress, as she and her maidservant followed His Majesty up into the royal box. There the party stood, the King with his hands on the rail, looking out over the course. And soon there came a flurry of activity: already, the first race was about to start and the crowd settled in eager anticipation.

But after that, the day held no pleasures for Betsy.

Races came and went, the crowds shouted, bets were laid, guineas won and lost. Yet through it all, not for a moment could she stop to watch the jockeys gallop, or the winners arrive at the post. Instead she moved among the race-goers, until she would have given a great deal merely to sit down. By mid-afternoon she had seen nothing of great interest, and no one who aroused her suspicions. Already the time was drawing near for the last race — The Roman Plate. The King, having taken a lengthy absence for dinner, had returned, and excitement was growing afresh. Many of the experienced jockeys had departed, she noticed, to be replaced by a more varied assembly of riders — and among them was Blunt, the man from the Egham bawdy-house.

Betsy had taken another turn about the jockeys' enclosure, where Mullin was making ready. Others were already mounted. She scanned the riders, then stiffened at sight of a man on a grey horse. Quickly she approached her fellow-intelligencer.

'Yes, I've seen him too.' Mullin was tightening his horse's girth as she drew close, and didn't look up. 'You keep your eyes on the royal party,' he went on. 'Stand near the box, where you can scream if necessary — or shout. Anything to attract attention if he gets near the King.'

'And you?' Betsy patted the animal, but her eyes stayed on Blunt, who was moving off towards the gate. 'Will you try to stay close to our friend from Egham, or — ?'

'Stay close to him?' Mullin echoed, turning to her. 'I intend to beat him. Then no one will be nearer to Royal Charles's person than Marcus Mullin!'

'Oh, cods,' Betsy breathed. 'Can't you forget your pride for once?' She dropped her voice. 'If that man's what we think he is, he's armed, remember. You may get yourself stabbed, along with His Majesty.'

'Then that's a risk I will take!' Irritably, Mullin gripped the reins. 'Let me do my part, Brand,' he muttered. 'You look to the King. Now, stand clear.' And with that he seized the pommel and swung himself into the saddle. Shoving his feet into the stirrups, he was about to ride away — then suddenly he froze.

Seeing his face, Betsy grew alarmed.

'What is it?'

'Prynn!' He was peering over heads, towards the river. 'It's him — and his friend too. They must have come by boat . . . ' He leaned down towards Betsy. 'You must watch them,' he hissed. 'The older fellow with the staff is Prynn; the other wears a pale blue coat. Get as close as you can, but for pity's sake don't let them see you.' He looked round quickly. 'I must follow Blunt. There's no time — just do it!'

And he rode off, following the remaining jockeys out of the gate. Blunt was ahead, and already his white blouse was lost among the other riders. Mullin, in red-and-white stripes, soon disappeared too, while the crowd surged towards the race track. So, without further delay, Betsy followed them, working her way around the edge of the throng.

Soon she was close to the royal box, the only woman among a group of men. Many wore swords, and among them were some she had seen in the theatres in London. Shading herself with her wide-brimmed hat, she eased her way through, ignoring the occasional ribald remark. Mercifully she was not accosted: all eyes were now on the riders assembling for the race. In a short time she had moved around behind the box, to the side facing the river. The steps were blocked by a couple of stern-looking guards, but they barely glanced at Betsy as she moved round. Soon she was close to the King's bodyguard, sitting stolidly on their horses. But to her relief none paid her attention, allowing her to skirt behind them towards the waterside until at last she stood among a crowd of a different stamp.

They were a ragged group of villagers and farm-boys, who had no doubt come to see The Roman Plate. They were noisy, filled with excitement, and some were drunk. Uneasily Betsy's eyes surveyed them, until at last she saw the men she had sought: a white-haired fellow leaning on a walking-staff, and beside him a younger, more portly man in a pale-blue coat.

The two stood slightly apart from the onlookers, their eyes on the course. Even from a distance, Betsy believed she saw tension in their stance; when one of them looked in her direction, she averted her face at once. Tense herself, she took a few steps closer until she could see their faces. Thomas Prynn — if indeed it were him — wore a dour expression. The other man appeared com-posed . . . But when Betsy's gaze travelled downwards, she stiffened. The fellow's left hand was at his side, but the other was in his coat — and she saw a bulge, which suggested a pocket pistol.

But there was no time for speculation, for the race was about to begin. Betsy saw the starter in his periwig, a white scarf held above his head. The jockeys were eager, crouching over their mounts, while the horses jerked excitedly at the reins. As the crowd surged closer she looked towards the Royal box: the aristocrats, too, had caught the mood of excitement. She saw the King leaning over the rail, a smile on his features — then the starter gave the signal, and they were off.

In the immediate thunder of hoofs, and amid the din of the crowd, Betsy was at first thrown into disarray. Men pressed about her, surging towards the track. To her left, she was aware of the guards keeping their line with some difficulty; their mounts were too excited. She turned to look for Prynn and his fellow, but they were lost to sight. Then, with relief, she glimpsed them again: neither man had moved. Both seemed intent on the race, and Betsy couldn't help following their gaze. The riders had sped off into the distance, the watchers craning their necks to see, but now the shouting and cheering increased again. In a flurry of colours, the pack turned about the furthest marker and began their return gallop. Emotions rose, as the thunder of hoofs drew nearer.

Betsy stood on tiptoe, trying to see through the throng. She thought she glimpsed both Mullin and Blunt's colours, though it was hard to be certain, so close-packed were the horsemen. Then, as they approached the final stretch at a furious pace, she found herself pushed forward by shouting watchers. She glanced towards Prynn and the other man, but could no longer see them. Heart pounding, she tried to force a way through, but the rough crowd gave her no quarter. She was shoved and jostled, and her hat came loose. Clutching at it, she called out.

'Sirs, I pray you, let a lady have some air!'

But all she got was a guffaw from someone near; by everyone else she was ignored. Struggling, she tried to free herself, while still the crowd milled about her. The shouts were reaching fever pitch, the winning post was within reach. The ground shook, the hoofs like a drum-roll . . . Then to her dismay, Betsy lost her balance and slipped. As she fell, she heard the cry that greeted the winner, while applause broke out on all sides. For a bizarre moment she thought herself on the stage of the Duke's Theatre, then all of a sudden she was alone, sitting on the grass, flushed and out of breath. In an instant the crowd swept past, hats and scarves waving: the race was over.

In undignified fashion she got to her feet, hat in hand, and looked about. She saw the jockeys circling, their horses blowing and snorting. Stragglers were still riding to the finish, but no one paid them much attention. Instead the crowd pressed around the winning post, some cheering, others giving vent to their disappointment. Betsy hurried forward, craning her neck. Her eyes went to the royal box, where the King and his friends too were applauding. Desperately, she began pushing her way through. Her throat was tight — even if she'd cried out, she knew no one would hear. Scanning the untidy press of riders she at last saw Mullin, taller in the saddle than most, struggling to control his horse. The animal was highly excited after the race, jerking the rein, but Betsy saw at once that, as she had feared, he was not among the leaders. They were holding back, as gradually the noise diminished. On the far side of the course, the starter was calling out; men hushed their neighbours, straining to hear. And then it was, with a sinking heart, that Betsy heard the words she had dreaded: the winner was . . .

'Silverfoot!'

The starter's voice rose clearly, prompting

a few muted cheers. 'Silverfoot has won by a head — the rider is Richard Blunt from Egham! Come forward, sir, and receive The Roman Plate from His Royal Majesty!'

And now she saw the winner in his white blouse, moving clear of the other men. Even from here she could see the grin on his face, as he raised his quirt to acknowledge the applause. Unhurriedly he walked his sweating horse forward, drawing rein before the royal box. Then he dismounted, and was lost to sight.

Breathlessly, Betsy whirled about; she could no longer see Mullin. Letting go her hat, she stuck her elbows out and charged. Soon she had gained ground, lashing out with abandon, forcing people aside. There were angry mutterings, and someone pushed her back, but she didn't stop. Eyes on the platform, she saw a flash of silver as the platter was manhandled by a servant. The King took it, turned and, with a smile, inclined his head towards the prize-winner, who had approached the front of the box. Attendants stood aside to let him near, while the noble personages applauded. Betsy was now only yards away, but she was too late, and she knew it. She drew breath to shout, but her hopes hung by a hairpin. Fleetingly she wondered if Mullin had got near enough to thwart the assassin. With a last effort she forced her way through, pushing and kicking, realizing she was causing a stir of her own. Men turned . . . and at last she shouted.

'Let me through! The King's in peril — danger to His Majesty!'

There was a shout, then another — then a gasp went up, that was almost a groan. From the direction of the royal box there was a cry, and something flew into the crowd. It materialized into a figure in a flowing black coat. Betsy barely saw him before he was on horseback. Then, before anyone could stop him, he cleaved through the throng, galloping towards the river.

Now there was chaos. Hands clutched at Betsy as if she were the assassin! She struck out . . . voices swelled about her, but the words made no sense. Flushed with fear, surrounded by men shouting, she peered up at the King — then, like waves, the crowd parted. Gasping, dishevelled and wet with perspiration, she could only stare at the sight.

Two men were on the ground, locked in struggle — one Richard Blunt, the other Marcus Mullin. Above them, unharmed, the King and his courtiers gazed down in bemused fashion. Then, from the crowd, men emerged to seize the combatants, dragging them apart. Panting, their faces twisted in rage, the two stared balefully at each other . . . Betsy saw splashes of blood, though it was unclear whose it was, then Blunt shouted.

'You hare-brained idiot!' he cried, eyes blazing at Mullin. 'He got away — and you let him!'

22

Heart in mouth, Betsy hurried to Mullin, who appeared unhurt: the blood, she now saw, belonged to Blunt. As men pulled him away he winced, grunting in pain. But one thing at least was clear: the King was safe. And since the races were now over, and by all appearances a brawl had simply broken out, his followers acted accordingly. In a short time Charles and his party were hurried away, while the mounted guards rode up to form a cordon around him. Coach doors banged, a whip cracked, and the royal conveyance lurched off, followed by a crowd of horsemen. Others were getting mounted and riding after them, watched by confused jockeys and race-goers, but all Betsy felt was immense relief. And as Mullin was being held by several men, at last she found her voice.

'Sirs, unhand my servant!' she cried, in her most imperious tone. 'He meant no harm to His Majesty. Let him go!' With that she took the captain's arm — and the performance worked. In surprise the men released him, whereupon Mullin shrugged them off, facing Blunt: and there was recognition in his eyes.

'By God, I know you,' he muttered.

But Blunt sagged. He was more badly hurt than Betsy had realized: blood spread from a wound in his side, soaking his clothes. With a groan, he sank to his knees.

'You're mistaken,' he breathed. 'When I saw that fellow get close to the King, I merely acted as any man would.' He glanced up at those who held him. 'I pray you, let go of me. I'm stabbed, and can do no one any hurt.'

There was a moment, then, with a glance at each other, the men released him. A circle had formed about the group, and now a heavy fellow in a buff coat pushed his way through.

'What happened?' he demanded. 'I'm the constable — answer me!'

'There was a madman, with a dagger.' Kneeling, one hand pressed to his side, Blunt peered up at him. Then he swung his gaze to Mullin, and an unexpected thing happened.

'This man tried to help,' he added. 'In the mêlée, he thought I was the assailant. You should let him pursue the fugitive — he's a good horseman.'

Betsy stared in surprise, from Blunt to Mullin and back. The captain's manner had changed: now he whispered urgently to her. 'He's a friend — see he gets help!' And with that, he squared up to the constable.

'He speaks the truth,' he said loudly. 'I, too, saw the one wielding the dagger. I can ride fast — let me chase him!'

'Well, I don't know . . . ' The constable frowned, but he was at a loss, as were those who stood about. Everyone of importance seemed to have disappeared with the King. Men exchanged glances, looking from the injured Blunt to Mullin.

'Good — then there's no time to waste!' Mullin looked round quickly. 'Where's my horse?'

'Take Silverfoot — give him free rein.'

It was Blunt who spoke — and a gleam appeared in Mullin's eye. 'I will,' he said. Then he strode towards the crowd, and his boldness was such, they parted immediately. Some yards away a boy was holding the grey horse's halter, which Mullin took from him. In a moment he had hauled himself into the saddle. 'That man needs a surgeon,' he said, pointing at Blunt. And with that he cantered off in the direction the would-be assassin had taken. Soon he broke into a gallop and was gone. With a sigh Betsy turned — to find all eyes upon her. Clearly feeling he had been upstaged, the constable was glowering.

'And who might you be, madam?' he enquired.

'Me? I'm . . . Hester Smith,' she answered.

'Wife of George Smith from . . . Yorkshire. I came to see our horse run; my husband's too ill to attend.'

'And that fellow?' The constable jerked his thumb in the direction Mullin had gone. 'Odd sort for a jockey, isn't he?'

'Oh indeed!' Betsy managed a smile. 'Too brave for his own good, I always say . . . But shouldn't we do as he said, and help this other stout fellow?' And with a look of concern, she moved towards Blunt. 'Can you walk?' she asked.

Without answering her, the man got stiffly to his feet. He swayed briefly, and someone moved to assist him, but he was waved way. 'I'll go with this good lady,' Blunt said. 'If one will kindly bring her horse, we'll make our own way . . . With your permission, madam?' He rested a hand on Betsy's shoulder, whereupon she bent close.

'Gladly,' she whispered. 'For I think you and I should converse, don't you?'

⋆　⋆　⋆

Night fell, and there was no word from Marcus Mullin.

In the tiny attic chamber at Mother Curll's, a single candle burned. On the bed lay the man who called himself Richard Blunt, while

291

Betsy sat beside him on a stool. The last few hours had flown by, but at last she could relax. The surgeon had been and gone, having sewn the fearful gash in the wounded man's side and ordered him to stay abed. His jockey's clothes were gone, his body washed and bandaged. Mother Curll, having been given a short account of events, had also left. As far as she knew a fight had occurred, and Danny Dark had gone after the man who'd stabbed her servant. Less cheerful than earlier, the bawd went off to oversee business. So now that all was calm, Betsy could speak to the injured man alone.

'He knew you, he said . . . ' She gazed into Blunt's face. 'Indeed, we both thought there was more to you than first appeared. Who are you, and what are you doing here?'

For a while the man didn't answer. His face was drawn and shiny with sweat. Briefly he met Betsy's eye, then looked away.

'I might ask the same of you,' he said at last. 'For you're no more Dark's cousin than you are Hester Smith, farmer's wife. That's no Yorkshire accent. Indeed . . . ' He sighed. 'He's not Dark either, is he? Unless I'm mistaken, he's Marcus Mullin!' When Betsy started, he gave a low laugh. 'Don't be alarmed. We're on the same side — just.'

'What do you mean?' she snapped. 'We

came here to . . . ' But she stopped herself, as Blunt gave a weak smile.

'You came here for the same reason I did,' he said. 'To catch a fellow who was bent on killing the King.'

'Then you knew that all along?'

In agitation, Betsy stood up. She was confused, fearful for Mullin's life, and no longer in sympathetic mood. 'Tell me what's going on!' she cried. 'If we're truly on the same side, as you say, then why didn't you reveal yourself? Indeed, if you knew what was afoot, why did you let matters go so far? The King could have been killed — '

'I think not, madam.' Blunt eyed her calmly. 'The traitor had to be allowed to make the attempt — caught blade in hand. Yet there were others close by, to protect His Majesty.' He paused, then, 'We meant to catch all of them: men whose names may be known to you. Thomas Prynn is one, John Phelps another — and one called Venn, who's no longer alive to trouble us.'

He fell silent, wincing. Suddenly, things began to make sense.

'Why, you're one of us!'

Betsy stared down at him. 'So, what's your number?' she asked, her anger rising. 'Thirteen, perhaps? For you've certainly been unlucky. The King may be safe, but you let a murderer escape, and got yourself run through doing it!'

But Blunt merely sighed. 'My number's thirty-four,' he answered. 'Our names don't matter, do they? Though you might ask me the name of the one we — Mullin and I, that is — allowed to escape. Would you care to know that?' And when she nodded, he told her. 'He has several guises. He sometimes goes as a novice priest: a bold choice for one such as he. He also passes as a Dutch seaman — but his name is Jerome Kyte. And if that sounds familiar to you, it should, for he's the son of John Kyte: one of the regicides of our late King, Charles the First!'

At that, a chill stole over Betsy. Old memories stirred . . . terrible memories of the King's revenge a decade back, on those who had ordered the execution of his father. As a young woman she had refused to witness the bloody acts of drawing and quartering at Tyburn, or to view the corpses of Cromwell, Ireton and the others, dug up from their graves and hanged in public. Many others had fled the vengeance of the Stuarts after the Restoration. In silence, she stared at the man before her, as he told what he knew.

'John Kyte died three months ago in Antwerp — a bitter and broken man,' he said.

'But his son burns with the same hatred — a hatred for which he would sacrifice his own life. That's how he fell into the hands of Thomas Lacy, another embittered republican — but one with the means to make use of our friend Jerome. The rest perhaps is known to you — do I hit the mark?'

Heavily, Betsy sat down. 'Lacy's dead,' she said quietly.

'Is he now?' The other grimaced. 'Then he'll not be missed, I can promise you that.'

But now she felt betrayed. All along, it seemed, another scheme was in place to capture Venn's circle — yet she, Mullin and Crabb had known nothing of it. 'Do you mean to tell me you knew all this before I . . . we were sent to the Dutch Provinces?' she demanded. 'For if so, a young girl's life could have been saved, and a man spared grievous hurt — '

'No — I swear I knew naught of your orders.' Blunt eyed her steadily. 'Have you still not teased it out?' he asked. 'You think me one of Mr Lee's men too, yet you're mistaken. We have worked in parallel, madam — like blind folk. Mere foot-soldiers, who aren't permitted to know the plans of our masters. Mine is the master of yours — two rivals who covet intelligence, and hide it from each other. So that when conspiracies are broken and traitors snared, one of them may claim the credit, to the other's detriment. It's all in the cause of influence, madam — and of the King's good favour. Now do you understand me?'

For a moment Betsy gazed at him, then slowly she got up. 'Well, perhaps I do,' she said. She moved to the door, but as she went out, she glanced back. 'Trust no one — isn't that your motto?' But Blunt turned his face to the wall, and made no answer.

She descended the narrow staircase, barely aware of the noises around her. Female laughter sounded from a half-open door, a male voice from another. But when she reached the hallway, someone was entering the front door, and in relief she hurried towards him. Mullin was back, and one glance at his face was enough.

'I lost him,' he said tiredly. 'The horse was spent from racing — the devil outran me. And by the time I'd ridden back to that cottage, the others had gone too. God help me, I've lost the whole lot of them!'

'Come, you're weary.' Quickly Betsy closed the door, then took his arm. But at that moment there was a voice behind them and Mother Curll appeared with her lantern.

'Danny?' She came forward, a frown on her face. 'What have you been about, eh? There's a man upstairs, sore hurt . . . '

'I'll deal with him, mistress.' Betsy faced her. 'If you'll let us spend the night here, tomorrow we'll be gone. I'll pay you for the room — will that serve?'

For a moment the bawd eyed her, then she nodded. 'As you wish . . . ' Her eyes went to Mullin. 'Save us, but when did you ever bring aught but trouble?' she added. 'Now I must look for another doorman, too!'

She went off, whereupon Betsy spoke low. 'You should come up with me. I've found out who Blunt really is — ' But Mullin stayed her.

'I've remembered,' he said. 'And I'll go gladly: he and I should talk. And after that, I intend to get drunk!'

With that he started up the stairs, Betsy following. And a moment later they were in the tiny attic room again, by the bedside of the one they now knew was a fellow intelligencer.

'Captain Mullin . . . ' The wounded man looked up. 'I hope you've taken good care of Silverfoot.'

'He's in the stable, none the worse for the gallop,' Mullin replied. At Betsy's bidding he sat on the stool, while she stood aside. 'And since you know my name, I'll use yours,' he added drily. 'I knew I'd seen you before.

You're Isaac Dowell — Lord Arlington's man.'

'And you're Williamson's,' the other said. 'It's as well neither of us killed the other, isn't it?'

'It's as well the man we fell over each other trying to catch didn't kill the King!' Mullin threw back. And when Blunt made no reply, he told him what he had told Betsy: how his pursuit of the conspirators had been in vain. By the time he had finished, the man Betsy now knew not as Blunt but as Isaac Dowell was looking grave.

'If I'd known you were here — known who to look for,' he said, 'we might have banded together.' Then in turn, he told his tale to Mullin; and when the captain learned who he had been pursuing, he was thunderstruck.

'John Kyte's son? By the Christ! I was one of those set to watch his father in Antwerp, a year back — until it was decided he posed no threat.' He frowned. 'Yet I never thought to trouble myself over his children . . . I didn't know he had any.'

'Just a son,' Dowell said quietly. 'As for your past activities in the Provinces, sir, they're known to me. My master's reach is long — I think you know what I speak of.'

'If you refer to Lord Arlington's wife, then I do know!' Restless now, Mullin got to his feet and took a few paces about the little room. 'She's a Dutchwoman,' he told Betsy. 'No doubt she's proved useful to her husband, on occasions.' He eyed Dowell grimly. 'Your master may be better informed than mine if, as I assume, Lady Arlington maintains her friendships among the Dutch,' he added. Then suddenly he stopped in his tracks. 'By God — Marieke Katz!'

Betsy froze . . . Then her eyes went to Dowell, and in an instant she saw it: Madam Katz, the clever burger's wife . . . She caught her breath, staring at Mullin. 'You mean, she knew what we were about from the start? Then, she's Arlington's woman!'

'Indeed, though not in the sense of her poor cuckolded husband,' Dowell said softly. 'She's an agent for de Witt — yet she's Downing's man at heart. She made use of a weak, lovesick fellow named Gorton — a former steward, who would do anything she asked.' Then, seeing the look on Mullin's face, he frowned. 'Do you mean to tell me he's dead, too?'

Mullin nodded. 'But now that's out, the fact remains we've failed — all of us,' he said bitterly. 'Kyte and the others are at large still, to make mischief again whenever they choose. While you and I — '

'No, it isn't over.'

Dowell spoke sharply, then winced in pain. 'Prynn and Phelps and their fellows — we needn't fear them,' he went on, breathing hard. 'They can be rounded up as soon as they break cover. But Kyte will keep apart, as always. He's without friends — indeed he shuns their company. He's but an instrument: vengeance for his father is all he wants — on Papists of any kind. That's why he posed as a priest, so that he could move among them.' He hesitated, catching Betsy's startled look. 'You understand me,' he added. 'And now that he's come to England, he may try again to get at the King — but not immediately. First — '

'First he will hide, while he chooses his moment.'

Moving to the bedside, Mullin peered down. 'And since the King returns to London soon, it will likely be there! Is it not so?'

The other gave a nod. 'I believe it is,' he murmured. 'I also believe there is one place he will go: his father's old house in Bishopsgate. It's empty and derelict, but it's the only bolthole he has.'

'Then we may yet move!' Mullin cried, and at once, his weariness left him. 'Tomorrow, at first light . . . by God, I'll ride like the wind, and get to London if it kills me. Then that murdering devil will taste *my* vengeance!'

* * *

But when the next day dawned, to Mullin's dismay matters took a different turn. For no sooner had he and Betsy risen, than a message arrived:

Joseph Williamson was in Datchet, and was awaiting them.

23

The spymaster was furious.

They stood in what was still Betsy's hired chamber at the Five Bells Inn in Datchet: she, Mullin and Williamson. Though it was barely three weeks, it seemed a lifetime since Betsy had faced this man in a room in Leadenhall Street and agreed to become his intelligencer. She had seen his impatience then — but she had not seen his anger.

'You, Girvan, are a disgrace!' he shouted.

Mullin, pale and tight-lipped, said nothing.

'A disgrace, sir!' Williamson repeated. 'As if the tidings I heard from Crabb weren't bad enough, I now learn that all our plotters have flown the coop. I can but thank the Lord that the King wasn't hurt!'

Betsy and the captain exchanged glances. It was but an hour since the two had woken up in Mother Curll's kitchen. Having stuck to his intention to drink himself senseless, Mullin had slept on the floor, Betsy in a chair. But even as they stirred the message had arrived, brought by a rider from Datchet. At his bidding they had ridden in at once, doubling up on Mullin's horse.

'Er, how is Wrestler — I mean Mr Crabb, sir?' Betsy asked quickly, trying her innocent look.

'He's well enough to perform his duties — just!' Williamson retorted. 'As for Eleanor . . . ' He glowered at Mullin. 'What happened in Delft was a dreadful business — as badly handled as any I've known! If I had time I'd demand your full report — '

'Then you do know we're wasting time — *sir*?' Mullin spoke up at last. He too was angry, and the worse for the brandy he'd consumed the night before. On first seeing Williamson he had tried to tell him of the events, but the man had brushed his explanations aside. 'And I would say, with every minute that passes,' the captain went on, 'the murderer Kyte is further away. Likely he's in London already — '

'I know that — now!' Williamson shouted. 'I already have men scouring the haunts of known Republicans. Every road out of London will be watched — Prynn and Phelps will be caught, at least. As for that other devil, the false priest — '

'Forgive me, sir . . . ' With a glassy smile, Betsy interrupted. 'But we believe we know where he is. There's a ruined house near The Spital Field, that once belonged to Kyle's father, Blunt says. He — '

'Who's Blunt?'

'I mean Dowell,' she corrected herself.

'Isaac Dowell — also called Richard Blunt.' Her fellow-intelligencer put in, hiding his impatience with difficulty. 'You'll know him as number thirty-four.' And when Williamson gave a start, he added, 'And if I might venture an opinion, sir, there are others, too, who have managed this business clumsily. Two hands, neither of which knew what the other was doing — do you take my meaning?'

'How dare you!' the spymaster cried. 'You need to be disciplined, sir . . . and besides, that's not a matter I'd discuss with you!' Then his agent's words sank in, he frowned. 'What . . . do you mean to tell me Dowell is here?'

'He was stabbed, saving the King's life,' Mullin said coolly. 'With the same blade that killed Eleanor and wounded Crabb. The man now lies at Egham, sorely wounded — it's his horse I rode in pursuit of Kyte. Now, would you care to hear my tale, or are you deaf to all but your own opinions?'

The spymaster opened his mouth, then closed it. He fumed for a while, then to Betsy's surprise turned to her. 'Why don't you tell it?' he said. 'And no embellishments, if you please!'

After a moment, she gave a nod. 'As you wish, sir. But may I sit? It's been a trying few days . . . ' She sank down on a nearby chair. Then, scarcely drawing breath, she delivered a concise report of all that had happened since she and Mullin had parted from Peter Crabb at Dover. That way, she hoped, there would be no more misunderstandings. When she had finished, she sat back and waited.

For some moments the spymaster didn't speak. Betsy sensed his mind at work once again, sifting and reasoning. At last he moved to the window seat from where Mullin had watched the King's arrival, and sat down stiffly.

'So it was late afternoon when Kyte gave you the slip,' he said, looking somewhat subdued. 'Why, he and I could have passed each other on the road!'

'Yet it isn't too late — I'm sure of it.' Urgently now, Mullin stepped forward. 'Last night I feared the fellow would head for Dover,' he added, 'but now, I doubt it. He's been thwarted, and he means to try again, so Dowell says, and I trust his instincts. I didn't get a proper look at Kyte — indeed, none of us have. And the man who can recognize him is too sick to travel. Kyte doesn't know London — he's grown up in the Provinces. Yet he will know of his father's house, by Bishopsgate. If we move swiftly — '

'Yes, very well.' Calmer now, Williamson

eyed each of them. 'That was quite a ride for a woman, Beatrice,' he said, after a moment. 'Dover to Egham, in two days . . . '

'I'm flattered you think so, sir,' Betsy replied. Then emboldened, she added, 'I hope you'll remember it when you come to pay me. I'm told you can be somewhat tardy in that respect.' Pointedly she looked at Mullin, who made a choking sound, quickly turning it to a cough. But at that Williamson frowned.

'Now you too try my patience,' he snapped. 'I meant there's more riding ahead — provided you come to London with me, that is. If you prefer to remain here in comfort, I could pay you off now — I'll even settle the reckoning for this room. However, if you wish to return . . . '

'I do wish it, sir,' Betsy said. 'Like Girvan and Mr Crabb, I've a desire to see Eleanor's murderer caught — to look him in the face, just once. With your permission, of course?' And she waited again, until the spymaster nodded.

'So be it,' he said.

Whereupon Mullin threw her a glance: and at last, the gleam in his eye was back.

★　★　★

306

Three days later, in the small hours of the morning, agents of the crown left the City of London by Bishopsgate, turned into Hog Lane and stealthily took positions about a large, broken-down house near The Spital Field. They were half-a-dozen men, and one woman. Marcus Mullin was in charge, and among the party was Peter Crabb.

Betsy had been heartened to see the young giant again. He was rested, his face less taut than when she'd last seen him. And, as promised, he had discarded his sling. 'The arm's usable,' he told her. 'But I take no chances — and anyway, my right hand's enough for this.' He showed her a light pistol.

Betsy shivered; the air was cold and she had had little sleep. Having been obliged to break her promise and endure the ride to London on a borrowed horse, she'd spent an uneasy night at the house in Leadenhall Street, where Crabb and Mullin also rested. Since their return, matters had moved swiftly. Williamson had laid his plans, and given Mullin the task of seeing them through: a chance to redeem himself in the spymaster's eyes. Crabb had insisted on being a part of it, and none would deny him. Now he and Betsy stood on a narrow, dirty street in the shadow of a wall, almost opposite the house where the fugitive was believed to be, though there was neither light, nor sign of habitation.

'I don't like it, Wrestler,' Betsy murmured. 'And I think even Mullin has doubts as to whether Kyte is there. Yet he's determined to lay siege to the place.' She peered into the gloom; the captain and the others were out of sight. 'And he's uneasy about me being here, of course,' she added.

'You'd have come anyway,' Crabb observed with a smile.

'And here you are — my protector once again.' Betsy returned his smile, drawing her cloak about her. 'So I'm safe. If you want to help the others, don't let me spoil it for you.'

But at that Crabb grew serious. 'I shan't be as careless as I was in Delft,' he said with a sigh. 'When we first took ship for the Continent, I never thought we'd end up back in London still chasing the man we set out to look for — the one who would murder Eleanor.' He shook his head. 'I confess to you, it's not a mission I'm proud of.'

'As I recall, you had misgivings from the start,' Betsy said. 'So did Eleanor. And I never dreamed that matters would unfold as they have done. It's more fantastical than a play!'

Crabb was about to reply, but at once there was a shout, and both of them looked round. From several points about the house, lights flared as Mullin's men lit their torches. At another command, they began to close in. In the gloomy street Betsy and Crabb watched, and soon came the crash of a door being forced. It was followed by more shouts: the agents had stormed in.

'I hope they've covered every way out,' Crabb muttered. 'As I hope I don't have nosy neighbours to deal with . . . ' He jerked his thumb at the houses nearby. 'If anyone asks we're constables, in pursuit of a thief who stole your purse,' he added. 'You're here to identify him.'

'I know, Wrestler,' Betsy said. 'Though I suspect at the first sign of trouble, people will stay indoors — it's that sort of parish.'

Crabb barely nodded; pistol in hand, he crouched. There were sounds of movement from the house but no further shouts, and Betsy's hopes wavered. Not that they had been high to begin with: somehow, she couldn't see anyone as cunning as Jerome Kyte letting himself get caught this easily. Nor, she suspected, did Mullin, in his heart. To cheer herself, she spoke up again.

'What of Thomas Pryn and the other conspirators?' she asked. 'Are they taken?'

'I don't know,' Crabb replied, without looking round. 'Though it should be only a matter of time . . . ' Suddenly he tensed. 'Now what's up?' He was gazing at the top of the old house. It was roofless, open to the stars; indeed, to Betsy's eyes the place offered little promise as a refuge. Even in the dark she could see broken-down walls and gaping window-frames.

'What do you mean?'

'See!' Crabb pointed. 'Someone's up there!'

Betsy looked — and saw a dark shape moving along the top of the wall. But even as they watched, it vanished.

'By the Christ, they've missed him!' Straightening up, Crabb glanced at her, and at once she nodded. 'You go, Wrestler,' she urged. 'Don't let him escape again!'

For a moment the young man wavered, torn between his desire to catch a murderer and to protect Betsy. But there was no time to lose, and to emphasize it she gave him a shove. 'Find Mullin!' she cried. 'Go on!'

So he went. And even as he ran towards the house shapes appeared, caught in the light of the torches. 'The roof!' Crabb called out. 'He's going to jump!'

There was an answering cry. Heart pounding, Betsy watched as someone ran out into the street. The man carried a musketoon: a short-barrelled musket, the sort horsemen used. He and Crabb exchanged words, then hurried off. Betsy looked up again — then her heart thumped.

From the end of a broken, jagged beam, a rope snaked downwards. A silhouette appeared, grasping it like an ape — and in a second, the figure had jumped from the wall and was shinning down at speed. All Betsy could do was watch as he neared the ground, leaped the last few feet, then disappeared.

'Cods!' She breathed. 'He'll get away . . . '

There was nothing for it: without hesitating, she stepped into the street and yelled from the bottom of her lungs. 'Here! He's down here!'

For a moment there was silence — then from the far side of the house came a shout, answered by another. Lights flickered again, then came rapid footfalls. From nowhere a man ran up, and to Betsy's relief it was Mullin.

'What the devil are you doing?' he snapped.

'He got down by rope!' Betsy told him. 'Look there . . . '

She pointed, and the captain whirled about. Men were calling to him. With an oath he sped away, calling over his shoulder, 'Get off the street — knock on a door, or something!'

But though she moved back to the wall, Betsy had no intention of doing any such thing. Eyes darting about, she looked for signs of the fugitive, but saw no one. Mullin's men were agile and well armed, but in the ruined house they were hampered. She heard men stumble over rubble, cursing. A torch fell to the ground and went out, and for a moment all was dark . . . until a black shape came hurtling out of the gloom straight towards her.

And the next moment, she was looking into the face of the killer.

'You!'

He stopped dead. But though his surprise was great, it was far less than Betsy's. For he wasn't a man: he was little more than a boy! She gazed at him — then softly she spoke.

'You tried to kill me.'

There was no answer.

'But instead you killed a girl, who was but your age!'

Still the boy said nothing. No stranger to good-looking males, Betsy found herself staring into pale, delicate features. And though the face was dirty and bore the marks of a desperate flight, it was almost beautiful. She caught her breath . . . then something bright flashed in front of her. Involuntarily she stepped back — and slipped.

'Then I will see it through now!'

Even as she fell, Betsy stared upwards.

Jerome Kyte was bending over her; and to her dismay he was smiling.

'Do you like my *chinqueda?*' He held it before her, turning it about. She saw the broad blade Crabb had once described, with its terrible, glittering edge. Her eyes met those of the one who wielded it, and in them she read her own death.

'She is Italian,' the boy said. 'Always faithful, and most excellent for concealment. Under a cloak, say, or a cassock.'

Betsy blinked: he had a Dutch accent! But of course, that was where he'd grown up . . .

'It was my father's,' he went on. 'He bade me draw it only to spill the blood of our enemies . . . '

Then his smile was gone. His hand went up . . . Betsy braced herself — until the night exploded in a burst of flame and noise that almost blinded and deafened her. There was a shriek, and the body of Jerome Kyte toppled forward, flattening her.

In horror she cried out, smelling rancid sweat: the sweat of the one who lay dying atop her, until it was replaced by a different odour. Gagging, she turning her head and retched . . . until all at once the body was lifted off her.

Mercifully the sickening smell of blood faded. With a jerk she sat up, her chest

313

heaving. Peter Crabb stood nearby, holding his arm in agony. Beside him lay the smoking pistol he had used, and dropped to the ground.

'By God, I've torn the wound again!' he gasped. Then he squinted down at Betsy. 'Are you hurt?'

Half-dazed she shook her head. There were running footsteps, and lights dancing towards her. Men crowded round; there seemed a horde of them. The one she remembered with the musketoon was brandishing it dangerously. She gazed about her, and flinched.

But a few feet away, the body of her would-be murderer lay on his back, eyes open. There was a gaping wound in his head where something unpleasant welled out, shiny in the torchlight. The *chinqueda* — the blade that would have ended her life — was still in his hand.

'That was a lucky shot, Crabb.'

The man with the musketoon bent down to peer at the corpse. 'If you'd let me fire my piece, we'd have been sure . . . ' He straightened up, looking round. The other men turned too, as Marcus Mullin hurried up. As he drew close he checked himself, taking in the situation quickly.

'Well, is no one going to help her up?' he said at last. Then he leaned down and offered

Betsy his hand. She took it, and allowed herself to be pulled to her feet. Her legs felt weak, but she was unharmed.

'You did well, Crabb.' Mullin was short of breath himself, but calm enough. 'You've kept your word and avenged Eleanor.' Wincing with pain, the young man looked away. 'As for you, madam . . . ' The captain faced Betsy. 'I imagine your part's over now.'

He glanced at the body, then round at his men. But they had drawn back, leaving the others alone. The three members of Mr Lee's Family eyed each other . . . and at last Betsy spoke.

'I imagine it is,' she answered. Then with a final glance at both men, she walked off towards Bishopsgate.

As she went she heard voices, saw windows open and lights showing. Faces peered out at her, and for a moment she almost felt like taking a bow.

24

Some days later, on a cold but bright afternoon, Betsy Brand entered the Star Tavern in Cheapside, and was shown into a private upstairs room. There was a single occupant seated at a table by the window. As she came in, the man rose and inclined his head.

'This is a surprise, Mr Lee,' Betsy said. She wore her favourite blue gown and a cream-coloured whisk, and her face was flushed from walking. 'I confess I was taken aback to receive your message . . . is anything wrong?'

'Not at all, madam.' Joseph Williamson, in his habitual black coat and periwig, gestured her to a chair facing him. As they sat he indicated a jug at his elbow. 'Will you take a cup of Rhenish with me?'

Betsy nodded her acceptance. 'I never thought to see you in such a public place,' she said, as he poured wine. 'Yet I'm glad — for I am curious to know how matters stand.'

'They stand well,' Williamson answered. 'In brief, two days ago a house in Coleman Street was raided, and a great deal of seditious material seized. But more importantly, a man who was hiding there was also taken: Thomas Prynn, of whom you know. He lies now in a place that's also known to you: the King's Bench. He has much to answer for.'

At mention of the prison, Betsy lowered her eyes. 'And what of the other man?' she ventured. 'Phelps?'

'Dead.' Without expression, Williamson took a sip of wine. 'He tried to shoot his way out, and paid the price. But what matters is, that web of treachery is broken. Of course there may be others, but . . . ' He shrugged. 'The crown's reach is long.'

Still wondering why the spymaster had asked to meet her, Betsy took a drink too. She hoped it was to pay her what was owed. The last few days, though filled with glad reunions — with Tom Catlin and Peg in particular — had been difficult. Money was still in short supply, and Catlin still troubled. As for her fellow-intelligencers, she had not seen Mullin or Crabb since she had left them in the street by The Spital Field, beside the body of the murderer Jerome Kyte.

'And our work is endless — though you've grasped that already, I think.' Williamson was eyeing Betsy with an intense look. So, seizing the moment, she decided to talk business.

'I don't wish to be importunate, Mr Lee,'

she began, 'but I must touch upon the subject of my wage. I believe I've done my part in breaking the conspiracy. Captain — I mean, Girvan — certainly thought so.'

The other gave a brief nod. 'That's one reason I asked you to come. I believe the two of you worked well enough together. I'd like to ask you to consider the offer I made when we first spoke. In other words — '

'I fear not, sir.'

Betsy spoke more sharply than she'd intended. 'Or at least, not in the near future,' she added, forcing a smile. 'I . . . I find I'm not a good traveller. I'd hardly left London before my little adventure. As for the duties a female intelligencer might perform, I found them limiting — and more dangerous than I'd anticipated.'

'Nonsense!' the spymaster retorted. 'From what Girvan says, you thrive on danger.' He put on a mirthless smile. 'Don't tell me you prefer to return to a life upon the stage?'

'That's precisely what I prefer,' Betsy replied. 'I'm an actress, sir, who's about to play a new role.' She spoke the truth. The day before, she'd had a meeting with her employer and mentor Thomas Betterton at his house in Long Acre. Though displeased by her lengthy absence, the great actor was

318

more than willing to let her return to the Duke's Theatre; however the role she coveted was now gone to another actress. Instead of Lady Waspish, she would play the comic role of an ageing bawd. She thought to model it on Mother Curll.

'Is it truly so?' Williamson gazed at her, and when she nodded, a frown appeared. 'Then you disappoint me, Beatrice. Of course I'll settle my account with you, if you desire it. Though I'd hoped you might agree to defer payment until later, in which case a larger sum could follow. Do you understand me?'

'I do, sir,' Betsy answered firmly, 'yet my mind is made up. So if you'd kindly let me have what I'm owed?' She waited, until at last Williamson put a hand in his coat pocket, drew out a small pouch and tossed it on to the table.

'Well, then you'd better count that,' he said shortly.

Betsy opened the pouch and shook gold coins out on to the table top. Counting them did not take long at all. 'Twelve pounds?' she looked up. 'That is all?'

The spymaster shrugged.

'For this, I risked my life?'

'You know there are always risks,' Williamson said. 'Crabb's lucky to be alive; Girvan too, for that matter.'

'As am I,' Betsy replied. 'I was nearly murdered — '

'Yes, I've had their testimony,' the other broke in. 'I thought to do you the honour of a private meeting, instead of merely sending your payment by messenger. It's not a courtesy I extend to other agents . . . ' He trailed off, and put on a somewhat different smile. 'But then, you are not like the others. It occurred to me, should you wish for preferment, we might come to another sort of arrangement. A more personal one, perhaps, that would no doubt give pleasure to us both.'

And with that he leaned back and regarded Betsy deliberately, whereupon her heart sank.

'Now it's you who disappoint me, sir,' she said quietly. 'And more, I doubt it would afford me any pleasure at all.'

There was a moment, then Williamson sat up smartly. Betsy thought he would fly into a rage, but instead his face had become a hard mask.

'Then you'd better take your money and be gone,' he said icily. 'Perhaps I've overestimated you. And, I might add, madam, that your first mission was somewhat less than a success. It has put me to considerable expense: horses, the cost of rooms . . . I've even had to arrange for the man Blunt to be conveyed to London by coach to recover from his wound. He'll be unfit for weeks.'

'Yet the King's life was saved, without him even noticing it.' Betsy's temper rose quickly. 'What if the assassin's blade had killed Dowell — or Mullin? Forgive my calling him that, but I was Mistress Mullin for a while. It's difficult to forget.'

Williamson gave a weary sigh. 'I thought you understood enough not to expect thanks,' he said. 'Loyalty is its own reward — or should be. Others have given their lives — '

'I know it,' Betsy broke in. 'I watched Eleanor die!'

The spymaster said nothing.

'I saw her die — in my place,' she went on, trying to master herself. 'So I need no reminders, sir. I expect only fair payment for my service . . . ' Suddenly she gave a start. 'I also asked you to pay a sum in advance, to my sister in Chelsea,' she added quickly. 'You agreed to do so.'

'Did I?' A puzzled frown creased Williamson's brow. 'I cannot recall such.' With a nod, he indicated the coins lying on the table. 'In any case, you have your payment now. What you do with it is your affair.' He stopped, as without warning Betsy rose to her feet.

'You lied to me!' she cried. 'You promised to do what I asked, as I tried to do your bidding! I was almost stabbed — not to mention nearly drowned, assaulted, half-starved and — '

'You grow tiresome, Beatrice.' The man's frown was back. 'You carried out your task and you've been paid. Had you been willing to work for me again, we might have discussed new terms — yet you've spurned my offer.' Then he leaned forward, and raised a warning finger. 'But let me remind you of something else,' he added. 'Everything you've learned since you entered my service — everything you've seen, heard and done — must remain utterly secret. On pain of death, I told you, and I repeat it now.'

Still on her feet, Betsy gazed back at him. One word sprang to her mind: betrayal. There were many varieties, she decided; some great, some small . . . With almost a shiver she recalled Marcus Mullin's words, in a chamber in Neiuwpoort. To steady herself she lifted the cup, took a final drink of wine and set it down with a thud. Then she scooped up the gold coins and thrust them into her gown.

'The Children of Judas . . . that's what some call us, is it not?' she said. 'I find it apt — more so now, than I ever expected.'

'No, you are wrong.'

The spymaster looked at her coldly. 'The Judases are traitors — men like Venn, Prynn and Phelps. And those devils abroad:

regicides who fled to save their miserable hides, like John Kyte, and madmen like Thomas Lacy! They're the ones who must be dealt with — by whatever means available! Do you think your life so important, that it be set above the safety of England and her sovereign?'

'Perhaps not,' Betsy answered. 'Yet I was foolish enough to think I was trusted — even valued. Instead, those of us who laboured in the Low Countries found we'd been marked from the start, merely because one of the King's ministers and his own deputy don't trust each other! And who like boys, strive to outdo one another! Where does that rank in the scale of betrayal, sir, can you answer that?'

Stung, Williamson sprang to his feet, but he was too late. Betsy had delivered her parting line, and had no intention of letting anyone spoil it. Before the man could speak she was at the door. It banged shut, and all the spymaster could do was listen to her wooden heels clumping down the stairs.

Once outside, she began walking; there seemed no other way to work off her anger. She passed the Saddlers' Hall, turned left into Old Change and then right, skirting the south side of St Paul's. The sounds and smells of London were about her, as familiar as her own heartbeat. Breathing hard she threaded her way up to Ludgate, then left the City. Soon she had crossed the Fleet Bridge and passed St Bride's — and at last, above the rooftops rose the Duke's Theatre with its familiar cupola. Still she didn't slow her pace until she had opened the side door and entered the pit. There at last she stopped, drew a breath . . . and blinked: the place was deserted. Then she remembered — it was Sunday.

With a sigh, she sank down on a bench and gazed at the empty stage. The festoon curtain was up, but the great candle-hoops had been lowered to the floor. At the rear, the sliding flats of the last scene played were still in place, but there were no actors. As always, without cast or audience the place was as dead as a mausoleum.

'Betsy Brand, is it you?'

She looked round to see a figure standing by the scene-room door. Then recognition came: Hannah Cleeve, the widow whom Betsy had helped to the post of wardrobe-mistress, came forward with a look of surprise.

'Why, you look like you're lost!' she exclaimed.

'I did forget myself, Hannah.' Betsy managed a smile. 'I've been away, you know — '

'That I do!' Hannah broke in. 'Who don't know it? Some said you was sick, some that you'd gone into the country.' She lowered her voice. 'Me and a few others, we thought you might have got yourself into trouble — you know, Nelly Gwynn sort of trouble. Woman's bane . . . '

'What, you thought I was with child?' Betsy blinked. 'No, I swear not.'

'That's well . . . ' Hannah nodded. 'So, you're all right, then?'

'Yes, I suppose I am.' With a glance round the auditorium, Betsy stood up. 'And now I should get myself home. I'm to rehearse tomorrow; you'll need to find me an old dress fit for a bawd.'

'Those I have aplenty,' Hannah said wryly. 'Back home, I mean . . . ' She gave a start. 'Here, I knew there was something: a fellow left a message for you.'

'For me?' Betsy raised her eyebrows. 'When?'

'Yesterday. I have it somewhere . . . ' Hannah rummaged in the pockets of her loose frock, then produced a folded paper, unsealed. 'I can't read, so I don't know that's in it,' she said, thrusting it at her. 'But I won't forget the fellow who brought it: big as a mountain, he was. Built like a castle and handsome to boot!'

Betsy stiffened. 'I thank you, Hannah,' she said, and took the letter. Then with a nod she went out.

In Water Lane she stopped, gazing down at it. To her surprise, her hand shook a little. But without further delay she unfolded it, and read:

I leave on Monday for foreign shores, but nights find me at The Rose in Covent Garden. Will you take a farewell glass with me?

It was signed 'A Captain of Horse.'

She stood in the lane and read it again, then crumpled it and thrust it into her pocket. Head down she walked up to Fleet Street where she halted. Her first instinct had been to tear up the paper and cast it away; now she knew she would do no such thing.

In fact, she found herself smiling.

And that was why in the evening, with a link-boy to light her way, she walked by Wych Street and Drury Lane to Little Russell Street, which led to the Great Piazza of Covent Garden.

There on the corner of Brydges Street stood the notorious Rose Tavern, haunt of rakes and rogues of all kinds: a fitting abode for Captain Marcus Mullin. Soon she was entering the noisy, smoke-filled interior — and the first person she set eyes on was Peter Crabb.

'Wrestler!'

Her face lit up, as did Crabb's — and at once he was elbowing his way through the topers to stand before her. The moment he drew near, Betsy put her arms about his huge body and squeezed.

'I'm most glad to see you,' she said, and stood back.

'Have a care . . . my arm's newly stitched.' Somewhat flushed, though more with embarrassment than pain, the young man smiled at her. 'We didn't get chance to say farewell, the other night, did we?' He looked over his shoulder. 'He's in the back . . . Will you come with me?'

'I will,' Betsy replied, whereupon the two of them made their way to the rear of the crowded room. The place stank of stale beer, wine and strong tobacco. Men drank, spat, laughed and shouted, and at sight of Betsy a few threw out ribald remarks — but a look from Crabb was enough to quell them. Soon they had reached a crowded table, where they stopped. At the same moment a familiar figure seated by the wall raised his head, then to her alarm cried out, 'By God, it's my wife! Now I'm caught!'

Marcus Mullin jumped to his feet, bumping into the man beside him. All those at the table were men: gallants and carousers of the sort to be found anywhere in Covent Garden. In surprise, they looked round, and laughter broke out.

'Caught is it, Dark?' one shouted. 'Damn, I wish I'd someone like that to capture me!'

'And I!' another cried. 'Why, I'd never leave the bedchamber! If you seek a rum cull, madam, I'm your man!'

'She don't seek one,' Peter Crabb said. The fellow looked round, then upwards, and gulped.

'No she don't . . . and I pray you'll excuse me, sirs.' With a tipsy leer, Mullin pushed his way through the seated men, clapping some on the shoulder as he disentangled himself. 'I'll join you again,' he said loudly. 'Next week perhaps . . . who can say?' And with that he turned his back to them and drew close to Betsy. Her instinct was to back away from him, drunk as he appeared, until she looked into his eyes.

'At your service once again, madam,' he said gently. 'Shall we find a more salubrious spot to talk?'

★　★　★

They sat in a small back room, quieter than the rest of the tavern. The only other occupants were an elderly gentleman and a blowsy-looking trull, fumbling each other in a corner. But after a while they too departed, leaving the three intelligencers alone. Soon they had exchanged such news as there was, though little of what the men said was new to Betsy. Not wishing to dwell on it, she gave them a very brief account of her meeting with Williamson. But at that, Mullin grew animated.

'The damned skinflint!' he grumbled. 'I had to wheedle to get my own money out of him, and still it wasn't all I'm owed. I told him I'd not had a penny in four months, and strike me if he didn't deny it! In the end I took payment for three, and bade him insert the remainder somewhere dark and unpleasant!'

Betsy glanced at Crabb and saw his look of amusement. 'I hope you got paid, Wrestler,' she said. 'After all you went through. And I'm very glad to be able to thank you again for saving my life.'

'I've been paid in full,' Crabb told her. 'Mr Lee needs a few like me, and he knows it. Besides, I come cheaper than gentle-folk.' He gave her a shy smile.

'You see we're the best of friends now?'

Mullin jerked his thumb at Crabb, then picked up his mug. 'I hope that pleases you.'

'It does,' Betsy answered. 'Especially since each of you once swore to kill the other, as I recall.'

But Mullin waved a hand in the air. 'That was the Dutch wine talking,' he said breezily. 'Why, even the Rose's ale is an improvement.' And as if to prove it, he took a generous pull. But, as he set his mug down again, he eyed Betsy keenly. 'It's fortuitous you got my message in time,' he went on. 'I had nowhere else to leave it, save at the theatre. I depart tomorrow — for the Low Countries again. Though not, thank heavens, Delft. It seems my talents are in demand at the Hague. Things are somewhat fraught there, I fear.'

'You're still certain there will be war?' Betsy asked quietly, to which the other nodded.

'Unavoidable,' he said, with a glance at Crabb. 'Early spring, as I said . . . ' He looked away. 'And for what? So another preening monarch can plunder the bog of Europe?'

'Let's not speak of it now, Captain,' Crabb said mildly. 'Should we not toast our gallant companion instead?'

At that Mullin slapped a hand on the table. 'Quite right!' Raising his own mug, he knocked it against Crabb's. Both men drained them to the last, then set them down.

'And before we part, madam, there's one other thing . . . ' A sly smile appeared on the captain's face. 'We've shared our displeasure about Williamson,' he added, 'yet I've news that may cheer you — indeed, I'm certain it will. It . . . well, it concerns a horse.'

In surprise Betsy met his eye . . . and caught a familiar gleam in it. She looked at Crabb and saw a knowing look there too. 'How so?' she enquired.

'Not just any horse, I should say . . . ' Once again, Mullin seemed rather pleased with himself. 'I speak of the one I rode from Dover to Datchet, then raced — a spirited beast. I was sorry to part with him, but needs must.' He grinned. 'In short, madam, I sold him to a dealer in Smithfield. He fetched a good price, I might add. Then I do enjoy a haggle.'

'You sold the other hired horse?' Betsy's mouth fell open. 'That was bold, sir, if not criminal.'

'Do you think so, after all we did?' Mullin shrugged. 'I told you Williamson would pay the reckoning, and so he has, albeit grudgingly. A sum will be sent to the stable in Dover, so no man's been ill-served. Except that skinflint, our master.' He grinned broadly. 'I enjoyed watching him rage when I told him the price of both our horses.'

'But how did you explain their loss?' Betsy asked. And when Mullin merely kept grinning, she looked to Crabb. 'Wrestler, won't you tell me?'

'Well, from what I heard, your mare was stolen in Egham,' the young man answered haltingly. 'The captain's mount was lost on Hounslow Heath. A fearful place for horse priggers, is that . . . ' He threw Mullin a look. 'You should be more careful in future, sir.'

'That I should.' Mullin put on a sober look. 'Still, what's done is done, so now I'll come to the nub of it.' He reached into his coat and drew out a small package. 'That matter is, I thought you had a right to a share in my good fortune, madam,' he went on. 'A small token of my appreciation — and our friendship, of course. After all, one of the horses I sold was yours, so to speak.'

In silence, Betsy took the packet.

'It's a trifle — a scrap of lace,' Mullin went on with a casual air. 'But good stuff . . . Flanders, of course. It'll serve to trim a collar, or cuffs.'

'I thank you,' she said.

'Best tuck it away before you go,' Crabb put in. 'Some thief will have it off you otherwise.'

'I will . . . ' She eyed him, then Mullin. Nothing more was said: it was time for her

332

exit and all of them knew it. So she rose and tucked the gift into her bosom. After that it only remained for the men to stand too and bid her farewell. It seemed unlikely they would meet again; and though Betsy was about to leave the two with whom she'd shared so much, she would not stay. When Crabb said he would see her safely to the street, she nodded. At the door, she looked back to see Mullin still on his feet. He smiled and made her a low bow; then she turned and went out.

In Brydges Street, the link-boy was still waiting. Drawing her whisk about her, Betsy took farewell of Peter Crabb with a hug and, without speaking, left him.

Then she was walking back down Little Russell Street, facing straight ahead.

Epilogue

Tom Catlin was in the parlour when Betsy returned to the house in Fire's Reach Court. As she came in, he glanced up from reading *The London Gazette* and nodded a greeting.

'Was your sister in good spirits?' he asked.

'She was.' Avoiding his eye, Betsy moved to a couch and sat down. Then, putting her hand down her gown, she pulled out Mullin's package. It was wrapped in coarse frieze. She frowned. In the moment of parting, she hadn't noticed how heavy it was.

'What is that?' Catlin enquired with mild interest.

'A gift, from a friend.' Rather hurriedly, she began opening it. There were several folds to unwrap before the small strip of lace was revealed. She picked it up . . . then caught her breath, while Tom Catlin gave a start. Both stared in amazement, at the shower of gold coins that fell out and clattered to the floor.

'A gift?' The doctor stood up. 'Then this friend is most generous . . . not to say wealthy.'

Betsy didn't reply. She gazed at the gold guineas and half-guineas lying scattered on the floorboards. Some were still spinning, glinting in the firelight. There were more than a score of them . . . twenty pounds, at the least. Finally she looked up to see alarm on Catlin's face — and at once she understood.

'Now, you don't imagine I've been selling my favours?' she asked drily.

'No — why would I?' Catlin frowned at her. 'And how could you think so harshly of me?'

She swallowed. 'Your pardon . . . I don't. I was . . . this money is . . . well, it's a shock.'

'So I observe.' After a moment, the doctor moved to a side table. 'You'd better take some sack,' he murmured. He poured out a glass for each of them, while Betsy stooped to pick up the coins. Sitting down again, she set them in her lap and counted them carefully: twenty-four pounds in all.

'Cods,' she muttered under her breath. The price, she knew at once, was well over half of what the horse would have fetched — even when the seller was Marcus Mullin. 'More likely it's the whole sum,' she breathed, then looked up. Tom Catlin was holding the glass out to her.

'Let me explain this later,' she said, rather shakily. 'For now, I'd like to present you with ten pounds. I know I'm late in keeping the promise I made you before I went away, but I do so now, in the hope it will stave off your creditors. Shall we call it a year's rent in advance?' She took the glass from him, and drank it down in one gulp.

Speechless, Catlin stared at her.

'I swear it's my money,' Betsy said. 'And that I've done nothing wrong to get it . . . nothing *very* wrong, anyway. I want you to have the sum — this is our home after all. Peg's and mine, I mean. We'd simply hate you to sell it.' She paused. 'Please don't be tiresome: take it as a favour to me.'

Still Catlin didn't speak. His eyes went from Betsy's face to the money in her hands, then back. 'But . . . what of your father?' he said at last. 'Surely he needs this more than I?'

'Ah yes . . . ' Betsy put a hand to her brow. It was damp, but then the room was quite warm. 'I neglected to tell you,' she went on, thinking fast. 'My sister has raised a good sum from a family friend . . . it will go some way to helping our father in his plight. Together with the amount I will give her, I think matters will resolve themselves.' She smiled suddenly. 'Indeed, I'm planning another visit to Chelsea soon, to talk of our good fortune — see the money is well spent, and so forth. All in all, it should be a happier time ahead.'

'So it would seem.' Glass in hand, Catlin moved slowly back to his desk. At one side was the familiar stack of unpaid bills, weighed down with a pebble. He glanced briefly at them, then sat down. 'By the heavens, Betsy,' he muttered.

There was a footfall on the threshold, and the door swung open. Peg stalked in, sleeves rolled and cap at one side.

'Before you retire, I'll need two shillings for the butcher's boy tomorrow,' she said. 'Does Master think he can scrape up that much?'

She stared insolently at Catlin and, when he didn't answer, turned to Betsy. But when her eyes fell on the money, she faltered.

'Good Christ!' she blurted. 'Where did that come from?'

For a moment neither of the others spoke. Then as the women's eyes met, Peg's hand went to her mouth. 'Your pardon . . . ' She caught her breath. 'Someone's died — is that it?'

'No one's died, Peg,' Betsy said. 'At least, no one that I knew. So there's no need to ask pardon.' She smiled up at the servant, then picked out a half-sovereign and held it up.

'Take this for the butcher's boy,' she said. 'And tell him to be sharp about giving you change. Then take what's left, and use it to pay off whom you will — the ones who won't

wait, I mean.' Still smiling, she faced Tom
Catlin.

'And out of that rent money, sir, I hope
you'll take some to your wig-maker,' she went
on, 'and order something better than that
. . . doormat you're still wearing. I'd hoped
when I went away, to see the last of it.'

There was a short silence. Then shaking
herself out of her inertia, Peg stepped forward
and took the coin from Betsy.

'Leave it to me,' she said, and sniggered.
'As for the wig-maker, he'd be less than
pleased.' She jerked her head towards Tom
Catlin. 'Hadn't you noticed? That's not the
same one he had on — it's new! Talk about
cheap, eh?' And with that she gave a shout of
laughter, and went out.

Betsy looked at Catlin — not at his face,
but at the top of his head — and saw that it
was true.

'Well, at least the fuel's of good quality,' she
murmured. She turned and looked into the
fire — whereupon a coal cracked and hissed,
letting out a spurt of blue flame.

'Gas,' Catlin said.

Then he turned away, and took up his
paper.